Finding Faith

Finding Faith

A NOVEL
By Andrew Barriger

Writers Club Press
New York Lincoln Shanghai

Finding Faith

Writers Club Press
an imprint of iUniverse, Inc.

For information address:
iUniverse
2021 Pine Lake Road, Suite 100
Lincoln, NE 68512
www.iuniverse.com

This is a work of fiction.
Any resemblance to actual people, places, or events is entirely coincidental.

ISBN: 0-595-26309-7 (Pbk)
ISBN: 0-595-65576-9 (Cloth)

Printed in the United States of America

Dedication

To Siren,
the inspiration

To Todd,
the courage

Table of Contents

Foreword

It is my pleasure to introduce the work of a new writer, Andrew Barriger. I'm not so much interested in presenting a synopsis of the story, but the art and talent behind it. Barriger takes a chance with his readers by engaging in word play, which is the mark of a confident writer, and one who knows his craft well enough to engage the readers beyond the story itself. But it doesn't detract from the telling of the story; rather it enhances it, and readers will no doubt recognize that Barriger is a "good" writer without knowing exactly what it is that sets him apart.

I also want to note that while many new writers begin their careers hoping to glean readers, Barriger already has readers. He's just now getting around to making his work available to a wider audience. In fact, while this is Barriger's first published novel, it is not his first novel at all. In the coming months, he will be bringing out several of his works in varied genres, as well as continuing to publish chapters of this present story.

Another mark of a good writer is to create a setting so believable, that readers might be tempted to find it on the map. Such is the setting for this story. Is it based upon a real place? Maybe. Maybe not. Even so, it comes alive here, with its own unique population, backdrop, even landmarks. Though it is far from the kind of story Stephen King would write, I'm tempted to compare Barriger's ability to create place with King's ability to create place and to set it in a recognizable era. In fact, readers will be able to smell the food coming out of the oven, taste the meals set before them, hear the music being played, maybe even recognize the characters coming down the street.

Another mark of a confident writer is the ability to write simply, rather than attempt to dress up an ordinary work in fancy syntax and vocabulary. As a technical writer, myself, I've long since valued the ability to actually communicate with my readers, rather than to intimidate them with complex sentence structure and those foreign word cognates that unnecessarily clutter up perfectly good English. Barriger does this naturally, in my estimation, and his prose never feels forced. Situations develop in his story, his characters respond according to their traits. Telling a story is like signing a contract with the reader. "You can trust me to stay true to the characters," says the writer, and if the character behaves "out of character" the writer promises in this unwritten contract to show how it is logical in the end. There is nothing worse than a writer who breaks this unwritten contract, either by design or by lack of ability. So another mark of a good writer is that a reader can trust him or her to fulfill his or her obligation to the reader.

So sit back and enjoy this delightful story from an already accomplished writer.

—Ronald L. Donaghe, a reviewer for *Foreword Magazine*

Acknowledgment

This is my first published work, but it's my seventh manuscript. For the first time, I found I had a story I truly felt was ready to share. For all those other books, still awaiting for their "final edit," and those yet to come, I want to take a moment to thank the real people who have helped and supported me over the years:

Captain Siren X. Redbloom (and her alter-ego, Lisa Stager), friend and most trusted confidant, without whose support and encouragement, wit, and wry humor I may never have started writing novel-length literature,

Todd "Saffie" St. Pierre, friend, business partner, and causer of trouble, the one who helped me find the courage to be who I am and the muse to tell the truth's tales,

My family, from whom love is unwavering and unconditional, who make even the most difficult of life's transitions seem simple and effortless,

Ron Donaghe, instant friend, the guy who finally got me off the bench and into the land of the published with one simple statement: "Dude, you rock!",

And to the myriad of others who helped me hone my writing skills since my earliest years, most especially, Hal, Dave, Anne, Liz B., and Cathy H.

A writer is more than the sum of his experiences, but without experiences, a writer is nothing.

With gratitude and admiration, this one's for you.

Andrew Barriger
November 2002

CHAPTER ONE

What a Day for Picking Daisies

The open sunroof allowed a bright glow to warm his skin as Taylor Connolly deftly maneuvered his car in and out of mid-afternoon traffic. What a day it had been.

A few scant hours earlier, the day could have gone either way. Taylor had spent the last two months arguing a high-profile sexual harassment case levied against one of the biggest companies in town. A woman had filed the case arguing that the head of personnel had told her the only way she would be hired was if she cared to offer something to encourage him. He had even been kind enough to indicate the kind of encouragement he had in mind by unzipping his fly. Taylor had never seen a better case of *quid pro quo* sexual harassment, with one minor flaw—it was her word against the manager's.

At the eleventh hour, as the case gained media attention, several other women came forward to testify they had similar experiences. The evidence remained testimony only...until three days ago. That was when an anonymous phone call tipped Taylor that someone had found video on the internet.

Taylor introduced the evidence the following day and it was damning. The manager's face was clearly seen, as were certain other parts of his anatomy. From the angle of the picture, it was clear what had happened—whomever had made the phone call had turned the manager's computer teleconference camera in such a way that it would be able to capture the action in the office.

The company attorneys had been furious, but knew their case was lost. The jury was out for all of two hours before rendering their verdict. So it was that on the nineteenth of March, Taylor Connolly had a fairly sizable judgment to his name and his Jaguar X-Type was weaving its way down the freeway, bound for his flat in one of the trendy new developments on the other side of the city.

At three o'clock on the afternoon, traffic wasn't too bad. Another half hour, maybe an hour, and it would be virtual gridlock. Taylor wondered for the umpteenth time just where his tax dollars that were supposed to go to improving the traffic system actually went. Then he passed a small construction zone and watched the men standing around an orange pylon and put the thought from his mind.

Taking the exit to Fifth Street, he deftly crossed two empty lanes of traffic to hang a right on Washington. Three blocks up and another right and he was on Jefferson, less than a block from home.

His flat was in a converted warehouse. Given that it was not technically the best part of town, the lowest level had been turned into a parking garage, managed by an attendant from some third world country. As an employment attorney, Taylor would be the last to ever consider discriminating against someone, but it still struck him as funny that they always seemed to have a new gate attendant and he or she never seemed to be someone from the U.S.

Today was no different. Taylor pulled up to the gate and the attendant recognized the sticker in his front window. The gate to the guest lot opened and Taylor pulled the car hard to the left, aiming for the owner's garage. The door opened automatically as he approached and he pulled inside, parking his Jag next to his roommate's Range Rover, in the designated spot.

Quickly closing the sunroof, he pulled his suitcase and jacket from the seat next to him and slammed the door behind him. Pressing the lock button, he folded the key into the remote and dropped it in his pocket. The elevator waited a few feet away and carried him swiftly to the third floor, where his apartment was one of three.

As the door opened, the first thing he noticed was the sound of music coming from inside. He quickly took inventory and saw that nothing seemed out of place—the alarm was off, so if someone was there, it wasn't forced entry. Molly, his golden retriever, lay basking in the sunlight pouring in through the giant windows in the living room. She took notice of him coming through the door, but didn't otherwise look disturbed, nor eager to get up. Lazy dog.

Taylor set his briefcase down next to the antique hall rack, then hung his jacket on an empty hook. His roommate's winter jacket hung on the other hook. Walking down the hall on the oriental runner, his shoes made no sound. He passed the kitchen and again saw nothing out of place. It wasn't until he reached the living room that he found the first clue that something actually *was* amiss. There, on the couch, was someone's shirt...and it didn't look like Ryan's. As he followed the trail of clothes, Taylor found them to be more intimate...pants, socks, underwear. The destination was obvious.

He would never remember what he saw first—the fact that the young man was laying on *his* pillow, or the way his legs wrapped around Ryan's butt. Either way, the image was indelibly burned into his memory, as was the look of panic on Ryan's face when he realized Taylor was standing there watching and that no amount of creative explanation would get him out of having committed the mortal sin.

"You must be Taylor," the kid said, looking out from under Ryan's frozen chest. "Don't worry, we're almost done."

Taylor felt his face flush with anger and embarrassment as he remained motionless in the doorway. His hand gripped the handle so hard, it nearly bent.

"Taylor, don't freak," Ryan said. No one had moved—he remained on top of the kid, both of them watching Taylor. Taylor stood in the doorway, fully dressed, frozen in place, watching the naked visage of the man he had spent the last two and a half years with having sex with someone else.

"I won the case," Taylor choked, having no idea how to respond to the situation he faced.

"Congratulations," Ryan said, still unmoving.

"I think I should go," Kid said from under Ryan. "The mood is gone." Ryan pulled back, reaching to pull a sheet around him. As he did, Taylor turned and walked back into the kitchen, seeing it as the only room that hadn't been disturbed by Ryan's actions.

In less than a minute, Kid had collected his clothes and hurriedly dressed. He stopped at the kitchen where Taylor sat with a stupefied look at the small table.

"Nice to finally meet you," he said, then turned to go as Ryan followed him to the door. Taylor heard Kid say, "Call me," as the door closed behind him and Ryan turned the bolt.

He waited at the door to the kitchen, a bathrobe covering his nakedness. "You're home early," he remarked after several minutes of silence.

"I won the case," Taylor repeated.

"The internet video did it, huh?"

Taylor nodded. "The jury awarded punitive damages of several million dollars."

"And you get a percentage of that?"

"Yeah," Taylor said. His eyes remained firmly fixated at some invisible object on the table that looked a whole lot like his boyfriend on top of another guy.

"Taylor, I'm sorry," Ryan said finally.

At that, Taylor looked up, meeting him squarely in the eye. "No, don't do that, Ryan. Don't say that. The only thing you're sorry about is that I came home early. How many times have you done this?"

Ryan sighed, never moving from where he leaned in the doorway. "A few," he admitted. "You've been gone so much and I needed someone here."

"So you got some kid?"

"He's twenty," Ryan defended.

"You're almost thirty! He's a kid." Taylor stood and walked to the sink. "I've only been on this case for a couple months and I'm not gone that much."

Ryan shifted, but stayed in the doorway. "I met him when classes started last fall. He kept coming on to me. One night, when I knew you were going to work late, we went to dinner. One thing led to another..."

"And you've been carrying on like this for months while I was too busy to notice," Taylor finished. "For Christ's sake, you even let him use my *pillow!*"

Confusion showed on Ryan's face as Taylor stormed from the kitchen. He pushed past Ryan to the guest room where he disappeared for a moment, then reappeared carrying one of the pillows from the guest bed.

"*This* is now my pillow," he said, gesturing to the blue clad object.

"Okay..." Ryan agreed, unsure of how to proceed.

"You know, I knew something was going on," Taylor said, waving the pillow in front of him at Ryan. "You got distant again, like you did a year ago with that intern you met. You promised me then that it would never happen again."

"I know, Taylor, I know," Ryan breathed, putting on his best sympathy face. "I tried really hard to resist him."

"Yeah, I'm sure you tried hard," Taylor said, stuffing the pillow under his arm. He pushed past Ryan to the rack where his jacket hung.

"Where are you going?"

"Away," Taylor said as he picked up his briefcase and grabbed the jacket.

"Don't go angry. You'll drive too fast and get in an accident. Let's talk about this and see if we can work it out."

Taylor swung around, nearly whacking Ryan with his briefcase. "I've already worked it out. You're going to collect your stuff, including *his pillow*, and be out of here by the end of the week."

Ryan straightened up a bit, brow furrowing. "This place is partly mine, too. I'm not just leaving."

"I'll buy you out. Just get your stuff and get out. I never want to see you again."

Water formed at the bottom of Ryan's eyes. "Taylor, don't do this. I don't want to lose you."

Taylor turned for the door. "Save it for your kid. Or maybe last year's intern. I'm through being your afterthought." With his free hand, he unbolted the door, opened it, and then slammed it shut behind him.

He'd won the case.

As Taylor's butt hit the fine Italian leather of his car, he realized he hadn't even been gone long enough for the seat to get cold. How could he have been so stupid? He knew what was going on. Ryan had been distant for weeks, only feigning interest in the progress of the case when Taylor would come home from the office late. Their coupling had been perfunctory at best, as both of them ignored the obvious problems.

All Taylor had ever wanted was a normal life. He realized, as a gay man, that was a bit of a challenge but he didn't think it was so much to ask. Why couldn't he find a man who wanted him—and only him?

He met Ryan in college and they had been friends for several years. They both knew they were gay, but Ryan was the first to come out, opting for the club scene and the wild life. Taylor had been less interested, meeting a few guys here and there, but never finding the emotional depth he craved. After a couple years, Ryan had appeared to calm down and they got together.

A little over a year ago, while Ryan was still in med school, Taylor noticed him receiving a lot of pages and phone calls at odd hours of the day and night. A little investigation later, his fears were confirmed and he confronted Ryan. Ryan admitted to having been seeing a fellow intern from the hospital. Several tense weeks later, he was able to convince Taylor to stay and that he would not do it again. Taylor, still having the dream of a loving relationship, took him at his word.

How stupid could I be? Taylor thought. *Apparently that stupid,* he answered himself. Isn't that a sign of insanity, when you ask yourself a question and start getting answers?

With a groan, he jammed the key into the ignition and started the car. Like the cat it was named for, it roared to life, then purred softly. Pulling back on the gearshift, he backed out, then squealed out of the garage. Damn right he was going to drive fast—he didn't pay all this money for a Jaguar to drive it like an old Chevy.

Two quick turns and an optional stop sign later, he was once again on the freeway, headed out of the city. Traffic was heavier and he couldn't drive as fast as he had hoped. Leave it to Ryan to cheat on him during rush hour!

As he settled into the left lane of the freeway, he caught a glimpse of himself in the bright sunlight streaming in through the open sunroof. His blond hair had streaks from the sun it had been getting in the unusually warm weeks of March. For once, they were real streaks, not something his stylist had added for him. Though not yet tan, his skin had at least lost the pale of winter, making his bright blue eyes stand out that much brighter. And he realized he had no tears—he had known what Ryan was doing, he just hadn't been prepared to have it thrown in his face so obviously.

Maybe it was better this way. Though the defendants might opt to appeal the case, it was equally possible they would accept the judgment as a way to save face in the community. Either way, sooner or later, Taylor was going to come into some money. His options were opening up. The case had notoriety, and that notoriety would extend to him. He'd done well since graduating law school four years before, but this would really open some doors.

Traffic settled into a routine as it streamed out of the city. Admittedly, they were going about seventy, but that was about ten miles an hour slower than Taylor generally preferred. Powerless to speed it up, he decided to call his best friend and see what she was doing for the evening. Since he had already started heading toward her house, he figured it would be a good idea to call ahead.

Pressing a button on the steering wheel, he said, "Genevieve," and the car's phone system dialed. He had tried to program it to take "Gen," as he usually called her, but it always seemed to get confused. He had toyed with programming it with her most hated nickname, "Pussycat," but decided it wouldn't be worth her wrath if she found out.

"Hello?"

"Hi, Gen, it's me."

"Hey, you. Long time, no talk. How's the case?"

Taylor swerved as another car tried to cut him off. He flashed the other driver an evil glance, then tapped the accelerator to push past her.

"I won it today, actually," he answered, focusing on Gen's question.

"Woo-hoo!" she exclaimed. "Go Taylor, Go Taylor! Why don't you sound excited about it?"

"I just broke up with Ryan."

There was a silence from the other end of the line.

"Gen?"

"Honey, you have got to work on your celebration technique. What happened?"

Taylor sighed. "We got the verdict right after lunch. I was in a mood to celebrate, so I thought I'd go home and change and be ready to take him out when he got in."

"Uh-huh," Gen prompted. Traffic was moving a little faster as the city receded in the rearview mirror.

"So, I walked in to find clothes all over the living room and Ryan all over some kid in the bedroom."

"Oh, God, not again," Gen said. She hadn't been thrilled when Taylor had let Ryan stay before, pointing out "once a cat pees on the carpet, he's likely to do it again." Taylor didn't love the analogy, but understood the thought. He hated that she was right.

"Yeah," Taylor confirmed.

"So what did you do?"

"The kid left and we had a fight. I told him I wanted him to get his stuff and be out by the end of the week."

"Good for you!" He could always count on Gen to support his decision, as long as it agreed with what she thought.

"I feel like crap."

"You'll get over it. This will be for the best, you'll see."

"Easy for you to say."

"Have I ever been wrong?" Taylor was forced to admit her track record was pretty good. "Where are you now?" Gen asked.

"Where do you think?"

"I'm guessing you and my car are about fifteen minutes away."

Taylor laughed. "Traffic sucks. I'm going with seventeen minutes."

"Fair enough. I'll be ready when you get here."

"Thanks, Gen."

She hung up the phone and the car disconnected the signal. Traffic had thinned down noticeably as Taylor got closer to "the sticks." He had grown up in the suburbs, but had moved to the city when attending law school. Ryan had insisted they stay in the city "because that's where all the guys are," and Taylor hadn't really cared. Gen had tried to get them to move out to the small town where she lived, even going so far as to point out the couple of other gay couples living around town. Ryan had no use for the Sticks and convinced Taylor to stay in the city. Naturally, boyfriend won out over best friend.

Naturally.

Three days later, they stood surveying the devastation. The flat was a mess. Taylor had stayed with Gen, slipping home briefly on Wednesday to collect some clothes and a few other items of interest, including Molly, who he did not trust Ryan to care for. On Wednesday, there had only been a couple boxes strewn here and there where Ryan packed his things. Saturday morning, the story was completely different. Gone were the sofa, the loveseat, the bed, several large pieces of furniture, the dining room table, the stereo, and most of the knick-knacks. Left were the leather chair, the TV (which was too heavy to lift easily), some of the guest room furniture, and a few odds and ends.

"Wow, he really cleaned out," Gen said, surveying the landscape.

Taylor only sighed.

"Was all that stuff his?"

"He's a med student," was all Taylor need say. "It's just stuff and stuff can be replaced…just like a cheating boyfriend."

"You can do without another cheating boyfriend," Gen said, walking into the kitchen. "Hey, he left your spice rack," she called over the bar into the living room. Taylor loved to cook and she had given him the Crate and Barrel spice rack for his birthday.

Taylor picked up the things Ryan had left on the floor, absently finding a place for them as he tried to tidy the room a bit. Molly went to her rug—also left behind—and stretched out in the sun, never one to be too concerned with human goings on.

Gen came back into the living room. "Looks like most of the dishes and pots and pans are still there."

"Yeah, he wasn't big on cooking," Taylor agreed. "He hated cleaning up the mess."

"What are you going to do?" she asked.

"I don't know. I've got money—I can put everything back for a couple grand. It's not a big deal." Taylor lowered himself to the big oriental run, leaving the chair free for Gen to take. Instead, she sat down on the rug across from him.

"Do you want to live here?" she asked.

Taylor stared at the floor, dejection on his face. No matter how hard he tried, he still felt rejected and betrayed, both by Ryan's cheating as well as the state of their shared space. If he was to be honest with himself, he would admit that living in a warehouse had never quite felt like home, but he'd always been able to overlook that fact by knowing Ryan would be there waiting for him. Without Ryan…

"I don't know," he said. "It's convenient to be ten minutes from the office. I can be to the clubs in about as long. It's a better investment than renting."

Gen looked him in the eye. "You spend too much time at the office, you hate clubs, and you don't have to rent to live somewhere else."

Taylor looked up, only slightly surprised by her characteristic directness. "I suppose you have a better idea?"

Pete and John helped carry the last of the boxes to the car. There had been no point in hiring movers, or even in renting a truck. Ryan hadn't left that much stuff. John's wife, Sandy, and Gen had packed the kitchen while Taylor, John, and Pete moved the few large things to Pete and John's two trucks. Pete's girlfriend, Anita, had stayed with the vehicles to make sure no one decided to help themselves to any of Taylor's stuff. Ryan had already done quite enough of that.

As the two guys wrestled the sideboard out the door, Taylor followed with two drawers full of clothes from the dresser. Pete grumbled from the lead while he walked backward toward the elevator and tried not to trip.

"Good thing you've still got a couple straight friends to do the heavy lifting," he called back to Taylor.

"Ha ha," Taylor replied. "You were the only guys available on short notice."

"We would have been happy to wait another week," Pete countered. For his complaining, Taylor knew he was only kidding. They had been friends since law school, when Taylor was still more or less in the closet. When he

had come out, Pete's only response had been, "duh," and they went out and
had a beer. They had seen each other through a series of x-friends, each
being there to consol the other when the relationship went south. Pete had
been with Anita for about a year and a half—a record for him—and long
enough that Anita remembered the first time Ryan had cheated, too.
Talking them into helping with the move had been easy.

"Watch the door, Petey," John called, returning their attention to the
task at hand. Like Taylor, John was an associate at the law firm and had
helped on the harassment case he had just won. They had met three years
ago when they both joined the firm shortly out of law school and had
become friends despite their differences. John was a corporate lawyer and
tended to see things from the side of the business rather than the person.
It made him an excellent balance to Taylor's more liberal leanings and
helped Taylor to understand what the defense was likely to use to counter
his arguments. John's wife had taken to Taylor immediately, enjoying his
fresh outlook as a change from the often stodgy lawyers John was around.

Pete dropped the sideboard down low enough to let it clear the elevator
doors, then they turned it on its side to fit it in the tight space. Taylor
enjoyed the irony, not for the first time, that the elevator in the converted
warehouse was barely big enough to move a piece of household furniture.
Continuing to balance the drawers, he reached out to touch the button to
lower them to the garage level.

"I still think you should've made him give your stuff back," John
repeated, continuing a "discussion" they'd started earlier in the day. "It
wasn't his and he had no right to take it."

"It's just stuff, John," Taylor said again. "It would have just reminded
me of him and I wouldn't have anywhere to put it anyway."

"You should at least make him pay for it. What kind of attorney are
you, anyway?"

"A liberal one," Taylor shot back.

"Damn straight," Pete said.

"I don't think so," Taylor countered.

They all laughed as the doors opened and Taylor felt glad. That was exactly what he wanted—to keep laughing and not let the world get him down. There was more to life than places and things and he was convinced there were still good people in the world. For a lawyer to believe that, he thought, he must be doing well.

Anita waited in the guest lot, next to the trucks and cars they were using to move Taylor's stuff. At Gen's insistence, they were moving his few remaining possessions to her house to store in her basement. Taylor would live there while he looked for a new place and sold the flat. Gen was one of the few women he would consent to live with because he knew she understood it was friendship only and that nothing would happen. She had broken up with her last boyfriend about six months before and had been taking it easy since then. He hoped her outlook would rub off on him and help him to relax in this post-Ryan world.

"How much is left?" Anita asked. Her raven black hair caught in the light breeze and blew away from her olive skin. She had been patiently staying with the cars while everyone else brought the boxes and other items for her to sort between them. They had decided her skill in packing was best put to trying to get everything in one trip. The fact that it let her spend a couple hours soaking up some sun didn't hurt, either.

"Two more drawers like these," Taylor said, "and a couple boxes from the kitchen. That should be it."

Pete and John loaded the sideboard up onto the truck while Anita put the drawers in the loaded back seat of Gen's Mazda. Taylor's Jag was already loaded down with the contents of several closets and some of the kitchen cupboards. Between the front seats of the two cars, there should be just enough room left for the remaining contents.

Sandy appeared carrying one large box while Gen had the other. Gen looked over to Taylor. "Those other drawers are it, kiddo," she said.

Taylor nodded. "I'll be right back, then," he said, walking back through the garage to the elevator.

Once in the flat, he took a moment to survey the space. Gen had left the cupboard doors open in the kitchen to allow them to confirm everything was removed. Taylor closed them all, stopping to give them each a final inspection. He repeated the process with the hall closets and the guest room. In his room, he stopped, looking around the vacant space. The finality of his decision hit him in that brief second. He was alone.

As he stood there, he saw not the image of Ryan's treachery, but of the happy times they had shared. He remembered the first time he had been in the room, its brilliant white walls and honey oak floors inviting him to call it a home. Living in the warehouse district, converted or not, never seemed homey, but when Ryan had stared at him expectantly, awaiting his response, only one response had been possible. Taylor was a new attorney, almost fresh out of law school at the time, and it had been tight. Ryan had basically no income, thanks to med school, so he had supported both of them for a time. Then, as cases brought income, they had been able to live more extravagantly, buying expensive furniture and expensive cars. Ryan's Range Rover had been vintage, but Taylor's Jag was brand new. It wasn't the most expensive Jag he could get, but it was still pricey. Ryan was almost done with his residency. In a few short months, he would be a full-blown doctor and would start work in the lucrative field of cosmetic surgery. He no longer needed Taylor, nor his pocketbook.

Still, when he looked, he saw the happy times—chasing each other around the apartment like kids, bringing home Molly and teaching her not to relieve herself on the hardwood floors, sitting cuddled together in front of the warm fireplace, making their own warmth later...

Gen rounded the corner, looking at him through the open door. He was standing in the middle of the bedroom, facing the door, the two drawers at his feet. She gauged the expression on his face, reading it for what it was.

"Ready to go?" she asked, pulling him from his reverie.

"Yeah, I suppose so," Taylor said, reaching for the drawers. Gen picked up one of them, leaving only one for him. Wordlessly, Taylor closed the closet doors, then followed her out, stopping only to activate the alarm and lock the door.

That evening, they sat at Gen's long dining room table, sharing a couple pizzas.

"Moving just isn't moving without pizza," Pete said through a mouthful of food.

"Aren't we supposed to be able to hire people to do this stuff for us?" John asked.

"We have to do something to stay strong and agile," Taylor said. "We can't just sit behind our desks all day."

"Yeah, do that and you'll wind up with a belly like Pete," Anita said, poking Pete in the gut.

"Hey!" he defended, poking her back.

"So, Gen, you ready to have a man in the house?" Sandy asked.

Gen laughed, nearly losing the mouthful of pizza she had. "Sandy, it's not a man, it's Taylor."

"Hey!" Taylor yelled, echoing Pete.

"I sometimes have that same feeling," Sandy agreed.

"Wait a minute!" John said, getting into the game. "We don't have to sit here and take this."

Sandy nodded. "You're right, you have to get up and do dishes."

John seemed about to argue, but realized the futility of such a decision as he met his wife's gaze. With a nod, he picked up the empty boxes and filled them with the discarded paper plates. Taylor collected the glasses and Pete followed with odds and ends from the table. The girls got up and made their way to the living room, waiting for the guy's return.

Gen's house was an old Victorian style, with spacious rooms that tended to flow together to make the space warm and inviting. The floors were all dark hardwood and her decorating style was an eclectic combination of Victorian, arts and crafts, and modern. Partly with Taylor's assistance, she had followed some of the more recent trends toward bold, rich colors on the walls, giving the rooms a lively, contemporary feel in balance with the classical styling.

The large living room had ample seating for the six weary movers as they enjoyed their first moments of relaxation after the busy day. The two couples had paired off while Gen and Taylor each took one of the comfy overstuffed chairs.

"City or country, Taylor?" Anita asked.

Taylor shook his head. "I don't know yet. I've gotten used to the pace of the city, but I'm originally from the 'burbs, so it wouldn't be a big stretch for me to get out of the city for a while."

"I'll have him planting fields in no time," Gen said. Her dark eyes flashed mischievously at him as she sat curled up like a cat in her chair. Her coffee brown fingers even had long white nails at the ends, curled as though claws ready to strike.

"The city isn't bad," John said, "but it is nice to drive away at night and leave it behind. Sandy and I lived in the city for a couple years and it was okay, but we enjoy the peace and quiet our neighborhood offers now. "

"There's just not a lot to do out here," Pete complained. "Most of the people I know who live out here wind up driving into town whenever they're bored. So, you trade peace and quiet for a lot of driving. I'd rather be able to just walk."

"That's only 'cause you don't drive a Jag," Sandy said. Pete shot her a look as they all laughed. Choosing to ignore her jab, he turned back to Taylor.

"Any bites on the flat?"

"A couple," he said. "The good news is the neighborhood has appreciated a lot since we moved in. Most of the surrounding buildings have been converted or are in the process now, so it's not like the one or two buildings there were when we moved in."

"It'll sell. Ironically, this is the best time of year to try to unload property. You'll be fine and you'll have more to choose from when you're ready to buy," John said, ever ready to examine the situation from a business perspective.

Sandy could see Taylor was getting tired. She turned to John, "Well, honey, we still have to drive ourselves home, so we'd probably best be going."

Anita picked up on the cue, turning to Pete. "I'm sure Gen and Taylor would like to finish unpacking. We should go, too."

The friends rose, following Taylor to the door. They shook hands and exchanged hugs and then they were gone. Silently, he closed the door and followed Gen back into the living room.

"Well," he said, "That's that."

"Honey, you'll be fine," she said, slipping more into her homegirl accent.

"You sure?"

"I promise."

CHAPTER TWO

A Bagel and Two Hot Crossed Buns. Hold the Bagel

Taylor awoke to a room bright with sunlight, awash with spring colors he didn't recognize, and a blond head resting on his stomach. Blinking, he pushed the sleep from his eyes to make sense of his surroundings. On second viewing, he saw the lime green and banana yellow color scheme Gen had chosen for her guest room. Sensing his return to the land of the living, the head rose and two amber eyes gazed down on him. Molly gave a small whimper, a reminder that, though she was a good dog, she wasn't a saint.

"Okay, Mol, we can go outside," Taylor sighed. His mouth was dry and tasted horrible and he felt the same call of nature as poor Molly. In a moment of pure selfishness, he went into the bathroom and saw to both problems.

Putting away his toothbrush, Taylor inspected his appearance in the mirror. Running his fingers through his hair, he managed to shift it around and eliminate the most obvious signs of bed head. His beard definitely needed a shave, but he decided it would make him look roguish for the morning. After all, aside from taking Molly for a walk, his only other pressing task was mowing the lawn.

The irony of needing to mow the lawn was not lost on him. The flat had no lawn—he hadn't mowed a lawn since he lived with his parents, the summer between undergrad and law school. Gen hadn't asked him to do anything but take care of his own messes as a part of his tenancy. He had insisted that he had to do more than give her the paltry rent she'd asked for, so she told him he could manage the lawn. He then immediately tried to think of a reason why he couldn't take care of the lawn, but nothing was forthcoming. Gen went on to point out that he could mow the lawn without his shirt and start working on that tan. Taylor decided to cut his losses and let the subject drop.

Molly sat politely outside the door, tail wagging just slightly. She had originally been Ryan's idea, but had bonded to Taylor immediately. He knew virtually nothing about caring for a dog, but learned fast. Fortunately, Molly was a patient teacher, rarely doing anything wrong and always there when he needed her. He tried to return the favor whenever possible. He pulled on an old T-shirt and shorts and once again stared into the amber eyes.

"Come on," Taylor said, and she took off down the stairs. Like his former home, Gen's house had hardwood floors covered in oriental rugs. He tried to walk softly to avoid waking her, but Molly's toenails still clicked here and there between carpets.

At the front door, she waited staring at the handle. Taylor double-checked, but it was still only seven-thirty. He hadn't made her wait any later than normal. Sliding his bare feet into an old pair of running shoes, he unlocked the door and stepped into the cool morning air.

For all the joking, mornings in a small town truly were better than in the city. It was quiet, peaceful, with no smog, no traffic. Gen had told him that he didn't have to lock the doors every time he left the house—her neighborhood was very safe and she knew all her neighbors. They would watch the house and let her know if anything suspicious happened.

Hooking the leash to Molly's collar, he led her to the part of the yard Gen had designated for "dog doody." She had a dog until about a year ago, so she was comfortable with their needs. And, she reasoned, since Taylor had to keep up the yard, he would keep up with withdrawing Molly's deposits.

Molly, possessing an unerring sense, realized this was her new spot and quickly took care of business. That done, she looked expectantly to Taylor, hope clearly visible on her face.

"Yeah, I'd kind of like to have a look around, too," Taylor agreed to the unspoken question. Molly immediately hopped up, pointed for the sidewalk. As one, they started walking, heading in the direction of "down town."

Taylor marveled at the picturesque community. He felt like he'd stepped back to the fifties, with humble houses set back from a tree-lined street, a couple blocks from a modest downtown of soda shops, restaurants, and a small theatre. Taylor was born in 1972. All he knew of the fifties was what he had seen on TV and in the movies, but this town was a dead ringer for it.

As he walked, he noticed some of the neighbors were also up and about on the early spring morning. A couple kids even chased each other as their dad washed his car in the driveway. All waved as they saw Molly and him, and he waved back. People rarely waved in the city, either too busy, too aloof, too indifferent, or just plain too wrapped up in their own concerns.

The two kids stopped their play long enough to run up to Molly. For her part, Molly had virtually no experience around children, but she accepted their frantic petting valiantly. Their dad stopped his washing and joined them at the end of the drive.

"Hi, I'm Rob," he said, holding out a hand.

"Taylor," he answered. "And this is Molly."

"Hi, Molly," the little girl said, continuing her petting.

Rob indicated the girl, saying, "This is my daughter, Amanda, and her friend, Sally. New in town?"

"Yeah," Taylor confirmed. "I'm living with my friend, Gen, for a while."

"Oh!" Rob exclaimed. "You're the guy with Jaguar. Nice car."

Taylor was momentarily confused that someone had taken note of his car. In his circles, it wasn't particularly noteworthy, other than he had opted for red where most had either silver, green, or blue. As he glanced up and down the street, however, he realized most of the driveways had American cars in them.

"Thanks," he said, at once proud and self-conscious.

"What do you do, Taylor?"

"I'm an employment lawyer," he answered, glad to be off the topic of the car.

"You work in the city?"

"Yeah."

"Cool. I'm in advertising. I work in the Morgan Stanley building. If you ever need a ride, let me know."

Taylor nodded and smiled. "Thanks, I'll remember that. Same for you."

"Cool. Where you headed this morning?"

He gestured to Molly, who had opted to lie on her side to allow both girls better access to scratch her belly. "We're just out for a walk to get the lay of the land."

"You're heading in the right direction," Rob confirmed. "Be sure to check out Downey's Bakery when you get downtown. Great way to start the morning."

Taylor nodded, ready to keep moving. "Thanks," he said. "Very nice to meet you."

"Likewise," Rob said, shaking his hand a second time. He turned to go back to his car while Molly got back to her feet, realizing the time for attention had passed. They resumed their walk, stopping two more times to meet other neighbors along the way.

By the time they got to Main Street, it was eight o'clock and they'd only walked four blocks. Taylor shook his head, still very much adjusting to the relaxed pace of the community.

Finding the bakery wasn't hard. Downtown was only four blocks long, and at eight a.m. on Sunday morning, the bakery and the church were the only places open. The church stood at the opposite end of the street, while the bakery was almost exactly in the middle on the other side. Self-consciously, Taylor looked for a crosswalk before realizing that there really wasn't one on the two-lane road.

There were two cars outside the bakery, but both patrons left as Taylor got to the door. He tied Molly's leash around a convenient light post, the swung open the old wooden screen door to enter the warm store.

The air outside was in the upper fifties to low sixties—warm enough that shorts were comfortable, cool enough that it was nice to be walking rather than standing still. The bakery was a good ten to fifteen degrees warmer, and the smells of fresh bread, donuts, and other baked goods permeated the humid air.

Behind the counter, a young man expertly hefted a tray of fresh bagels from a cart and dumped them into a waiting basket. Taylor watched as he carefully let the round rolls slide down just fast enough to clear the edge, but not bounce onto the floor. The tray empty, he put it back on the rack, then dusted his hands on his white apron where it covered his athletic gray T-shirt.

"Mornin'," he greeted warmly. "What can get I for ya?"

The breadth of the selection before him momentarily overwhelmed Taylor. Rolls, bagels, sticky buns, donuts, cakes, breads, sandwiches…he didn't know where to start.

"Uh, how about a wheat bagel and light cream cheese?" Taylor said, eyes still intent on the selection. A good start—healthy, easy on the waistline.

The guy quickly turned to pull a bagel from the appropriate basket and walked to the back of the bakery to retrieve some cream cheese. "Nice day out there, huh?" he said, making conversation. Taylor continued to be amazed by the friendliness of the people in the town.

"Yeah, looks like it'll be a great day," he agreed.

"Hope so. Some guys are talking about setting up a baseball game out on the field tonight."

"Sounds good," Taylor agreed absently, thinking he should bring something back for Gen, too.

Sliding the bagel and cheese into a small bag, the baker asked, "Anything else?"

"Yeah, I should get my friend Gen something," Taylor said, uncertainty in his voice as he looked between the sticky buns and the donuts. Gen never had to worry about her figure, eating virtually whatever she wanted with impunity.

"Gen Pouissant?" the guy asked.

Taylor realized he shouldn't be surprised that someone in the town would know Gen, both because the people here seemed so open and because Gen tended to get noticed wherever she went. "Yep, that Gen."

The guy on the other side of the counter broke into a broad lopsided smile and reach into one of the display cases to pull out a chocolate covered croissant. "Trust me, this is what she'll want," he said. "You can tell Pussycat I sent it to her."

"You're willing to take your life in your hands and call her that?" Taylor asked, genuinely surprised to hear someone else dare speak her most hated nickname.

"I'm her pusher. I keep her chocolate cravings satisfied," he said. Again, the lopsided smile crossing his face.

"I guess you're a valuable person to know," Taylor agreed.

"Probably so." He held out his hand over the glass display case. "Tom McEwan."

Taylor took the hand, answering, "Taylor Connolly."

"Pleased to meet you, Taylor," Tom said. "New to town?"

Taylor nodded. "Yeah. I'm staying with Gen for a while."

"Oh! You're the Jag guy. I saw you drive through yesterday."

Frowning in confusion, Taylor said, "My car seems to have gotten a lot of attention."

Tom smiled and shrugged. "We just don't see a lot of them around here. It's a small town—you'll get used to it."

"I'm trying," Taylor agreed.

"Let me get you a bag to put all that in," Tom said, returning to the back of the store again. As he did so, Taylor got a better look at him. The apron hid his athletic form, as the counter did his tan legs poking out from under khaki shorts. He was shorter than Taylor, maybe five-six or five-seven, with medium-brown hair cut short but not too short, and warm slate-gray eyes. His height, smooth skin, and lack of much of a beard made it hard to judge his age. Taylor realized his face was both tan and slightly flushed from the warmth of the bakery, but the way it lit when he smiled was thoroughly disarming. Taylor reminded himself he had only been apart from Ryan for less than a week and this was definitely *not* the time or place to be shopping for anything but baked goods.

Tom returned with a brown paper bag and handed it across the counter to Taylor.

"That's your dog outside, right?"

"Yeah," Taylor confirmed.

"I put a little something in there for her, too. Wouldn't do to send you home with stuff for you and Gen and leave her watching you eat."

"Thanks," Taylor said, genuinely surprised at the thoughtfulness. "What do I owe you?"

Tom shook his head, again flashing the smile. "This one's on me. Just tell Genny I said hi."

"You sure?" Taylor asked, uncomfortable with not paying.

"Yep. Go enjoy the day while you can. You can catch me on the next round."

"Okay," Taylor agreed, walking to the door. "Thanks again and nice to meet you."

"Same here," Tom said, smile still there. "See you 'round."

Taylor pushed open the door and walked back into the warming morning sun. Molly stood as she saw him and waited patiently while he untied her leash. As he turned to head back toward the house, he caught a glimpse of Tom again out of the corner of his eye. He had waited to watch as Taylor collected Molly, but turned back to the racks of bagels as Taylor walked away.

Making his way back to the house, Taylor waved to many of the same neighbors he had on the trip out. Make eye contact, say hello, go on about what you were doing. It seemed so simple, but escaped so many people. He found he really enjoyed it and had a smile permanently etched on his face by the time he pulled open the storm door to walk back in the house.

"Mornin'!" Gen called from the kitchen. As he hung Molly's leash on a nearby coat hook, Taylor returned the greeting, then removed his own shoes and padded into the kitchen.

Passing into the room, he found Gen looking about as good as he did, wearing a navy blue T-shirt and plaid pink pajama bottoms. Her eyes locked onto the bag as he set it on the table.

"Where have you been?" she asked expectantly.

"I took Mol for a walk and we went downtown," he said, using the novel name for the tiny town.

"You went to Downey's?"

"Yep. Quite a selection—lots of goodies to choose from."

No longer able to resist, she pulled open the bag. One of Taylor's favorite things about their friendship was the casual familial aspect and the lack of inhibition.

"Tom said to be sure to tell Pussycat hello," Taylor ventured, taking an unconscious step backward.

Gen actually laughed. "Leave it to Tommy," she said, smiling. She pulled her small bag from the larger one and retrieved its contents to a plate. "These are *the best* chocolate croissants you will ever eat."

"Are you going to let me try it?"

She momentarily glared at him, then reluctantly offered one *small* piece. Taylor, also addicted to chocolate, quickly appreciated the bittersweet flavor and smooth consistency. He made a mental note that he would have to go back to the bakery and get a croissant for himself, fat content be damned. And he *did* owe Tom for this morning's breakfast…

As Gen continued to scarf down her croissant, he reach into the bag and retrieved his much more healthy bagel and cheese. As an afterthought, he glanced into the bag again and found the other small package Tom had deposited at the bottom. Unwrapping it, Taylor found it contained three small dog biscuits. He gently set the paper and biscuits on the floor, where Molly quickly scarfed them up.

Gen watched the action with interest, her upturned eyebrows asking the obvious question.

"Tom saw her sitting outside, so he put a couple biscuits in the bag for her."

Gen nodded. "He's thoughtful like that." She looked as though she might have something else to add, but said nothing.

"So, how does he rate getting to call you Pussycat?"

Gen nearly choked as she took a long swig of milk from the glass she had poured upon seeing the croissant.

"We were having dinner one night about a year ago. We were discussing embarrassing nicknames we had been given in our youth. He finally managed to whittle mine out of me after one too many stiff drinks. Pussycat Pouissant. Certainly not an elegant variation, but then they never are."

Taylor nodded, unable to argue the point. "But you let him get away with using it?"

"Oh, he only uses it around people who already know. I'm sure once he figured out who you were, he knew it was okay."

"You've talked about me?"

"Only that you would be living here for a while. It's a small town."

"I'm learning that. Tell me, what was his nickname?"

Gen laughed out loud. "Oh no, I'm not going to open *that* can of worms. If you want that info, you'll have to get it right from the horse's mouth."

"Oh, come on, Pussycat…"

Gen's eyes narrowed dangerously. "Don't push it, Connolly. You may have brought me chocolate, but it only lasts so long."

They both laughed and Taylor smartly stuffed a big bite of wheat bagel into his mouth, stifling any further argument.

Though the lawn was fairly good sized, the mower still made relatively short work of it. The temperature had pushed into the low seventies, and the sun beat down from the cloudless sky. Taylor chose to follow Gen's suggestion and left his shirt hanging over the rail of the front porch while he let the sun help cure his winter whiteness. Even with the occasional chocolate binges and the stress of his relationship ending, Taylor managed to maintain a good, well-toned body and he realized it was something to be proud of.

Molly relaxed in the shade of the porch, wisely staying out of the grass until Taylor had a chance to clean up some of the clippings. Gen sat in the porch swing, enjoying her first iced tea of the season and the view of her friend's exertions. Though their friendship was platonic, it couldn't hurt to enjoy the view, she thought.

As he finished blowing the clippings from the sidewalk and driveway, Taylor cut the leaf blower and put it back in the garage. Walking up the steps, he recovered his T-shirt and pulled it on, falling into the swing next to Gen. She reached down to the floor beside her and retrieved a glass of iced tea for Taylor.

"Hear you go, honey," she said, holding out the glass.

"Thanks," Taylor breathed, catching his breath. Though he really hadn't had to exert himself, he also hadn't gotten a lot of exercise in recent weeks. He stifled a yawn as he looked out on the neighborhood in the warm afternoon sun.

"So, what do you think? Better than the city?" she asked, clearly indicating the neighborhood specifically and the town in general.

"I like it," Taylor said. "I'm still adjusting, but it's a welcome change."

"I think you could fit in here pretty well."

Taylor eyed Gen wearily. "Really? I'm not sure. I heard about my car no less than three times this morning. Everyone seems pretty taken with it."

Gen laughed. "It's just new. New and different always gets attention here. It doesn't last long, though. Something else comes along and yesterday's new thing is today's old thing. I was the new thing once, you know."

"You?" Taylor asked.

"Oh yes," Gen confirmed. "This town is very inviting, but not very diverse. When I moved here, I was one of the only black people and the only black person in the 'greater downtown' area. Everyone was pleasant, but it took them a little while to warm up to me."

"They seem okay now," Taylor said.

"Oh, they are now. It's been a while, you understand. That's what I mean. You're new now, but soon enough, you'll just be the guy with the Jag, among other things."

Taylor looked back out over the yard. "You think they're ready for other things?"

Gen nodded. "In that, you're not the first. There are several other gay couples around town, and probably a few more who manage to stay below the gossip radar. I'll have to introduce you to the people I do know, though."

Taylor was surprised. The idea of other gay people in the town went against his morning observations of the Ozzie and Harriet nature of the community. While he would be glad not to be the only person, it still had a contrary feeling.

"You're really pushing to keep me out here in the sticks, aren't you?" Taylor said with a sidelong grin.

"Just stacking the deck in my favor," Gen shot back.

Unsuccessfully trying to squelch a big yawn, Taylor downed the last of his iced tea and stood. "After my long day, I'm going to take a nap," he announced. Molly looked up at him, but made no effort to move, as did Gen.

"Have a good one," Gen said.

Taylor returned the glass to the kitchen, then made his way upstairs to his room. Gen had slipped into his room and made the bed, ever one to abhor disorder. His pillow, covered in a sky blue case, stood out against the greens and yellows of the room. For once, he didn't care, deciding it was *his* pillow and it didn't have to fit in. Sliding across the bed, he wrapped himself around the pillow and quickly fell asleep, the breeze of the warm afternoon blowing softly over his back.

He awoke to the visage of two golden eyes staring directly at him. He jumped in spite of himself, slowly pushing back from Molly's persistent gaze. Dusk had set in and she was no doubt ready for an evening walk.

A quick glance to the clock told him it was seven-thirty. Gen had mentioned she was going to the store and the relative quiet of the house told him she was probably already gone.

Pushing himself up, he returned his pillow to the head of the bed and straightened the covers. Molly rose expectantly, tail wagging. Running a hand over the scruff on his cheeks, he turned to her and said, "Give me five minutes."

The steam from the shower felt wonderful, but Taylor knew better than to give in to it with Molly waiting outside. Quickly, he scraped away the whiskers and ran some soap through his hair. With a rinse, he stepped out and pulled on his clothes. Running a hand through his hair, he decided it was good enough to take Molly on her walk and left the bathroom.

She again stood, though a little less eagerly than before. Whoever thought dogs couldn't communicate had never met Molly—her message was obvious: can we go *now*?

Taylor donned a pair of running shoes, then led the way to the front door. He'd pretty much given up on running, but they were still the best for walking. He'd learned the hard way the value of wearing good shoes, especially on the uneven streets of the city.

Dusk was the dinner hour for the small community. As Taylor walked toward downtown, he found everyone in their houses or glimpses of them sitting on wooden decks behind the house. He didn't mind the more peaceful walk, as it gave him a chance to consider his own situation.

He'd been able to more or less avoid thinking about Ryan for the past week while the move occurred. Gen had done a brilliant job of providing distractions, keeping him busy around the house, around town, and generally wherever she could cook up something to do. Several of his other friends had given him a hard time about moving to the sticks, but they had all made plans to come and visit, too. Having grown up in the Midwest, a half hour drive hardly seemed like anything to Taylor, but he understood how those used to the convenience of minutes in the city might be intimidated.

The images of Ryan and the kid were still there, but thankfully, had started to become blurry. A few more weeks and he might be able to forget altogether. Maybe.

Their relationship had always been tumultuous. Taylor had met Ryan as an undergrad. Neither of them was out and both pretended to lead "normal" lives. Shortly after graduation, Ryan had announced he was gay and he wasn't going to hide it anymore. He had looked at Taylor expectantly, but Taylor had been unable to bring himself to say the words. Ryan went on, spending virtually all of his free time going from one bar to the next. Fortunately, he had the good sense to be safe about it, but it definitely wasn't the lifestyle for Taylor.

They lost touch for a couple years, during which time Taylor came to grips with who he was and wafted in and out of several unsuccessful relationships. They ran into each other by accident one afternoon while Taylor sat at an outdoor eatery waiting for a friend to join him for lunch. Ryan was walking by on the street and happened to look down at just the right moment to catch Taylor's eye. They talked for a couple minutes until Taylor's friend arrived, then exchanged numbers. To Taylor's surprise, Ryan called that night to see if he wanted to get together.

The time that followed was like a whirlwind and still brought a smile to Taylor's face. They were both poor, he nearing the end of law school and Ryan continuing on in med school, but they still managed to eek out a life, finding the cheapest possible way to still have fun. When he graduated law school, they decided to get a place together and found the flat. It was more Ryan's idea, but Taylor would have lived virtually anywhere to be with him. All he had ever wanted was to find someone to be with and Ryan seemed to feel the same way.

It lasted for about a year. Then, shortly before the holidays, Taylor noticed Ryan grow more and more distant. Where their relationship had always been carefree and happy, Ryan became broody and sullen, claiming everything was fine, but rarely smiling or initiating contact with Taylor. Suddenly, his cell phone, which he never used a lot, rang much more often and he always had to "call back later." Taylor wondered if something was going on, and had it confirmed when a note fell out of the laundry one night.

Ryan never really bothered to deny the relationship, but promised it would end. Taylor was devastated. He had always believed trust was the only thing he could really offer and it was the only thing he could ever truly hate having broken. They spent several tense weeks while Ryan convinced him he truly was sorry and it wouldn't happen again.

Another year and a few months passed and then Taylor got the big discrimination case. All of a sudden, he wouldn't get home until late and had to disappear out the door early to be gone again all day. At first, Ryan seemed okay with it, but then the same distance reasserted itself and Taylor knew trouble was brewing. He just hadn't expected it to be so obvious.

The truth was, even after what had happened, he missed Ryan. That was probably the most unfair thing—he had done nothing wrong, but he had to take the action and he had to live with the disappointment. Even now, he realized Ryan would just go out and find himself someone else to be with—maybe even the Kid. Taylor would be the one to carry around the pain.

Without even noticing it, they had reached the town and walked one side of the street. Traffic remained very light, so he led Molly across to the other side to walk back. A couple of restaurants had their doors open and he heard the eager conversations going on inside. Several even appeared equipped for outdoor dining, but they didn't have it setup yet.

He passed the bakery, smelling the telltale yeast of tomorrow's goods already rising. What a great way to tempt people to come back, he thought to himself, seeing the empty shelves that would be full in a few hours. Even at this hour, several people moved around arranging things for the coming day. Neither of them was Tom, so Taylor never broke stride.

There was an alley beside the bakery. It was nearly dark, so all Taylor could make out was a dumpster around the corner, but nothing else. He picked up the sidewalk again on the other side, passing a used bookstore.

"Taylor!"

He stopped, hearing the voice behind him. Molly heard the voice as well and back stepped to stand at his side. From inside the alley, Tom appeared, carrying a bat and mitt. He wore a gray T-shirt and denim shorts, with a worn white ball cap on his head.

"Out again?" he asked.

Taylor nodded. "It's a nice night and she likes to walk whenever we have time."

"I was just heading down to the ball field," Tom explained. "It's just a casual game. Care to join us?"

"I don't really play," Taylor said.

Tom nodded understanding. "You wanna just come watch? It'll give you a chance to meet some of the other people our age around here."

For the second time, Taylor wondered how old Tom was. He was almost thirty, but his fair complexion made him look younger. He wondered if Tom suffered from the same thing, along with his shorter stature. He realized he really had nothing else to do for the evening and it *was* nice out.

"Yeah, I'd like that," he said, heading back in the opposite direction.

Main Street led down toward a small river. Just before the river was the fire station, probably originally positioned for the easy access to a water source. A bridge connected the two shores. The other side held a good-sized park, complete with baseball diamond.

Tom led the way onto the field, stopping at the bleachers where everyone was gathered. As promised, there were a bunch of guys and several girls, some playing, some watching. Tom introduced them, though Taylor quickly lost track of who was who. The only person he recognized was Rob from down the street, who he had met that morning.

Under the bright lights of the field, they started the game. Tom was first up to bat. Even though they were only having a "friendly game," Taylor saw the teams were evenly divided and had something approaching colors. Tom's team wore light shirts—grays and whites—while the others were in blues and blacks. It helped him to tell the difference.

As Taylor watched, he once again wondered about this guy he had just met that morning. He reminded himself that the people of this town were inordinately friendly and he might just be a nice guy trying to help the new guy meet people.

As Tom lined up for the pitch, he glanced quickly at the bleachers and Taylor saw him make eye contact. The crooked smile appeared again and he cracked bat against ball, sending a pop fly to center field. Running to save his life, he made it to second base, where he stopped, waiting for the next move.

CHAPTER THREE

Meeting Faith

"Hey, do you have time to run to the store?" Gen called up the stairs.

Taylor walked out of his bathroom just in time to catch her call from the landing.

"Yeah, I can go. What do you need?"

"I left a list on the fridge. You're a lifesaver. I'll be back this afternoon!"

"See ya," Taylor said, hearing the door slam shut behind her.

Shaking his head, he picked up the clothes he had left on the bed and threw them in the hamper. For once, Molly wasn't skulking near the bed, so he guessed Gen had already seen to her morning needs.

The week had gone by with stunning speed. As he expected, Taylor was now the new rising star in the employment discrimination field and the firm had been inundated with calls from other people who felt they had a case. He was glad for the work, but it left him feeling bone tired when he finally made his way out to Gen's each night. Even though he felt like he should do something social last night, he had finally admitted to himself all he really wanted to do was crawl between the sheets and read a good book. He'd made it to eleven o'clock.

Fortunately, his social life wasn't a complete disaster—Gen was seeing to that. She had insisted that they needed to have a small gathering for some of their friends. Taylor had reluctantly agreed, not sure he was ready for a major social event. And no matter what Gen said about it being small, it would be a major social event.

He headed down to the kitchen, interested to see just how small the gathering would be. Pulling the list from under the magnet of Lucille Ball stuffing her mouth with chocolates, he unfolded the sheet. He leaned against the refrigerator to allow it to support him.

Cheese—mozz., ched (orange), jack; green and red grapes, cantaloupe, three boxes of crackers (the baked kind); Velveeta and picante sauce (mild), tortilla chips; beer, Pepsi (reg. and diet); Bailey's, Skyy (2), Kahlua, orange juice, champagne; three lbs. boneless chx. breast; white rice (instant okay), green leaf lettuce, apples, raisons; yellow cake mix, milk choc. frosting (not whipped!), brownie mix, vanilla i.c.; dinner rolls from Downey's.

Taylor wondered which Army division Gen had invited over for the evening. On his best day, he would barely make a dent in that menu, but he knew better than to argue. The last item on the list caught his attention—he hadn't seen Tom McEwan since the game on Sunday evening. He had joined them at a local bar for after game drinks, but really hadn't gotten to talk to Tom much more and ultimately had to head back before it got too late.

Taylor was still conflicted on what the situation with Tom might be. There was no question he was friendly and clearly appreciated Taylor being at the game. The invitation had been more than merely polite—he had taken a couple chances during the game to stop up and make sure Taylor was enjoying himself. At the same time, he hadn't called or dropped by, and Taylor still knew virtually nothing about him except he dumped bagels into a basket with great aplomb.

Shaking himself from his reverie, he patted Molly, then headed out the back door to the detached garage where he and Gen had made enough room to park his Jag. It was about eight-thirty on Saturday morning. Even Taylor knew enough about grocery shopping to know it was better to go early and beat the crowds than to wait even another half hour. He resolved he'd stop at the bakery on his way back from the supermarket.

The red Jaguar backed out of the garage as though it had lived there for years, slowing only to make sure none of the neighbor kids were up riding their bikes on the sidewalks yet before backing into the street.

The supermarket, Safeway, was in the "new section" of town, the other side of the neighborhood from downtown. The planners had decided it would be less obtrusive and invasive to locate it out near the freeway, rather than taking away from the scenic beauty of the town proper. Taylor saw no reason to argue their logic. The city's seeming endless urban sprawl was reaching out toward the smaller towns a few miles distant and slowly sucking them in. Keeping the development nearer the freeway would hopefully help deflect the downtown from being absorbed in the megapolis so near and so far from them.

As always, Taylor's car drew attention as he skillfully navigated the streets, making him feel self-conscious. Though there were plenty of affluent residents in the town (Gen being a prime example), few seemed inclined to have fancy cars. Though Taylor made a point of driving carefully, he knew there was little he could do to avoid notice.

Pulling into the Safeway parking lot, he took the first spot he saw, which also happened to be second from the front. As he got out, several women turned to see who was driving the car that had become the talk of the town. He flashed them a self-conscious smile and said, "Good morning." He grabbed the handle of a shopping cart, both steering it away from his bumper and commandeering it to collect Gen's list.

Gen had brought him to the store when he first moved out, helping him get some of the food items he wanted for himself. It was the only other time he'd been in the store. As he'd hoped, the place was not yet busy, so he opted to just walk every aisle, learning the layout and appearing a little less lost about where everything was.

As he maneuvered the shopping cart around the end of one aisle, he slammed into another cart, jolting him from thoughts of what else he needed to do to prepare for the party.

"Excuse me," he said, genuinely embarrassed.

"Oh!" the woman exclaimed, apparently having been elsewhere as well. "My fault—no need to apologize."

"I wasn't paying attention," Taylor admitted.

She smiled warmly, looking directly at him. "That's okay," she said. "Hey, aren't you the Jag Guy?"

The way she said it, Taylor mentally saw the words in capitals, like it was a title. "Yeah, that's my car."

"Nice car," she said. "That must make you Gen's friend."

Again, Taylor was not surprised in the least that someone else already knew about him. There was no doubt it was a small town. "Yep, that's me. Taylor Connolly," he introduced.

"Hi, Taylor. I'm Faith. Faith Roberts." She held out a slender hand, never taking her eyes from Taylor's face.

"A pleasure to bump into you," he said and they both laughed.

"So," she continued, "You're new in town, huh? How long have you and Gen known each other?"

"We've been friends since undergrad," Taylor explained. "She's helping me out while I find a place to live."

Faith nodded. "Oh, so you're just friends?"

Taylor blushed slightly at the implication that he would be dating Gen. "Yeah, just friends. Roomies."

"How nice for both of you," Faith said. "What do you think of our little town?"

Taylor smiled. "I really like it, actually. It's a great change from the city."

"You were living in the city," Faith remarked, both a question and a statement. "Did you live alone?"

"No, I had a roommate there, too," Taylor said, not willing to volunteer too much information. "And my dog, Molly."

Faith smiled. Her dark blue eyes were like sensor probes from behind her gold-rimmed glasses. "What a nice name for a dog. What kind is she?"

"Golden Retriever. She's a really great dog."

"So, what brought you out here?"

Taylor thought for a moment, deciding how to answer the question. "My roommate had to move away. I didn't want to live alone in the city."

"Understandable," Faith agreed. "Well, I shouldn't tie you up; I'm sure you have a lot to do. Maybe we'll run into each other again soon."

Taylor caught the pun and laughed easily. "I hope so," he said, turning his cart away. "Have a good morning," he said, heading down the next aisle.

"You, too," Faith said, successfully piloting her own cart down the aisle he had just left.

Taylor shook his head, replaying the conversation in his mind. He definitely felt like he'd been debriefed under the guise of a casual conversation, but that was okay. He'd revealed what he felt comfortable with while keeping other aspects of his life to himself. While no longer "in the closet," he'd never felt it necessary to advertise his personal life to everyone he met. Ryan had tried to get him to put a rainbow sticker on the Jag when he got it and Taylor had turned the idea down in no uncertain terms. "Who I sleep with is hardly something I need to advertise on the bumper of my car," he'd said, ending the discussion. Ryan had put one of the more subtle elongated stickers across the back window of his Range Rover and Taylor had said nothing. He didn't really care what other people did, as long as he was comfortable with his own life.

Taking care not to run into any other shoppers, he finished collecting what he could of the list. Several items required a second pass on a couple of aisles, but he collected everything Gen wanted, save the dinner rolls from Downey's. As he headed for the checkout, he saw Faith standing in one of the lines farther down. He decided he didn't feel like answering any more questions, and so took a slightly longer line at the other end of the store, feigning interest in a copy of Better Homes and Gardens. To his surprise, the issue dealt with "the 30 best chocolate recipes for French Pastries." Thumbing through, he realized several would be ideas Gen would enjoy, so he deftly tossed it on the conveyer when his turn came. Chocolate really was a great way to keep Gen happy, and he liked it, too.

While he waited for the checkout girl to scan his items, Faith pushed her cart down the aisle in his direction. He mentally prepared himself for more questions, while offering a casual smile and a nod of recognition. She raised her eyebrows at the size of his order.

"You guys like to cook, huh?"

"Yeah, we're both into it a little," Taylor said, smartly sidestepping the fact that it was for a party they were having that night.

"Sounds good," she said. "I'm a big cook myself. Anyway, have a great day, Taylor. Say Hi to Gen."

"Thanks, I will," he said, watching her walk off to the door.

"You're Gen's friend?" the girl at the register asked.

"Yeah," Taylor answered.

"The one with the Jag?"

Taylor's attention shot up from the counter to look her evenly in the eye. He didn't speak for a second, then said, "Yeah, the one with the Jag."

"Great car," she observed, swiping the last of the groceries over the laser.

"Thanks," he said, hoping his lack of conversation would cause the conversation to drop.

"You know Faith, too, huh? Looking for a house?" She swiped his credit card, waiting for the machine to spit out a receipt.

"A house?" Taylor asked, confused.

The girl looked back, hand reaching for the receipt. "Yeah. She's one of the best realtors in town."

"Oh," Taylor said, making a mental note. "I hadn't realized that. I just ran into her—literally!"

"How 'bout that. Well, if you decide to look for a house, she'd be the right person to talk to," the girl said. Taylor took a moment to note her name, "Suzy," on her badge.

He signed the slip, handing it back to her along with the pen she'd given him. "Thanks for the tip, Suzy," he said, using her name. "Have a great day."

"You too, Taylor," she said, telling him that she'd caught his name, too, either from Faith's comment or from his credit card.

Feeling even more like the center of attention, he pushed his cart away, walking the proverbial green mile to the exit at the other end, outside which sat the car that had gained him so much attention. As he walked, he caught the gazes of several other women in his peripheral vision and heard their whispered comments after him. He grinned a bit at his inner secret, but also cringed at the idea that he might be the new most eligible bachelor in town. The thought reminded him that he needed to stop at the bakery on his way home…and hopefully get to say hi to Tom again.

The easiest way to the bakery was essentially to go back the way he had come. So, Taylor stopped off at the house and dropped off the groceries he had collected, putting the perishables in the refrigerator. Gen still wasn't back, so he got back in his car and headed up the street.

It was just after ten and town was getting busier. Most of the businesses opened their doors around that time and the warm sun again had people eager to be active. Ten was a little late for a bakery, though, so there were plenty of spots open in front. Taylor pulled up right in front of the door, turned the car off and went inside.

Several other people were already in the store. He hung back, waiting while Tom and a girl helped them. Tom noticed him immediately and gave him a short nod while he closed and folded the bag of bagels he had prepared. The lady handed him a twenty and he handed back the change.

One other person was ahead of Taylor, so he busied himself looking around the store. He had only been in one other time and hadn't paid much attention. Now he noticed the pictures of various scenes around town, a few he even recognized, various patrons, some little league teams…one of the more recent pictures caught his attention. There, next to a bunch of kids he judged to be ten years old or so, was Tom.

"Sir?"

Taylor didn't pay attention to the girl's voice as he looked closely at the picture of the team. Sure enough, Tom stood there in a red jersey, smiling with the rest of the group.

"Can I help you, sir?"

The second time, he realized she was speaking to him and turned back to face her. Tom had noticed his close attention to the picture and the smile was back.

Before he could speak, Tom turned to the girl. "That's okay, Emmy, I'll help Taylor. Go ahead and pull that last batch of bread out, okay?"

"Sure, Tom," she said. Taylor guessed her to be about fifteen. She turned back to Taylor, eyes bright and said, "Tom will be right with you, sir." She held his gaze a moment longer, then turned and headed to the back, ponytail swaying behind her.

Tom handed back the change to the woman ahead of Taylor, saying, "Here you go, Mrs. Jensen. You have a great day."

She thanked him, calling him Tommy, then excused herself around Taylor with a bright smile. As the screen pulled shut behind her, Taylor stepped up the counter.

"How are you today?" Tom asked, smile broadening.

Taylor felt his old confusion, but stifled it in favor of staying upbeat. "I'm great, how are you?"

"Real good, thanks," Tom answered. He gestured to the picture that had held Taylor's attention. "I see you found the picture. That's last year's little league team. We won the county championship," he said proudly. "I coach them Tuesdays and Thursdays."

That helped explain why Taylor hadn't seen him around. "You must be a good coach. You sure did well last Sunday."

Tom shrugged self-consciously. "It just takes practice. You should come by sometime and I'll have you playing like a pro in no time."

Taylor turned back around. "Sounds like fun."

"We're playing again tomorrow night, too. You're welcome to bring Molly down again."

"Sounds good."

Tom nodded. "I'm guessing you didn't just stop by to talk baseball. What can I get for you?"

Yes, I did, Taylor thought. "Gen wants two dozen dinner rolls."

"Two dozen!" Tom exclaimed. "Having a party?"

Blink! went the light over Taylor's head. "Yeah, we are—tonight. Care to come by?"

Tom looked genuinely disappointed. "I wish I could. I'm getting together with my study group tonight. We have a big exam on Monday."

"Exam?" Taylor asked. Uh-oh, maybe he was younger than he thought.

"Yeah, I'm wrapping up my teaching cert over at the college. I got my bachelor's in English, but there isn't a lot of work for a writer around here and I'm not ready to move to a city." He put the two bags of rolls in a paper grocery bag. As an afterthought, he tossed a couple other things in with them. Taylor didn't catch what had gone in the bag, but he suspected it would be good.

"That's cool," Taylor said, again unsure of how old Tom was.

"We could hang out later in the week, though. Maybe you'd like to have the kids teach you how to hit a ball."

"How old are they, ten?"

"Around that," Tom confirmed, setting the bag on the counter.

"They'd make me look silly."

"You're only silly if you feel silly," he philosophized.

Taylor sighed. How could he turn down an invitation? It wasn't exactly a date, with twelve ten year-olds there, but it was better than nothing. "Okay," he said simply.

"Okay," Tom said, smiling back. "Six o'clock Tuesday evening at the same diamond we play on."

"It'll give me an excuse to leave work at a reasonable hour."

"See? I'm helping you out."

"I'm sure," Taylor deadpanned. "How much?" he asked, gesturing to the bag.

Tom made a show of looking inside, like he didn't know what was there. "Let's see…two bags…two bucks?"

"For real," Taylor said.

"A buck?"

He threw a ten on the counter. "You can catch me next time," he said, returning the smile.

"Taylor, that's too much," he argued.

"You're a hungry college student," Taylor said, backing out the door. "Buy a pizza!"

"See you tomorrow," Tom said.

"Where do you want to meet?"

"You can come here. My apartment is upstairs. Seven-thirty."

"I'll be there," Taylor said and let the screen close behind him.

He felt almost giddy as he set the bag in the passenger seat and pulled the door closed behind him. He'd left the sunroof open, as usual, so the seat was almost burning hot. Inserting the key in the ignition, he saw Tom's smile as he agreed to come over tomorrow and Tuesday. It was a feeling he hadn't had in a long time and he hoped it lasted.

This time when he walked in the kitchen, Gen was hard at work starting preparations for the food. She had her Cuisinart on the counter and was pouring olive oil into some mixture that appeared to include some of the apples, judging from the peels.

"Hi there," she greeted warmly. "Back from the bakery?" she asked, noting the bag.

"I got the rolls," Taylor said, setting the bag on the table. He could barely contain his curiosity to see what else Tom had put in the bag. He hadn't wanted to look in the car—too obvious. Reaching in, he set the rolls on the counter, then looked to see what else was there. As expected, there was a croissant for Gen. He nearly cheered as he saw another chocolate croissant along with what looked like a cheese croissant and some biscuits for Molly.

Gen turned off the Cuisinart, looking over her shoulder to see what Taylor was doing. "Tommy sent home some samples, huh?"

"Chocolate," Taylor said simply.

"He's such a good pusher," she said. "He knows how to keep us coming back."

Taylor wanted to say he thought it might be a little more than chocolate, but held his tongue. He really had no idea the situation between Gen and Tom and he didn't want to say something he'd regret later.

"I ran into Mel Grady at the drug store," Gen said. "She said you met Faith Roberts this morning."

Taylor's eyes widened. This town's grapevine had to be wired with optical cable for the speed rumors traveled.

"I met her at Safeway, about an hour ago."

"Small town, kiddo," Gen said, laughing. "Faith is a good person and a good friend. If you do decide to settle down here, she'll be the person to find you a place. A word of warning, though, she's also probably the town's most eligible bachelorette."

"I got that impression," Taylor admitted.

"We'll avoid inviting her to dinner for a while."

Taylor groaned. "It's almost like coming out all over again."

That brought even more laughter from Gen. "Honey, don't worry about it. Like I told you, you're not the first here. It'll work out."

She turned back to her work, pouring the contents of the Cuisinart into a bowl.

"What've you got there?" Taylor asked.

"Apple dressing."

"For the salad?"

"Yep. One of the tastiest salads I've ever had—greens, apple slices, raisons, walnuts, and an apple vinaigrette. Mmm, mmm, good."

"May I?" Taylor asked, gesturing to the bowl. She picked up a spoon and gave him a small sample.

"Wow," he agreed.

"Did you *expect* any less?" she asked, moving her head with *attitude*.

"No, ma'am," he said.

"Now, take your croissant and get that lawn squared away, mister. I'm gonna need you in the kitchen this afternoon."

"Yes, ma'am," Taylor said. Gen nodded with mock authority, then turned to the next cooking task. He slipped up the back stairs to his room, changed, then went back out into the warming late morning sun.

Gen's chicken rice and vegetables was a hit—no one left a spec of food on his or her plate. She had opted to only bake the cake, and the ravenous group made short work of it, then helped clean the kitchen. Afterward, they retired to the living room, enjoying Gen's selection of classical blues music in the relaxing glow of a couple lamps and several candles.

"I'm not sure I'm going to be able to move to go home," Pete moaned from one of the chairs. Anita sat on the floor in front of him, resting her head on his knee.

"Don't look for any help from me," she said.

"No one ever leave's Gen's hungry," Sean observed.

"Sean may have to sleep in the guest room tonight," Matt, his boyfriend, commented from the table where he sat playing cards with Gen, and two other dinner guests, Chad and Mike. Catcalls came from around the room.

"Good luck, Mattie," he said.

"I don't know, Sean," Chad interjected. "Matt spent a lot of time in the con queso. You might be safer a ways away."

Taylor sat in the other chair, next to Pete, quietly observing his friends' interaction. He had always prided himself on having a diverse group of friends who all enjoyed being around each other as much as around him.

As though sensing his reflective mood, John spoke from his position in front of Sandy on the floor in front of the couch.

"Still enjoying the sticks?" he asked.

Taylor laughed. "So far, so good. Gen is bound and determined to convert me."

"How will you ever meet anybody?" Chad asked.

"Gen assures me the town isn't completely dry."

Sandy looked up from where she had been massaging John's shoulders. "That reminds me—I met a guy the other day who you might be interested in."

"Oh?" Taylor asked.

"He's just wrapping a Master's in advertising and marketing. We're bringing him into an associate position at the firm. He looks like a mover and shaker from what I've seen of his work."

Taylor looked down, thinking of Tom…and Ryan. "I'm not sure I'm in the market yet," he said.

Gen watched him from the far end of the table, but said nothing.

"Well, keep it in mind," Sandy said. "I'd be happy to set something up."

"You might have to come back down to the city, though," John piped up.

Taylor laughed. "I'm still there every day, remember," he said.

"I hear you've been getting a lot of business," Pete observed.

"Not the business he needs to be getting," Chad said over his cards.

"Just 'cause you're frustrated doesn't mean everyone is," Mike said, snapping him around.

"At least my boyfriend didn't stand me up to go to *Canada*."

"At least I have a boyfriend to stand me up," Mike fired back.

Taylor watched the discourse with amusement, but turned back to Pete. "And, *yes*, I've pulled in some new business, Petey."

"I knew I should have done something different," Pete said. "Property law just isn't that lucrative."

"It'll work out," Taylor said.

As the last of the group made their way out the door, Taylor let it close slowly behind them. Thankfully, a combination of gay men and straight women lent itself nicely to leaving the place in pretty good shape. He and Gen picked up the remaining items and carried them off to the kitchen. Taylor let Molly in the back door. She had, as usual, been the model of good behavior, never begging or causing trouble. She had spent most of the evening in the kitchen, sitting patiently in front of the doorwall.

"That was fun," Taylor said.

"Always is," Gen said, putting the last of the dishes in the dishwasher.

"They're quite a group, aren't they?"

"*We're* quite a group," she corrected. "You're not getting out of this group."

"True," Taylor agreed, closing the back door.

"How are you feeling?"

He turned to face her, caught off guard by the question.

"What do you mean?"

"I mean, how are you feeling? Since you've been here, you haven't said a whole lot about your feelings. You just broke up with a long-term boyfriend. How are you doing?"

While Gen was always compassionate, he hadn't expected her to broach the subject—at least, not yet.

"I'm okay. It's a process, you know."

Gen nodded. "Yeah, I do know, but I've been around the block a couple more times than you."

"I'll be okay."

Again, she nodded. "Just don't retreat too far. I know you're not a big dater, but it won't hurt to take people up on offers now and then. You should consider getting together with Sandy's friend and her and John."

"I'll consider it. I'm just not ready yet."

Gen smiled, turning off the light and leading the way to the stairs. "Just don't wait too long. He's not going to feel the pain like you do and putting the pain on yourself isn't going to fix anything. It's just going to cause you harm. The sooner you get past it, the better for you."

Taylor said nothing, accepting the advice and concern for what it was. He knew Gen cared. Gen had always cared—that was why he always went to her first. From his travels about town, he was getting the impression more and more that she treated everyone that way and he had immense respect for that. Gen was truly his best friend and he knew it.

At the top of the stairs, they parted ways and went to their separate rooms. Molly followed him, but didn't come in the room, opting to stretch out on the floor outside the door where she could monitor both rooms. Taylor left his door ajar in case she changed her mind, then turned the light off. After seeing to his evening bathroom responsibilities, he pulled back the covers and lay on the soft sheets of the bed.

Though it was only mid-April, they were enjoying unseasonably warm weather and he took the opportunity to sleep on top the covers. The night had been good and he was glad to have seen everyone, but in some ways, it had created more questions than it answered.

He knew why he wasn't interested in Sandy's offer—he already had someone who he was interested in. The question was whether that person was interested in him. His instincts said yes, but he'd been wrong before. He wasn't even sure if Tom was gay…and he had a track record of being attracted to straight men, too.

He'd heard stories about rebound relationships. Maybe he should tell Gen about Tom. He didn't want Tom to be a rebound relationship, no matter what.

For tonight, though, it was late and it was time for him to get some rest. He had two...meetings...set up with Tom in the next few days. Surely the situation would start to resolve itself one way or another in that time. In the meantime, his only immediate responsibility was getting some sleep. As the darkness surrounded him, he saw Tom's smiling face...and he smiled back.

Chapter Four

A Hit and a Miss . . .

The back door opened slowly as Gen hesitantly peeked inside.

"Taylor, are you home?" she asked, uncertainty in her voice.

"Yeah, I'm in the living room," Taylor called, getting up to join her in the kitchen.

"You're home early for a Tuesday afternoon," she said as he took a big gulp of his glass of water. "Big date?"

Taylor choked, water dripping down his chin and onto the dark green T-shirt he was wearing. He reached out with his left hand to catch most of it.

"I'm going to play baseball," he said, giving Gen a dirty look.

"With whom?" Gen asked, voice incredulous.

"Tom McEwan, from the bakery," Taylor answered, shaking his hand in the sink to dry it as he reached for a towel.

"Honey, baseball is a *sport*," Gen said.

"I know that," the slightest hint of irritation in his voice as he dried himself off.

"Okay, just making sure. I didn't want you to be confused and expect it to be—"

"Gen!"

"Okay, okay, you know it's a sport..." She set her bag down on the table, turning to pull some orange juice from the fridge. "I've just never known you to play sports."

"I won two track awards..." She looked over her glass at him. "...in high school."

"Exactly."

"The point is to teach me, anyway. It's just Tom and a bunch of ten year-olds."

"And the point of you learning to play?"

Taylor squirmed under her unwavering gaze. She smiled and looked away.

"Right. Have a good time. I'll leave a light on for you." Chuckling to some inner joke, she got up, picked up the briefcase and made her way up the back stairs.

Taylor grimaced, realizing the cat was pretty much out of the bag. One of the reasons he and Gen were so close was they could virtually read each others' minds. He knew she knew he was interested in Tom and she knew he knew she knew...and he stopped right there, before he got a headache.

Another thought occurred to him. For all the time he had known Tom, he hadn't actually openly admitted to himself that he was interested in him. How could he be interested? He barely knew him. Yet, once the thought had passed, it was impossible to recall.

A glance to the clock on the stove said the time was five fifty-two. No time to walk now, he'd have to drive...the Jag. In the weeks since he'd lived at Gen's, his car had gone from being "a car" to "a Jag." He could feel eyes on him wherever he drove...even imagining them there on the freeway to work. He told himself it was ridiculous, but he couldn't shake it.

"Molly!" he called. She had sacked out next to the chair where he was sitting in the living room and hadn't gotten up when Gen got home. For a young dog, she was remarkably lethargic sometimes. Fortunately, she was very good about coming when called, and she trotted into the kitchen.

"Time to go for a ride," he said, grabbing the spare leash off the hook by the door. He held the door and she followed him to…the car…jumping happily onto the towel he had spread across the leather of the back seat. She sat so her head was just high enough to see out the side window, but otherwise was stretched out on the seat. Taylor opened the sunroof and lowered all the windows so they could enjoy the warm spring air. The days were already reaching into the upper seventies to low eighties, making it very comfortable.

The park was only a two-minute ride away by car and the near complete lack of traffic in town made it a breeze. Taylor pulled into a convenient spot near the front, seeing a number of kids and several parents already standing near home plate. Taylor felt just slightly conspicuous, but his sense of adventure forced him out of the car. He opened the back door and Molly jumped out and waited patiently beside him. He hooked the leash to her collar, and then led her over toward the diamond.

Several of the parents had already turned to take note of his approach. The evening breeze was coming toward him and heard several muted comments about "Jag Guy." As he got closer he recognized one face in the crowd—Rob, from down the street. He offered a smile of greeting as Taylor and Molly walked up.

"Hey, Taylor, how's it going?" he asked, holding out a hand.

"Great, Rob, thanks," Taylor said, giving the hand a firm shake.

Tom gestured to the two other parents. "This is Hank, Freddie's dad, and Trudy, Michael's Mom," he introduced, then turned to the parents. "This is Taylor Connolly. He's a friend of Gen Pouissant's. He's living with Gen while he finds a permanent place to live. He was telling me the other day that he doesn't know how to play baseball and I told him the team would be happy to teach him."

Rob shook his head, giving Taylor a friendly pat on the shoulder. "Good luck, man. Tom's a great teacher, but they're still ten."

"You're a glutton for punishment," Hank said, following Rob to the cars.

"You'll be fine. Just keep the tip of your bat up," Trudy said, sounding motherly. She turned to Tom, "See you at seven-thirty," she said, then followed the two men. As Tom watched, their cars took off from the parking lot. Trudy's had another kid in the back seat, while Rob and Hank each drove off alone.

"Ready?" Tom asked.

"Yeah. What do I do?" Taylor asked.

Tom looked from the kids to Taylor and back again. "Actually, why don't you just relax on the bench for a minute. I'm going to get the kids warmed up, then we'll bring you in as a relief hitter."

"I don't know how much relief I'll provide," Taylor said.

"A little comic relief, at least," Tom said, giving him the smile.

Taylor harrumphed as Tom turned to the team and gave them all their start up pep talk. He walked around the protective fencing behind home plate, took a seat, and tied Molly's leash around the bench, making the knot just tight enough to make sure she wouldn't be able to take off. She had always been the picture of good behavior, but he could never be sure what to expect, especially in a new setting.

The kids broke into teams, half taking position on the field, the other half lined up to bat. Tom stood on the pitcher's mound with one of the boys, talking to him quietly as he helped him select a pitch. At once, the boy threw the ball and the girl at bat hit it toward second base. She dropped the bat and ran for first base, making it just before the second baseman was able to toss the ball to the first baseman.

"Safe!" Tom called.

And so it went for the next twenty minutes. Taylor was mildly interested to learn that the girls on the team actually were nearly as good as the boys, if not quite as strong and so not able to hit quite as far. They were clearly at the stage where they were more coordinated. For his part, Tom spent time at each position and Taylor watched his technique, getting to the level of the player, coaching on his or her terms. The kids really brightened when Tom focused his attention on them. Taylor knew the feeling.

As the time came to switch between positions, Tom called a break. Everybody ran to the cooler of water Tom had setup and drew glasses one at a time. Tom took a minute to walk over to where Taylor and Molly waited in the evening sun.

"So, how are we?" he asked.

Taylor nodded. "Looks good from what I've seen. They seem to play well together."

Tom smiled, but differently than when he looked at Taylor. "They're good kids and they have a good time." He pointed to the diamond. "Ready to show us what you've got?"

Taylor grimaced. "No pressure, huh?"

"You'll be fine. Come on, they'll love it."

He led Taylor to home plate, picking up an adult bat he had brought for the training session. As he walked up, the kids stopped talking to watch.

"Okay, guys, let's see what we can do. This is my friend Taylor," Tom announced. Taylor liked the sound of it.

"Hi, Taylor!" the team said in unison. Apparently, elementary school still taught them how to speak as one.

"Hi, guys," Taylor answered, a shy grin playing across his face.

"Taylor doesn't know how to hit a ball," Tom explained. Taylor nearly made a comment, but was able to restrain himself. "We're going to show him today. Jacob, I want you to be the catcher. I'll pitch. Emily, you come up and show Taylor how to hit. The rest of you can go out and be ready to catch the ball when he hits it—it's going to go farther than we're used to."

As the kids ran to their positions, Tom gave Taylor a little wink and walked to the pitcher's mound. Emily handed him a hard batting hat and put her hands on his hips to turn him sideways to the pitcher.

"You're right handed, right?" she asked.

"How did you know?" Taylor inquired.

"Your watch," she said, indicating where his watch hung on his left wrist.

"Oh," Taylor said, resting on the bat like it was a cane.

"Okay," Emily said, all business. She picked up a bat and stood next to him. "You want to try to hit the ball with this part of the bat. Don't reach out, just let it come to you. Keep your eye on the ball and swing the bat like this." She swung the bat in one smooth motion. Taylor was impressed that a ten year-old girl was showing him how to play baseball.

"Got it," he said. In truth, he had hit a ball before, but it had been a very long time ago.

"I'll stand over here and watch," she said. "I'll let you know what to change if you miss."

"Thanks," he said.

"Ready over there?" Tom called.

"Yep!" Taylor answered, assuming the position. Tom tossed the ball and Taylor swung…a clean miss.

"Strike one!" Jacob called from behind him. Despite himself, Taylor gave him a dirty look, but recovered quickly as Tom pulled another ball from the bucket.

He lined up the pitch and threw another. Taylor swung…and missed.

"Strike two!"

Emily walked over from where she was standing by the fencing. "You're reaching," she said. "Let the bat find the ball. Just watch the ball and hit it."

Taylor had no idea what she meant. What else would he be doing? He felt like…well, a ten year-old, except all these ten year-olds could play baseball.

He again held his bat at the ready and Tom lined up. The ball came in at him, but too close and he jumped back at the last minute, narrowly avoiding being hit.

"Ball one!" Jacob called.

"Sorry! Sorry!" Tom called. This time, Taylor shot him the look and he mouthed, "sorry!" again, then picked up another ball.

"Last shot," Jacob commented.

Determined, Taylor again held his bat at the ready. The ball came at him.

Crack!

It sailed toward the outfield with considerably more force than Taylor had expected. The kids all took off after it, apparently not expecting it to go so far, either.

"Run!" Emily ordered from beside him. Taylor took off, remembering to drop the bat as he ran. He sailed over first base, on his way to second. One of the kids picked up the ball and tossed it back toward second base, but he didn't have the arm to get it all the way. Taylor crossed second, running all out for third. Another kid got the ball to second and the second baseman threw it, but not fast enough. Taylor's shoe touched the base just before the ball hit the glove.

"Safe!" Tom said.

Taylor heaved a couple quick breaths. He was in decent shape, but hadn't run in some time. He looked at the dust he had kicked up and then turned to Tom, who was rewarding him with the smile he was used to seeing. Tom turned away, his attention back at home plate.

"Okay, Emily, bring him home."

Bring me home, Taylor thought, but his attention was still at the Pitcher's Mound. Tom wound up and tossed the ball gently—more gently than he had for Taylor. He really did care about the kids.

Emily hit it on the first try, sending it sailing right over Tom. She ran for all she was worth as Taylor took off for home plate. The kids snapped to, ready for Emily's hit, but not fast enough. Taylor's longer legs offered him the speed advantage he needed and he hit home plate. He turned and saw Emily making her way toward third, the ball chasing after her. The third baseman missed and had to run after the rolling ball. Emily kept running, her small legs pumping like pistons, determination strong on her face. The kid at third base got the ball, but it was too late—Emily crossed the plate, arms wide over her head. She ran straight to Taylor and threw them around his waist.

"You did it!" she exclaimed. Her demeanor was once again that of a little girl and she was happy to see him succeed.

"So did you!" Taylor said, returning the hug. Tom called in the rest of the team to break back into their normal practice positions while he walked to Taylor.

"I knew you could do it," he said. "You just had to have the chance."

"That was fun," Taylor admitted.

"I've gotta work with them for a while longer. You gonna hang around?" Tom's eyes never left Taylor's, the question a bit more urgent than just whether he would watch the team.

"Yeah, I've got all evening," Taylor said.

"Great! If you want, we can hit a few more after they're done."

"Sounds good," Taylor said. He returned to his bench, gently scratching Molly behind the ears. She glanced at him, only moving her eyes and brows, not impressed. He watched her expression, then poked her in the side.

"Okay," he said, "So I'm no DiMaggio. It's still better than you could do."

She gave him the tiniest hint of a snarl, again convincing him dogs understood more of what a human said than anyone thought.

The game went on as it had before, the kids alternating between batting and fielding. Taylor knew just enough to have a good idea of how they were doing and it looked like they were doing pretty darned good. The sun continued its downward path in the sky, finally resting behind the trees, another day put to rest. Parents had started to show up and joined Taylor in the stands. Thankfully, none of them seemed to feel it necessary to ask him about the car for once.

As Jacob called, "Strike Three," the last kid was finally struck out and the fielders ran in. Tom, who was standing with the pitcher, gave him a pat on the back and sent him running in as well. Some of the kids stopped for more water while others went to meet their parents. Within five minutes, most of them had left.

Emily walked up to Taylor, trailed by Amanda, whom Taylor knew from down the street. She held out her hand.

"Good job today, Taylor," she said. "You'll be batting a thousand in no time."

Taylor smiled, both at the confidence of the young girl and the attempt she made to boost his ego.

"Thank you very much, Emily," he said. "I couldn't have done it without your help."

"Boy, is that the truth," Amanda said, rolling her eyes. Rob had come up behind her and had his hands on her shoulders.

"Amanda!" he exclaimed, then gave Taylor an embarrassed look. "Sorry."

"No need," Taylor said with a wave of his hand. "She's right."

"Come on, girls, time to get some dinner," Rob said, smacking them both on the butt to get them moving. "See you, Tom, Taylor."

At last, the kids and the parents were gone. As Rob pulled away, Tom stood before Taylor. "How 'bout we use the last of this sunlight and give you a little more practice. Then, pizza."

"Great plan," Taylor said, jumping to his feet.

They rounded the fencing and Taylor picked up the adult bat and helmet. He stood at the ready as Tom pitched. This time, he made contact on the first try.

"Good shot. Try not to hit too hard—wherever they go, we have to go find them and it's getting dark."

"Got it," Taylor said. The last ball had gone far, so Tom ran to retrieve it while he could still remember where it was. As he picked it up and ran back, Taylor was forced again to admire his athletic form.

"Ready to play on Sunday yet?" Tom asked, tossing the ball.

Taylor hit it low between first and second, where it rolled to a stop a few feet from Tom.

"I think I'm still a better observer than player."

"Can't learn if you don't practice," Tom countered, throwing another.

Again, Taylor sent it to virtually the same spot, a yard from the last one. Tom watched it, eyebrows raised.

"Not bad. You sure you haven't played?"

Taylor shook his head. "Not since high school, and even then, only in gym class."

Tom tossed another and Taylor put it with the other two. He gave Taylor a wide-eyed look of shock.

"That's amazing."

"Amazing good?" Taylor asked.

"Yeah, amazing good. See if you can hit it over here," he said, indicating the other side of the mound.

"How?"

"Watch the ball, then look in the direction you want it to go as you hit it."

"Okay."

Taylor hit the incoming ball, but it sailed right at Tom. He ducked and just in time as the ball passed where his head was a second before.

"Aggh!" Taylor groaned. "Sorry! You okay?"

"Yeah, fine," Tom said, looking at the ball out by second base. "Try again, only don't look at *me*."

Taylor laughed, mentally reminding himself *not* to look at Tom. He didn't think he had before…but he wasn't sure…

The bat connected and the ball went precisely where it was supposed to. Tom turned back to Taylor. "You're a natural," he said.

Taylor held out both hands. "I swear I had no idea."

"I'll bet," Tom said. The sun was well below the horizon and the stars were peeking out. "Ready for pizza?" he asked.

"Sounds good!" Taylor said. He picked up the kids' discarded equipment as Tom collected the balls on the field. Together, they loaded everything into Tom's car.

"The pizza place is just down from the bakery. You know the one?"

Taylor thought about the layout of the town and realized Tom must be referring to the small restaurant he had taken as an Italian place.

"Yeah, I know it," he said.

"Cool. I'll drop off my car and meet you there."

"Okay," Taylor said. He opened the door and let Molly hop inside. The night was a perfect temperature. He could let her stay in the car and not have to worry about her being too warm or too cold. He wouldn't have to worry about himself for that matter, either.

He followed Tom's car, a sandy-silver Jeep Grand Cherokee, into town. Tom turned at a side street and he realized it must lead to a different place to park for the apartment. After hours, the parking meters were inactive. Tom said no one really ever checked them anyway, but Taylor still felt compelled to put a quarter in during the day. City life was a hard habit to break.

He lowered the windows enough to leave Molly comfortable, but not enough for her to get out. In truth, he neither thought she would run nor that anyone would bother her in the small town, but it was better not to take chances.

Before he even made it to the curb, Tom came around the corner from the alley, still wearing his coach's uniform. He gave a little one-handed wave, walking quickly to meet Taylor.

"I hope you don't mind I didn't dress up," he said, smiling again.

"It's okay. I forgot my tux at home," Taylor agreed

The restaurant wasn't particularly busy, but Taylor reminded himself it was after the dinner hour for most people on a Tuesday night, so that shouldn't be a surprise. Tom made him order, so he opted for a simple conservative pepperoni pizza with breadsticks and diet coke. At the last, he glanced to Tom, who nodded.

Tom then leapt into a long oratory about the town, the kids, baseball, the bakery business, life, the universe, and everything. Taylor was briefly surprised at the breadth of his knowledge until he reminded himself Tom was an English major finishing his teaching certificate—more than just a baker. He was enthralled, but also a little disheartened—he wanted to learn more about Tom, not just make small talk.

The pizza came and they dug in, saying little in deference to their shared hunger after a long day and physical exertion. Tom made a sandwich of two pieces laid on top of each other, while Taylor opted to eat one piece at a time. He realized that he wasn't going to get as much pizza, but told himself he didn't really need it anyway, remembering being just slightly out of breath after his run around the bases.

"So," Tom said between bites. "You're an employment attorney. What does that mean, exactly?"

Taylor sighed, deciding how best to spin it. "Lately, it means I've been getting a lot of sexual discrimination cases. It basically deals in any aspect of the law pertaining to employer and employee rights."

"Why sexual discrimination?" Tom asked, brow wrinkled in interest.

"I won a big case about a month ago. I got the client a few million dollars in punitive damages."

"The DDX case?"

"Yeah," Taylor said, surprised he knew about it.

"That was you?"

"That was me."

"Wow! I remember watching that on the news. Congratulations."

"Thanks," Taylor said, a little embarrassed. He really didn't like talking about himself much, but hoped it would lead Tom to share some of his own experiences.

"How did you wind up here?"

Taylor shifted in his seat. He didn't want to lie to Tom, but he wasn't ready to be completely open, either. "My roommate had to move away. I'd just won the case and didn't want to live alone again in the city. Gen and I have been best friends for years, so she told me she thought I should move out here for a while—to get a change of pace."

"This *is* a change," Tom agreed. "Like it?"

"Yeah, actually I do," he said, smiling back. "What about you? How did you land here?"

Tom sighed, smile thinning for the first time. Taylor immediately regretted pushing. He looked away, obviously composing his own thoughts. As he spoke, his eyes met Taylor's again.

"As I said, I did my Bachelor's in English. I moved to the city to take a position as a technical writer. I worked at it for about two years, moving my way up through the company to become one of the senior writers."

Taylor nodded, silently prompting him to continue. "Problem was, I was bored to death. I hated the city. I'd grown up in a small town—smaller than this one—and I realized I wasn't cut out for that life. I wasn't made to sit in a cubicle or drive in traffic or play political games with employees."

"I'm not sure anyone is," Taylor agreed.

"I knew I liked working with kids. I'd coached baseball for a couple years while I was in college and thought it was really cool. I was coaching high school aged kids then, so it was a little different, but the same idea."

Taylor was keeping up, so Tom kept going. "With an English degree, my options were a little limited. I was talking with my Dad about it one night and he said I ought to just go get my teaching certificate. I told him I couldn't keep my job and go to school at the same time. He pointed out that I hated the job, so I ought to find a place where I could go to school and just work enough to cover my bills until I was done."

"So you checked the local schools," Taylor said.

"Right. The college had a program for people like me, but was quite a drive from the city. I got a paper and found the ad for a baker right next to the ad for the apartment. I convinced the owner I could do the job and she said she was glad to have someone so responsible to run things during the day."

"And you've been at it...?"

Tom nodded. "Almost two years. I have been doing student teaching while finishing classes. It takes a lot of my time during the week, but leaves me available during the very early morning hours and on weekends."

"You mean you get up, bake, then go teach, then come home and try to study, *and* you're coaching two days a week?" Taylor said, incredulous.

"Pretty much," Tom said, a weak smile creeping up again.

"And I thought I had it hard."

He looked Taylor directly in the eye, as though reading his thoughts. It was an uncanny feeling. "You must work some long hours."

"True," Taylor agreed, "But not like that."

Tom's smile broadened as he enjoyed the recognition. "It'll only last a few more weeks. Then, I graduate and start looking for a position. Once I'm tenured, I get summers off—that's not so bad."

It was Taylor's turn to laugh. "Okay, you've got me there."

Tom glanced at his watch. "I'm really glad we got to hang out tonight. I've gotta get home, though, so I can catch a few hours' sleep before getting up to bake."

Taylor rose, tossing a twenty on the table. Tom picked it up and handed it back to him.

"Hey, Mr. Fancy Lawyer, I invited you out tonight," he said, setting down two tens. "Besides, I still owe you."

Taylor laughed again, watching Tom intently. "As long as the next one is one me."

Tom shrugged. "Sounds good to me. You know Armand's in town?"

Armand's was a pretty classy restaurant—reasonable, but definitely a city place. Taylor realized he'd been had and appreciated Tom's technique.

"Yeah, I know Armand's. Have you seen that new movie about the government cover up of bioterror weapons?"

"No, but I saw the preview."

"Armand's and the movie—seven o'clock, Friday?"

Tom smiled broadly and Taylor became convinced it was a smile meant only for him—he hadn't seen Tom look at anyone else like that. "Works for me."

They walked out of Alberto's and stopped by Taylor's car.

"See you Friday," Tom said, holding out a hand.

Taylor took the hand and echoed, "See you Friday."

Tom turned and walked back toward the alley while Taylor hopped in his Jag and headed back to Gen's. He tapped the horn twice as he passed where Tom was just turning into the alley. Tom gave a little wave, then disappeared into the shadows.

Taylor pulled the car into the garage, then gave Molly a chance to answer nature's call before walking in the house. As promised, Gen had left the kitchen light on for him. He closed and locked the door, then checked Molly's water and food. Satisfied everything was in order, he nearly missed the note on the table.

Sandy called—dinner invite for Saturday. Has friend for you to meet. 7pm. G

Taylor frowned, considering the meaning. He remembered Sandy telling him she knew someone who she wanted him to meet. Still riding the euphoria of his evening with Tom, he wasn't inclined to want to meet anyone else, but at the same time John and Sandy were good friends and it might just be casual. Besides, meeting people couldn't be bad. *And*, he thought, *Tom and I still haven't had "the discussion."*

Taylor was fairly sure Tom was interested in him. What the dynamics of that interest might be, however, were uncertain. Taylor was patient and he was willing to wait to have those questions answered…but in the meantime, he shouldn't put all his eggs in one basket. He'd done that with Ryan and now look where he was.

Molly followed him upstairs, resting in her new favorite spot outside the door. Taylor checked his watch and realized for the first time that it was after ten o'clock. He hadn't realized they'd sat and talked that long. Gen's light was already out—ten was an early night for her, but not necessarily a surprise. He'd talk to her in the morning and find out what she thought. If there was anyone in the world he could talk to, it was Gen Pouissant.

Leaving the door just slightly ajar, he took off his clothes and slid between the sheets. The windows were open and the house was warm, but it felt great. He felt the slightest tingle in his arms, reminding him of his evening exertions. That in turn led him to think about Tom and for a few more hours, anyway, Tom was the only person he need think about.

CHAPTER FIVE

It's Just Dinner and a Movie

Taylor stood in front of his closet, arms crossed over his bare chest, a scowl on his face. What to wear? It was a gay man's nightmare—a night out with the guy he was interested in and no idea what to wear. Well, that wasn't precisely true—he knew the restaurant and the general look that would be acceptable. But should he go dressy, preppy, dressy-cas, chic, or some combination thereof? He didn't want to look *too* easy—after all, Tom might just be a nice guy. Taylor's eyes narrowed. Probability, 26.2%. Still, he didn't want to push—if Tom was gay, he must still be in the closet because he knew Gen pretty well and she hadn't said a word. For Gen to not say a word was practically a miracle in itself.

Black, Taylor's fashion mind said. Simple. Elegant. Sure to please. But what with it? Maroon? A bit devilish. A sly smile crossed his lips. Maybe. Hmm…slate blue. Kind of Regis, but might be okay with a black tie. White was right out—he'd just look like an attorney, and an old one at that. French blue was classy, but probably a little too dated for a first date…er, dinner and a movie. All black? *Yeah, maybe if I'm a vampire. I vant to suck your—*aaaghh!

Taylor buried his hand and pulled out a beige linen shirt. Comfortable, classy, not too much, just right. Turning to his tie rack, he selected a patterned silk tie with muted beige, maroon, and black colors. Perfect.

Shoes…Kenneth Cole, bright polished black leather. No contest. Laces, not buckles—a little more conservative.

He pulled on the clothes, hit himself with a dash of cologne, then checked out the reflection in the full-length mirror. Very datable. The recent sun had added some very nice streaks to his hair, but his stylist had added a few more for good measure. The gel held it smooth to his head, making the highlights show that much more. As an afterthought, he reached for his glasses. He usually wore contacts, but the glasses would make him look a little more studious…or a little older. He put the glasses back on the dresser and ran into the bathroom to install his contacts. In the bathroom mirror, he again checked his appearance—perfect.

He walked out, his shoes making a clip-clop sound on the floor, even through the oriental rug. Molly was sprawled in front of Gen's door—traitor. She had moved during Taylor's first round of clothes flinging, leaving his bed in a heap of also-rans. Taylor took the front stairs, hoping to slip by Gen's commentary.

"Forty-seven minutes and fifty-three seconds. Way to go, Slick," she said from the couch. She had positioned herself to catch him at either door. Taylor stopped cold as he saw her pink fluffy slippers and large bowl of popcorn.

"Staying in?" he asked casually.

"Yeah, since everyone else already has something to do," she said. "And don't worry, I'll put away the rejects in case the night goes better than you're expecting."

"It's just dinner and a movie," Taylor objected.

"Sure, honey, sure. You keep telling yourself that."

"He may not even be gay."

"So you emptied half your closet for a straight guy?" Her gaze was unflinching as she stared Taylor down.

"Maybe."

"You're going to be late."

Taylor looked at the clock. Six fifty-five. Time to get moving.

"Have a good night," he called over his shoulder, taking the back door to the garage.

"You too, Stud-boy."

Taylor groaned as he headed out the door. If Gen knew anything about Tom, she wasn't talking. He couldn't say he was real surprised—Gen was never one to talk much about her friends. But, if he wasn't gay, why would she let Taylor go on for so long? *Maybe* she *doesn't know*, Taylor thought to himself.

He backed the Jag expertly out of the driveway. In the few short weeks he had lived there, Gen's house had started to feel like home and he was thankful for that. It truly had helped him to forget about…that other guy. Taylor smiled to himself, then frowned as rain spattered the windshield.

"Rain!" he exclaimed out loud. "Naturally."

By the time he got to the bakery, it was a virtual downpour. He didn't actually know where Tom's door was, but Tom had apparently thought of that as well—he waited in the overhang of the bakery, just out of reach of the drops.

The parking spots were all empty, so Taylor swung his car around, leaving the minimum space between the bakery and the car. He nearly hopped out to get the door, but caught himself—it's just dinner and a movie.

Tom hopped into the car, slamming the door behind him to keep the rain out.

"Hi there!" he said cheerily, his "Taylor Smile" on his face. His warm gray eyes glistened in the lights of the town.

Tom had opted for a light charcoal gray sweater, a black sport coat and slacks, and polished black shoes with a heavy tread. Definitely more trendy than Taylor's tie. Damn.

"Hi, yourself. All set?" Taylor caught the subtle sweet smell of Tom's cologne, but couldn't quite place it.

"Yep. I don't have to bake tonight and I don't have to be in the store until ten tomorrow. I wasn't sure how late the show would go."

"Cool," Taylor said, feeling another charge of uncertainty. He'd cleared his schedule. Good sign.

He swung the car around, heading back for the freeway. The navigation system in the dashboard advised course corrections in a soft British accent as he drove, all the while keeping the display centered on where they were.

"Wow!" Tom said. "This is one of those built in GPS systems, huh?"

"Yeah," Taylor confirmed. "The only problem is it makes it really hard to say you got lost going somewhere."

"Does it control everything?"

"Not everything, but there are a lot of control options."

Tom reached out to touch a couple of the other keys. "Love the accent."

"You get used to it."

Tom shook his head. "No, I mean it's cool I'm an English major, remember?"

"Right," Taylor agreed. "Speaking of which, I forgot to ask how you did on your exam the other day."

Tom sat back in the plush leather seat. "We aced it, of course."

"Congratulations."

"Only finals left to go and I'm done."

Taylor glanced in Tom's direction, again catching the smile. "Then what?"

Tom shrugged. "Then I have to quit hiding out in the bakery and find a real job."

"Teaching?"

"Yeah."

The Jag made its way onto the freeway and Taylor's lead foot worked its magic. In no time, they were sailing along in the left lane, just under eighty.

"Wow!" Tom exclaimed, eye on the speedometer.

"Too fast?" Taylor asked.

Tom shook his head emphatically. "Not at all. I just can't believe it rides this smooth this fast!"

Taylor was still amused by the interest his car always got. He gave Tom a sidelong glance. "Wanna drive?"

"Now?"

"Sure." Traffic was light and Taylor swung the wheel to the right, pulling onto the shoulder. The Jag decelerated as easily as it accelerated and he slid it into park. Tom hopped out and ran around the front of the car. Taylor ran around the back, completing the fire drill.

Tom took a minute, examining the controls and getting his bearings. Several cars passed them, but no one slowed, assuming they were okay. Tom adjusted the seat forward a short distance, making up for his legs being shorter than Taylor's. He checked his mirrors, then hit the brake and pulled back on the console shift.

"It's got pretty good acceleration, so have—" Taylor was interrupted mid-sentence by Tom jamming the accelerator and flying onto the free-way. "—fun..." he finished.

"Taylor, this is *awesome*!" he said, the speedometer once again climbing to eighty.

"Just watch for cops," Taylor said. "This stretch is usually okay, but if you get pulled over, you're on your own."

"No problem," Tom said, his smooth tan hands gripping the wheel as he adjusted to the performance vehicle. Being used to an SUV, the car would feel completely different. Taylor remembered driving the Range Rover and never feeling really comfortable, even if it did allow him to sit higher.

He watched Tom as he stared intently ahead. The freeway out near town was boringly linear, but a few good curves would come up shortly as they neared the traditional suburbs outside of the city. Tom was clearly just enjoying driving, so Taylor said nothing for a few minutes.

"Maybe once I get my job, it'll be time to replace the Jeep," Tom said finally, relaxing back into the driver's seat at last.

"They cost about the same," Taylor confirmed, remembering when he had actually priced a Grand Cherokee a couple years before.

"Not really," Tom said. "I inherited mine from my grandfather. He passed away just before I started back in school. My Dad was an only child, my sister already had a good car, and mine was in bad shape, so they gave it to me."

"Would you even want to get rid of it?" Taylor asked. He was pretty sentimental about family heirlooms and usually expected the same of everyone else.

Tom glanced at him, barely taking his eyes from the road. "No, not really. It *is* nice to dream, though," he said, gently petting the steering wheel.

Taylor laughed, slowly feeling the tension from earlier in the evening fade away. "We'll have to arrange visitation for you."

"Wednesdays and every other weekend?" Tom offered.

"And half the holidays?"

"Sold."

Taylor slid farther down in the seat, letting the headrest support him. It was rare that he was a passenger in his own car. He'd only let Gen drive it a couple times. He realized it really *was* a comfortable car and it felt good to let someone else drive for once.

"So, you were saying you are going to start applying for teaching positions," Taylor prompted, returning the conversation to where they had been before the trade-off.

"Actually, I've already started," Tom said.

"Where are you looking?"

"Several places. I applied to all the local districts in the county, as well as sent my info back to my parents in case there was anything around them."

Taylor felt his nervousness grow again. "You're thinking of moving home?"

Tom glanced at him again, keeping his attention on the road. "Not really. It just makes my Mom feel better."

Whew! "Cool," Taylor said, maintaining his composure.

"I really don't want to move. I love the town and the people. I just need to see if any jobs are going to open up."

"What age group?" Taylor asked.

"I'm K-12 certified. I can teach at any level."

"You must know somebody."

"Several somebodies, actually. I'm just waiting to hear back from them."

"Any idea when?" Taylor realized he was starting to sound like one of the nosey women from the grocery store.

"Probably in the next couple of weeks," Tom said.

Taylor sat quietly as the lights of the city started to show before them. He felt perfectly comfortable letting Tom drive, but was a little concerned about Tom's teaching options. He definitely wasn't ready to be interested in somebody and have that person wind up moving away. He reminded himself that there was no need to worry until there was something to worry about.

"Are we doing dinner or movie first?"

"Up to you," Taylor said. "There is a show at eight and one at ten-thirty."

"I think I'm hungry. How 'bout dinner first?"

"Works for me," Taylor said. They had entered the city proper and exits peeled off to the right every now and then.

Taylor again watched Tom as he drove. His intimidation with the car was gone and he sat with his right hand over the top of the wheel, as though he drove it every day. Taylor smiled and Tom caught it out of the corner of his eye.

"What?" he asked, screwing up his face as the grin started to appear.

"You just look natural."

"Me, a Jag-u-ar driver?" he asked, pronouncing the name in the correct English form.

"Seems so."

"I wish," Tom said, laughing. "Maybe after I've been teaching for about a decade." He pulled off onto a different road, nearing the restaurant.

It might not take a decade, Taylor thought, but kept his comment to himself.

Taylor sliced through his prime rib like it was butter. As usual with prime rib, a small pile of fat was discretely discarded at the side of his plate, hiding just behind the skin of the nearly empty baked potato. He hadn't been sure whether to opt for the steak or something healthy in the salad area. Tom had ordered a New York strip with barely a glance. He felt vaguely guilty about skipping out on some of the best Italian food in town, but opted to follow his guest's lead. New York strip was too grainy, so he went for the rib.

Taylor watched Tom as he expounded on a book he'd read recently. He tried to focus on the discussion, not wanting to get caught up short, but he was simply enjoying the evening. Even when he had been with…that guy…he hadn't gotten to go out as much as he liked. That guy tended to want to frequent exclusively gay establishments. Taylor had no problem with them, but liked to broaden his horizons. Technically, Armand's was "mixed," but he knew it to be a little more of a gay hangout. It certainly spoke to Tom's leanings, but again, it wasn't proof and Tom had avoided any conversation that would lead to an admission. Taylor couldn't determine if his avoidance was on purpose or not.

Even though Tom did much of the talking, Taylor had paced himself, trying to make sure they would finish their meals at roughly the same time. He sliced his last piece of steak in two, taking one bite. Tom still had a bite to go, so he set down his fork and reached for the glass of Merlot he had been nursing from the bottle they'd ordered.

Tom was telling a story of the time his sister had insisted on joining his father and him on a camping trip in the mountains a few hours from their house. Tom was twelve and his sister was seven. His dad had planned the trip for the two of them, but his sister had put on a "mighty campaign" to come along, even turning down a "girl's shopping trip" with her Mom. Ultimately, both parents had relented, giving Mom a weekend to herself and Dad a weekend with just the kids.

"Dad had explained everything to her, but it wasn't until we got there that it really hit home. There was nothing to do, nowhere to go, and no TV. All we did was fish and hike and sit and talk. She was bored out of her mind."

"And you had her for two days?" Taylor asked, taking another sip.

"Yeah. We had a boat, so the second day we went up and down the river, trying to entertain her. Dad had brought an old guitar, so when we got back, we made a camp fire and sang old songs. Mandy did okay, but she never bugged us to go again."

Taylor eyed Tom over the glass. "You sang?"

Tom puffed up a bit with pride. "I sang *well*." He flashed Taylor the smile and put another bite of steak in his mouth.

Taylor considered the story—Tom seemed very at ease with talking about his family, something Taylor had never done as much. He loved his family and they got along well, but he'd never felt as close to them as he might.

"What about you?" Tom asked, prompting Taylor. He took the last bite of steak, giving him a couple extra seconds to compose his thoughts.

"My mom is an interior decorator and my dad owns an architectural design company. My younger brother, Bryce, just graduated last year with an MBA and is working for a bank in Chicago. We keep in a touch a bit, mostly by email, but he hasn't been out here to see me since he was a sophomore in college."

It was Tom's turn to watch him as he spoke and he felt his gaze. Taylor wasn't used to talking about himself and he found it vaguely disorienting.

He'd never been big on dating and talking about himself reminded him why—it made him nervous.

"So how much younger is Bryce?" Tom asked. Taylor was impressed that he picked up his brother's name—another sign of interest.

"Five years, to the month."

Tom did the math. "You said you're twenty-nine, so he's twenty-four." He nodded to himself. "I've got him beat by a year."

Finally! Taylor thought. Tom was a little younger than he might have guessed based on his behavior, but right around where he thought. "So," he confirmed, "you're twenty-five?"

"Yep," Tom said, suddenly a little self-conscious himself. Maybe he realized Taylor had thought he was older.

"That's cool," Taylor said, spinning it for him, "You don't act it. Since you said you'd already been out working before you went back to school, I figured you were right around my age."

"You can be seen with a baby like me?"

"As long as you don't have to be burped," Taylor said, laughing.

The waiter arrived, stifling any further discussion. "How was it?" he asked, indicating the clean plates.

"Very good," Tom said, a hand on his stomach.

"Room for dessert?"

Tom looked across the table to Taylor, who shrugged. "It's just after nine," he said, looking at his watch. "The movie doesn't start until ten-thirty, so there's time."

A sly grin appeared on Tom's face as he looked at the waiter. "What have you with *chocolate?*" he asked through thin eyes, brow raised, voice cunning.

"Ah, chocolate," the waiter said, matching Tom's wit. "Perhaps the Devil's Delight?"

"Lots of chocolate?" Tom verified.

"You might want to share it," the waiter said.

Taylor watched the discourse, immediately realizing that Tom had clued in to his shared addiction with Gen. He was very astute. Tom again looked to him, his right brow cocked in question.

"Let's split one," Taylor affirmed.

"One Devil's Delight, two forks," the waiter confirmed, carrying off the dinner plates. He returned to clear most of the table, leaving the white table cloth and their wine and water glasses. He offered coffee, but neither Tom nor Taylor were coffee drinkers.

"You really are a pusher, aren't you?" Taylor asked.

Tom laughed. "It's not such a bad habit."

The movie let out at quarter to one. For once, Taylor regretted living so far out—it would be almost one-thirty by the time they got home. Of course, Tom had studiously kept the key to the Jag, "offering" to drive for the evening. Taylor recognized that he was enjoying driving the car, and truth be told, he was enjoying letting him.

"So do you think the government could really get away with that?" Tom asked.

Taylor hopped into the passenger's seat and they were off. "I think the government could pretty much do whatever it wants," he said.

"But a cover up like that? Somebody would *have* to say something."

"The government has all kinds of secrets. Look at the hidden space aliens."

Tom shot him a look and Taylor laughed. "Kidding!" he said.

Tom shrugged. "Who knows? Maybe there really are hidden space aliens. We usually think the people who have come forward are kooks, but what if they're just like the people in the movie?"

"At least it was a good movie."

"Yeah, that's true," Tom said. "Julia was looking particularly good this round, wasn't she? The last couple of movies she's been in lately haven't done her justice."

Taylor squirmed a bit—he'd noticed the *girl*. Not necessarily a deal breaker, but a check in the strike column. He held up his end of the conversation, though. "Yeah, she was definitely doing better in this movie than that one last summer."

"I have a cousin who looks a lot like her," Tom said. "It can be really annoying when we try to go somewhere—'Aren't you that actress?' people are always asking. Of course, they don't believe her, either, figuring she just doesn't want to be bothered."

"I'll bet it makes it a lot easier to get dates, though."

"Definitely," Tom said. "She was one of the most popular girls in town when we were younger."

"That had to improve your popularity by proximity," Taylor said, taking the tack.

Tom shrugged, navigating the car onto the outbound freeway. "Maybe. I never dated all that much—it just wasn't my scene, you know?"

Yes! "Yeah, I was the same way. A few here and there, but college and law school seemed to get in the way. I've spent the last couple of years trying to solidify my place in the firm."

"Exactly. Between classes, coaching, and working, there just wasn't time to worry about anything else."

An awkward silence ensued as Taylor struggled with how to proceed with the conversation. He was dying to ask Tom about himself, but felt that if Tom had wanted to say something, he would have. He reminded himself that Tom was a few years younger and had lived a different life that had forced him to focus on self-sufficiency far more than Taylor had. Taylor had done well because it was his nature to do so—he kept on task and didn't distract easily. But, his parents had paid for his education and he had never had to scrape the way Tom had. Tom's perseverance was highly commendable and something Taylor viewed as a great strength.

At last, Tom spoke. "Have you ever been camping?" he asked, eyes still ahead on the road.

"My Dad sent me to a summer camp when I was eleven, but I wasn't really into it. All kinds of team activities and Indian crafts."

Tom pondered for a moment longer, his face uncharacteristically serious, two small divots where he thin brown brow was wrinkled over his nose.

"Do you think you'd be interested in trying it again?"

Taylor stared ahead, watching the constant pattern of the broken white lines separating the two lanes of the freeway. "I could probably be persuaded."

"Two Cadbury bars and a peanut butter cup?"

"Two Downey's chocolate croissants and a cookie."

Tom laughed. "Heck, that's easy. I'll throw in four and a brownie."

"How could I turn that down?"

"Resistance is futile."

They both laughed and Tom nodded. "I've got finals this week and I'm supposed to go to my parents' next weekend. How 'bout the weekend after that?"

"Let me check my calendar," Taylor said, paused a moment, then said, "Okay, I'm clear. What day do you want to go?"

"Can you get Friday off?"

"They owe me a break after that case. Shouldn't be a problem."

The smile returned. "Great. It'll be a blast. I'll get a list together of what you'll need. We can take the Jeep." He eyed Taylor.

Taylor took the bait. "You want to take the Jag, don't you?"

Tom laughed, a rich easy sound for him. "Yeah, but we really should take the Jeep. It has four wheel drive in case it gets messy while we're out there."

"I'll leave it up to you," Taylor said. "You know what you're doing better than I do."

Tom yawned involuntarily, the late hour getting to him. "'Scuse me! Way past my bedtime,"

"Sorry," Taylor said, feeling genuinely guilty.

"God, no, don't be. I've had a great time. As I said, I don't have to be to work until ten tomorrow. That means I'll roll out at about nine forty-five."

Taylor nodded. "Gen will probably have me up before that mowing the lawn. She's usually very quiet, but somehow she can really rattle pots and pans on Saturday mornings."

Tom laughed. "You got lawn duty?"

"I sort of volunteered," Taylor said. "I felt guilty not doing something and that's what she popped on me."

"At least it gets you outside. You don't want to look like it's still January outside, right?"

"True," Taylor agreed.

They pulled into town and Tom made the turn to take them behind the Main Street buildings. Taylor still hadn't done a lot of exploring, with most of his visits to downtown involving a stop at the bakery.

"I'll show you how to get to my place," he said. Taylor caught sight of his Jeep parked in a small lot immediately behind the building. He saw how the alley connected to the street beyond and the stairway leading up to Tom's apartment.

"This is it," Tom said.

He parked the Jag next to the Jeep. He stopped the car, but left it running, opening the door to get out. Taylor met him on the driver's side, standing next to the open door in the cool night air.

"I'd invite you up, but it sounds like we both need to get some shut-eye," he said.

"Yeah," Taylor agreed, thinking, *not really*.

"Busy tomorrow?"

Taylor was about to say no when he remembered the dinner at John and Sandy's. Damn! "Yeah, I have to meet some friends for dinner tomorrow night."

Tom looked slightly disappointed, but managed to hide it pretty well. "That's cool," he said, tone saying *not really*. Taylor found himself glad

Tom seemed disappointed—another sign of interest. "Still planning to come out for Sunday B-ball?"

It was Taylor's turn to offer a reassuring smile and nod. "Definitely."

Tom brightened. "Come on by around seven and I'll show you the place."

"Will do," Taylor said. He wanted to reach out and give Tom a hug like he would most of his other friends, but he still didn't want to push it. After all, they'd only known each other for a few weeks. He held out a hand.

"Thanks for a good evening," he said.

Tom shook the hand, confusion evident in his own eyes, the smile a little weaker.

"Thank *you*," Tom said.

He turned and headed for the stairs while Taylor went to get in the car. At the last moment, he hollered up to Tom, "Don't forget to give me that list of stuff for camping!"

The brightness returned to Tom's face as he remembered Taylor's acceptance of his offer. "I'll give it to you Sunday," he said.

"Great—See ya!"

"Have a good one," Tom said, then disappeared inside.

Taylor backed out, retracing the path around the buildings as he was uncertain of the status of the alley and whether the Jag would clear it. The town was completely quiet at one-thirty in the morning, everyone having long since gone to bed. For once, his car wouldn't draw any attention.

As expected, the kitchen light was on when he got home. Not as expected, Molly was nowhere to be found. Taylor saw another note sitting on the table.

Sandy confirmed 7pm. Bring Downey's dinner rolls. Hope you had fun! G

Taylor wrinkled his nose at the note. He really didn't want to go to the dinner tomorrow. He loved John and Sandy, but didn't want to be setup with some guy right now. As ambiguous as his evening with Tom McEwan had been, he felt it was headed in the right direction and he wanted to give it a chance. With a sigh, he reminded himself that he only had to be polite—it wasn't a marriage!

Turning off the light, he took the back stairs and found Molly planted outside Gen's door. She opened one eye to look at him, then promptly closed it and let out a breath.

"You'd better hope *she* can get Tom to send you biscuits," Taylor whispered at her. He thought she grunted in response, but it may have just been a creak in the floor.

As promised, Gen had cleared his bed and even pulled back the covers. He really didn't know what he'd do without her. Her support was as unwavering as any he could ever have hoped for and she took care of him like no one else in his life.

He gently closed the door, leaving it just ajar for Molly, then hung his clothes in the closet at the end where he left things that needed to go to the cleaner. After a brief pass through the bathroom, he slid under the sheets, enjoying the moisture the evening rain had left in the air. Warmth and humidity didn't bother him—it made him feel alive. He looked forward to it making him feel even more alive in two weeks, when he and Tom would be sharing a tent somewhere out in the middle of nowhere.

CHAPTER SIX

Saturday Night Neil

Taylor stood in front of his closet, arms crossed over his bare chest, a scowl on his face. What to wear? It was a gay man's nightmare—a night out with a guy who he wasn't interested in and no idea how to look bad enough. As with the night before, that wasn't precisely true—he knew John and Sandy and had an idea of the kind of guy with whom they would set him up. He could always wear flannel.

He struggled to remember why he had rejected various outfits yesterday—too old, too dated, too stodgy. What would be the right look to guarantee a lack of interest? Flannel. Okay, *other* than flannel?

Taylor stopped himself. He was mentally trying to sabotage the evening before it had even begun. Why? Because he was in love with Tom. Whoops! A short time ago, he could barely even acknowledge to himself that he was interested in the young teacher to be, now he was admitting he was in love? *Better to be honest*, he told himself.

Problem was, Tom hadn't given any indication he felt the same way. Taylor was sure Tom liked him, but he had no way to know whether that interest exceeded friendship. He didn't want to pressure Tom by asking him, nor cause him to feel uncomfortable by indicating his true nature unless it would be reciprocated. If Tom wasn't gay, he was still a worthy friend.

Taylor sighed. He'd known Tom less than two months. He was putting all his eggs in one basket again and he knew it. It was a bad idea and not fair to himself. Sandy had gone out of her way to setup the evening—the least he could do was be graceful and enjoy it. Maybe the guy would be a dud and he could just make polite small talk. Maybe he was the man of his dreams and would sweep him off his feet. Fat chance.

He buried his hand in the closet and came out with a white business shirt. Turning to the dresser, he pulled out a T-shirt, put it on, then pulled the shirt on over it. He grabbed a tasteful, if very muted tie, and wrapped it around his neck. An attorney, and an old one at that. If this guy was going to be so wonderful, he wouldn't care anyway. He pulled out a three button black suit and put it on. In the bathroom, he styled his hair back in a more conservative, less trendy style, parted on the side. The grooves created by the brush largely hid the highlights in his hair. He had told Sandy he wasn't ready to date, so at least he didn't have to make it easy, trouble or not.

Back to the closet, he hunted down a pair of shoes—wing tips. He chuckled to himself, remembering his quandary last night. Nope, no cool trendy clothes tonight. In his mind, Tom's smiling face watched the display with amusement. In reality, he knew Gen was waiting downstairs to do the very same thing.

Taylor checked himself out in the full length dressing mirror. He looked great—straight, but great. As an afterthought, he reached over and put on his glasses. "Who would want to date an old fart like me," he said to his image, then laughed and walked out the door.

As with the night before, Molly was sprawled out in front of Gen's door. She managed the barest hint of a greeting and Taylor shot her a disapproving stare as he trucked down the stairs.

Unlike the night before, Gen was not waiting in the living room. Taylor was surprised, turning his head to glance around the corner. She sat at the dining room table, surrounded by paper.

"Everything okay?" he asked, seeing that she was paying bills.

"Yep, just taking care of monthly maintenance."

"Cool. Well, it's about time I head over to John and Sandy's."

Gen eyed him, expression neutral. "Not trying very hard tonight, huh?"

Taylor raised his eyebrows at the blunt statement. "Tell me how you really feel."

Gen's brown eyes rose to meet his. "I think you're trying to avoid having a good time tonight in case Sandy's friend turns out to be someone you might actually like."

He stood there, somehow feeling vulnerable that she had figured out his plan so easily. Was he that transparent?

She waved a dismissive hand at him. "Don't worry about it. If he's worth anything, clothes won't matter. If they do, you're better off to move on."

Her words were still a backhanded comment that told him his outfit was unacceptable. Should he change? He already knew he wasn't trying, but was there something wrong with that?

Taylor frowned, indecisiveness evident in his expression. He stood, unable to move forward toward the car, unwilling to move back toward the stairs, at an impasse. Gen looked up, clearly recognizing the confusion she had created, and offered an embarrassed smile.

"You look good," she said, rising from her chair. "You just don't look like you normally do when you're on a date." She adjusted his tie and straightened a couple run-away strands of blond hair. "Maybe that's for the best. Look, I know you like Tom, and honestly, I think he likes you, but he's not out and I'm not sure he knows what to do about it. There's going to be some baggage there. You're going out for a nice evening with a couple friends and a friend of theirs. Enjoy it and don't put any pressure on yourself. If you're interested in whoever they've invited, go on a date—it's not like you're married, or getting married. It's just a date."

Taylor appreciated the pep talk. Gen had a way of interpreting what was going through his head without him even having to speak. He also caught the valuable piece of information she'd tossed him—she thought Tom was gay, too, but knew he wasn't out. Taylor felt a little spark of happiness at the idea that something might be possible with Tom, and that spark was enough to bolster his confidence for the evening. Gen was right, it was just a casual dinner. He clung to that idea and tried to put the rest of it out of his mind.

"Thanks, Mom," he said. Gen smiled broadly and pulled him into a hug, then pulled away and straightened his jacket again.

"Okay, now get moving. I don't want John and Sandy to think I failed to push you out the door."

"Yes, ma'am," Taylor said smartly, then leaned down and gave her a peck on the cheek and headed out the door.

Once in the car, he took the long way to the freeway, making a quick pass through town. He saw the light on in Tom's apartment above the bakery, but the bakery itself was dark, closed for the day. He smiled thinly, in spite of himself. *I think he likes you*, Taylor heard Gen's voice say, over and over.

She was right, though. If Tom wasn't out, he was going to be carrying some emotional baggage. *That's not a deal breaker*, Taylor thought. He knew he wasn't technically the most "out" person in the world, either. Though he had long since stopped denying his sexual orientation when the question was put to him directly, he still did not feel it necessary to advertise it.

He remembered again the sticker Ryan had put on the back of the Range Rover. It occurred to him that might also be how Ryan managed to find two other guys in the two years they were together. *Two others who I knew of*, Taylor said to himself. His smile soured. That thought hadn't really occurred to him before as he consistently tried not to dwell on the past.

Taylor had never wanted a lot of men in his life—he was satisfied with one man who cared about him. He was perfectly content to have his other gay friends be like his straight friends—just friends who he could enjoy spending time with, but not objects of sexual attraction. He thought it was healthy, though he knew several of his friends, Chad foremost among them, would think just the opposite. *To each his own*, Taylor thought.

The freeway loomed ahead of him and he stepped on the gas. As the red Jaguar sped ahead in the left lane, he remembered Tom's exclamation of surprise…and the way he had smiled as he drove the car. Taylor felt his own smile return. *I think he likes you.* Gen was never one to say something just to make him feel better—she was one of the few people who understood the long term damage a white lie could cause later. She told him what she thought, good, bad, or indifferent. If she had said Tom liked him, it meant she'd given it thought and had a fairly good idea she was right. *Maybe she talked to him?* Taylor thought. Could it be that Tom said something?

Taylor thought back—for once, Gen had let him sleep in, not banging pots or pans in her usual Saturday morning ritual. Had she slipped off to the bakery and talked to him about last night? Had he told her something more than it was dinner and a movie? *But it was just dinner and a movie,* Taylor defended. Except we already made plans to get back together again tomorrow night…and camping in two weeks…Tom had initiated both activities.

Thinking of last night also made Taylor think of the note from Gen last night—dinner rolls! *Crap!* Taylor thought. It was too late, anyway—the bakery was closed. He had spent the day trying to busy himself, not wanting to think of the dinner, not wanting to face Tom and have him see in Taylor's face what was happening this evening. He'd put a mental block about the note, which hadn't been hard because he was so tired when he got home last night.

The car ahead in the lane was driving significantly slower than Taylor's 80 mph, so he signaled and moved into the empty right lane. As he looked in his rear-view mirror, he noticed something in the seat behind him. A second glance revealed it to be a brown paper bag and Taylor smiled as he realized what it was. Gen had let him sleep in to force him to only have enough time to do his Saturday chores…leaving her an excuse to drop in on Tom. *So, she did talk to him. That little devil,* Taylor thought, giving her a silent approving nod. She'd bailed him out in more ways than one.

He reached the exit to John and Sandy's. They lived outside the city, in one of the new subdivisions that had sprung up with the economic prosperity of the late 1990's. Taylor slowed from highway speeds, navigating the roads to their house.

What to do about Tom? Gen was clearly right—if he was gay, and that was looking likely, he wasn't out. Taylor could understand that, on several counts. First, it was a social stigma some people just didn't want. Second, Tom had been forced to fend for himself for a long time. A relationship, especially one that would force him to face so much about himself, might simply have been more than he could handle with everything else he had to deal with. Third, he might just never have found the right guy. Living in a small town wouldn't have presented a lot of options and Tom didn't seem like the club type, either.

Taylor wondered if he would be the right guy. He remembered Gen's other comment, about Tom having baggage. Taylor knew he had some baggage of his own—a failed long term (or at least sort of long term) relationship, and very little dating experience outside of that. He might be slightly more experienced than Tom, but he knew the difference was minimal. He'd just have to play it by ear. Maybe the camping trip would help shed a new light on the situation. He definitely did *not* want to do anything this week with Tom's finals in process. The only thing he would do this week was hang out and provide friendly reassurance. In fact, the best thing he could do would be to make sure Tom spent time studying, rather than thinking about him.

John and Sandy's sub was one of the trendy "cookie-cutter" neighbor-hoods of like-appearing homes, in this case covered in brick, with copper and brass fixtures. Taylor thought the houses would have been nice if there had been more than twenty feet separating them. He made the required turns on the curving streets, then counted five houses from the intersec-tion and pulled up.

His friends' cars would be parked in the garage, so the presence of a car he didn't recognize told him the other guy must already be there. He won-dered what Sandy had told this guy about him—more or less? He hoped less. He hated meeting people and trying to live up to whatever expecta-tions had already been set. *Relax and have a good time.* He heard Gen's voice again and felt its calming effect on him.

Taylor pulled up next to the car, not wanting to block the other guy's exit in case things didn't go as well as Sandy might have hoped. As he hopped out of his car, he remembered to grab the rolls from the back seat. Passing the other car, he noticed it was a BMW. Black 325i, he observed, taking a second glance. *I guess that makes him BMW Guy*, Taylor thought, considering what the people in town would have to say about him.

The lights next to the broad double wood doors came on as he approached, telling Taylor they had been waiting for him. He double-checked his watch, but he was right on time. He was okay with being punctual, as long as he wasn't late.

The door opened to reveal John's smiling face. He and Taylor could almost have been brothers—John was also blond, though darker and without the sun streaks. His eyes were a light brown, in contrast to Taylor's light blue, and his mid-section bore the mark of someone who had been happily married to a good cook for a few years. He wore a light shirt and slacks—definitely more relaxed than Taylor's black suit. *Home dinner party,* Taylor thought. *Oops.*

"Evenin', Mr. Connolly, how are you?" John greeted, shaking Taylor's hand.

"Not bad at all, how are you?" Taylor replied. Inside, Sandy waited, talking to someone just out of his range of sight.

"Great, thanks," John answered. "I guess you missed the casual dress memo, huh?"

Taylor shot him a look, then smiled self-reproachingly. "I knew who was cooking. I could barely keep myself from wearing my tux."

"Ha ha ha," Sandy said, walking over to give him a hug and a kiss, and relieve him of the bag of rolls.

As she made her greeting, the other guy came around the corner and Taylor nearly gasped. He'd never seen a more physically perfect man in his life. He had dark olive skin and dark brown hair combed in a casual style that left it falling down from its part to frame his angular, chiseled face. His black eyes regarded Taylor from under thin brows and he smiled in a friendly way as he approached. Taylor realized they were the same height, or he might even be an inch or so shorter, but the other guy was in much better shape, with a well-defined chest tapering to a thin waist and long legs.

"Hello. I'm Neil Gardener," he greeted, holding out a hand.

Taylor took it. Neil's grip was firm, but not painfully so, and his hand was dry, but not calloused. Taylor hoped his own hand felt the same way, as he was a bit taken aback by Neil's beauty. The Greek gods would have had nothing on him.

"Taylor Connolly," he replied, trying to maintain an even voice.

"Nice to meet you. Sandy and John have said some very nice things about you."

Taylor choked. He'd blown Sandy off when she mentioned introducing them during the party and had taken no steps to get more information since then. He'd only come to dinner because Sandy and Gen had more or less conspired to force him to and he didn't want to be rude to Sandy.

"Same here," Taylor lied. He hated lying, but hoped he could be graceful. "Sandy said you're in marketing?" He also hated resorting to discussing a person's job, but again hoped it might help lead them into something else.

"Yep," Neil said, smiling, and released Taylor's hand. "Just wrapped up my Master's and joined Sandy's company. I understand you're the guy who successfully fought the DDX case a couple months ago?"

"That's me," Taylor confirmed, slightly embarrassed at the notoriety.

"That's great," Neil said. "You did so much to help squelch harassment, you have no idea. The repercussions have been going through every company I know of."

Taylor smiled. "It certainly got our firm a few more cases," he agreed.

John interrupted, guiding them to the living room. "We don't need to stand here at the door. Let's sit down."

John and Sandy had been married for a little over five years. Both were in professional jobs that offered them a comfortable living and their house was well appointed. The living room consisted of two leather sofas facing each other over a mission-style wood and glass coffee table and two wing chairs with ottomans at one end. The other end had a massive wood-burning fireplace surrounded by floor-to-ceiling mission-style bookshelves. The ceiling rose to what Taylor guessed to be about twelve feet—high enough that a library ladder had been installed to reach the upper shelves.

Sandy took one couch while Neil took the other. John turned to Taylor as he tried to casually ponder where to sit.

"Can I get you something to drink?" he asked.

"Gin and tonic?" Taylor asked.

"No problem. Since we're going casual here, would you like me to hang up your jacket?"

Taylor smiled at his friend's thinly veiled comment about his attire. He figured he deserved no less for the purposeful way he had chosen the formal outfit.

"That would be great," he said, letting the jacket fall off his shoulders. He handed it to John, then turned back to the room. Neil and Sandy were involved in a conversation while John saw to his needs. He decided not to be a prude and casually sat down at the other end of the couch where Neil was seated.

Neil glanced over and offered a warm smile, turning the conversation back from whatever they had been discussing. John lowered a glass into Taylor's field of vision, complete with sliced lime on the edge of the glass.

"Aren't you just the bartender?" Taylor asked, accepting the glass.

"I like my guests to be served well," he said, his own glass full of ice and an amber liquid—probably Irish whiskey—and sat next to Sandy.

"Sandy was just telling me you've been living outside the city," Neil said, turning the conversation back to Taylor. "How's that working out for you?"

"Pretty good," Taylor said, nodding. "I've been out for a few weeks now and I'm really enjoying the more leisurely pace. It has even encouraged me to get out of the office a little more so I can enjoy just taking my dog for an evening walk."

"The people are nice?" Neil asked.

Taylor nodded again. "Very nice. They've been sort of preoccupied with my car, but that's been waning lately."

"What kind of car do you drive?"

Taylor nearly rolled his eyes, but it was a fair question from someone who had just met him. "A Jag X-Type."

Neil's eyes brightened. "I *love* that car! It came out just after I bought my car. I wish I'd known it was coming—I might have waited. You like it?"

"Definitely. It drives like a dream and rides on a cloud. I had a pretty old Pontiac I'd inherited from my uncle while I was in law school. It was kind of fun to walk into the Jaguar dealership to trade in that old car on a brand new Jag."

"I'll bet," Neil said with a big smile. Taylor couldn't help but feel he was genuine, and that was genuinely disorienting. Sandy spoke up, interrupting any further thought.

"Dinner should be about ready," she said. "In honor of Taylor's recent success and Neil's new degree, I splurged and made lamb." She looked directly at Taylor, who broke into a broad smile.

"You make *the best* lamb," he said, then turned to Neil. "She makes the best lamb I've ever had."

"A good enough endorsement for me," he said, rising from the couch. The rest of the party followed Sandy into the dining room, where she had laid out a formal dinner setting.

"Wow," John said, impressed. "She wouldn't let me see what she had planned," he explained to the two other men. "She just sent me to the store with a list, then shoed me outside to work on the lawn and closed all the doors."

"It's the only way I can ever surprise him," Sandy said. "Please, sit and be comfortable. We're going to have soup, then a small salad, followed by the main course, and dessert."

"You secretly wanted to be a chef?" Neil asked, taking the seat opposite Taylor in the middle of the rectangular table.

"Only for the occasional special occasion," she said. She turned and passed through the door to the kitchen, then returned with two bowls, which she placed before Neil and Taylor. They waited while she brought in bowls for John and herself, then picked up a spoon and sampled the soup.

"Sandy, this is incredible," Neil said in appreciation.

Taylor took a bite and was forced to agree. Subtle flavor, smooth texture, neither too spicy nor too bland.

"It's just cream of vegetable," she said. "It's my grandmother's recipe."

"She must have been quite a cook," Taylor said.

Sandy smiled. "She did okay. Her brother was head chef at the Plaza in New York. He brought her a few of her favorite recipes for her to practice. Needless to say, none of us objected to having to go to Grandma's for dinner."

Taylor picked up a roll and lightly buttered it, wishing he could just dip it in the soup, but not wanting to be too much of a country bumpkin. After all, he'd only lived away from the city for a few weeks.

They progressed through dinner, leaving Sandy's fine china almost clean enough to eat off directly. She was as skilled a cook as she was gracious a host, seeing to her guests' every need, looking caringly after her husband, and enjoying her creation in the process. Dessert consisted of a chiffon cake laced with Bailey's Irish Cream, layered with cream frosting and covered in white chocolate shavings. She had used a light drizzle of chocolate syrup to add some color to the masterpiece, along with a very light dusting of dark chocolate.

As much as Taylor loved sweets and ate them with regularity, the cake was so rich that he only had one serving. Sandy watched as he finished and gently set his fork on the edge of the plate.

"Only one piece?" she asked with a smile.

"It was delicious," Taylor said, holding his stomach, "But I'm stuffed and that was really rich."

"But I can send some home with you?" she asked.

"Definitely. Gen would probably kick me out if you didn't."

They all laughed and John spoke. "Shall we head back to the living room?"

"We should help Sandy clean up," Neil said. "The cook shouldn't have to clean."

"Agreed," Taylor said.

Sandy shook her head. "Not a chance, boys. Guests are guests and I won't have them working for their dinner. You're guests."

"But—" Neil began.

"No."

"Okay," he said, his gaze again turning to Taylor. Taylor had noticed he spent much of the meal watching him. Of course, he realized that he had to have been doing the same in order to see the attention.

Neil was definitely not what Taylor had expected. Aside from his physical beauty, he had a warm, caring personality that Taylor found endearing. The corners of his eyes were perpetually wrinkled in a smile and he was attentive both to Taylor as well as his hosts. Whatever his reasons had been for agreeing to dinner, they seemed more than just the possibility of getting together with Taylor and he found that comforting. In his experience, his straight friends sometimes missed the subtler nuances of setting him up on a date—they thought that just because both guys were gay, that was all that mattered.

Neil had expounded a bit on what his experience and job responsibilities were, then segued the conversation into discussing their family backgrounds, asking thoughtful questions about Sandy's family, who were first generation immigrants from Germany who had escaped to the United States as children during World War II.

They followed John to the living room, where he offered everyone drinks. As the evening was winding down, Taylor opted to just have a tall glass of ice water and Neil asked for the same. Sandy was still nursing her glass of burgundy from dinner, and they reclaimed their relative positions on the sofas. Taylor felt much more at ease sharing the space with Neil—he felt confident that they had enough in common that they would see each other again.

"So Taylor," Sandy said, "Are you thinking you may stay out there with Gen for a while?"

"I don't know," Taylor answered. "I've been thinking about starting to look for a house. I met the top realtor in town at the grocery store a couple weeks ago."

"I remember that!" John said. "Tell Neil the story."

Taylor recounted his run-in, literally, with Faith Roberts. He explained her obvious interest in him, as well as the way the other women in the store had watched him as he collected groceries for the party.

"I know how you feel," Neil said. Taylor could imagine he did, with his Mediterranean good looks. "I've had that happen even in the city. I live in a very mixed part of town with a lot of single people. I feel like I'm always on display whenever I walk out the door. I've even done the ball-cap and sweatshirt routine some Sunday mornings when I go shopping."

They all laughed, commenting on how difficult it could be no matter whether in a small town or in a small community of a big city.

The clock chimed eleven and Taylor noticed John's eyes had grown a bit heavy. He knew Sandy had to have a pile of dishes to do and he knew there was no chance she would let them help. He had about a half hour drive to get home and was feeling a little tired himself, even though he had thoroughly enjoyed the evening.

"Well, we should probably let you wrap up for the evening," Neil said, as though reading Taylor's mind.

"No hurry," John said, smiling.

Neil smiled back. "Well, I have to get up in the morning and run the gauntlet at the grocery store. Taylor has to drive back out to his place, and Sandy has a kitchen full of dishes she won't let us help clean up," he explained.

"And you look like you're going to saw some lumber any time," Taylor observed, needling his friend.

"Eleven o'clock and he's a pumpkin," Sandy said.

Neil set his empty glass on the coaster on the table and got up. Taylor and Sandy followed him, then John struggled his way up and led them back to the foyer. He pulled Taylor's forgotten jacket from the closet and handed it to him while Neil and Sandy said their goodbyes.

Neil turned to Taylor, again holding out a hand. "Taylor, really great to meet you. I had a really great time tonight."

"Me too," Taylor agreed, realizing he honestly had enjoyed himself.

"I'm still new to this area. I wondered if you might like to get together for dinner on Tuesday and show me your town?"

Taylor was a little surprised by the invitation, but thought it might be fun to hang out with Neil again. He had turned out to be much more interesting and open than Taylor had expected and truly did seem genuinely friendly.

"Dinner Tuesday would be great," Taylor agreed, reaching into his pocket to retrieve a card. "Call me at this number and I'll give you directions."

"Good deal," Neil said, then finished saying his goodbyes and walked out the door. Taylor turned back to John and Sandy, who were both grinning broadly at him.

"Gen warned us you would try to be a poop," John said.

"I told you he was nice," Sandy said. "Why would I introduce you to a dud?"

Taylor took his told-you-so's like a man, holding the plate of chiffon cake Sandy had given him to take home. "Okay," he grumbled. "So he was a nice guy. We're having dinner on Tuesday. Satisfied?"

"It's a start," John said.

Taylor let a small yawn slip in spite of himself. "Sorry," he said. "I guess I really am tired. I should let you guys go."

"I'm really glad you came tonight, Taylor. It was good to see you," Sandy said, giving him a hug and kiss goodbye.

"See you, buddy," John said, shaking his head.

"Good to see you guys, too," Taylor said, then walked out the door himself.

He gently set the cake in the passenger's seat, then navigated his way back to the freeway, feeling proud of himself for having survived the evening with grace. He definitely hadn't been prepared for Neil—smart, witty, attractive, and apparently interested in him. What a week.

As he accelerated onto the freeway, he noticed a vaguely yeasty smell he had missed on the drive out, so preoccupied had he been with thinking about Tom. His brain stopped cold. Tom. He realized he had been so taken by Neil Gardener that he had virtually not thought about Tom all evening. He cracked a couple of the windows, both to eliminate the yeast smell as well as get some fresh air.

What had happened? He'd been thinking about Tom right up until he walked in the house…then he saw Neil, the God. There was no question he was attractive—he had such classical features and obviously took care of himself, he couldn't help but look good. Not that Tom wasn't cute—he was gorgeous in his own way—but Neil was movie-star material.

Taylor liked to think he was above only being attracted to someone based on physical characteristics. And, even in Neil's case, he realized there was more to it than just a great body. Neil was attractive, but he was also intelligent, warm, insightful, caring.

Taylor stopped himself. How could he have gone from barely being able to spare a thought for anything or anyone but Tom to counting Neil's finer qualities? What was going on with him?

He slid lower in his seat, letting his head relax on the headrest. There was virtually no traffic on the freeway and he decided to take it a little slower to avoid becoming a tasty target to some cop running radar.

He was still very interested in Tom. Neil was just magnetic. No, he was electric. He polarized the room with his very presence. Sandy and John brightened as they spoke to him, too.

Taylor's attention returned to some of the thoughts he'd been pondering about Tom on the drive out—the baggage that he would have as a man coming out of the closet. Taylor knew first-hand the pain that could cause. Neil was already out—that much had been clear from the conversation they had carried on throughout the evening. Moreover, Neil was unabashedly interested in him. Of that, there was no doubt—Sandy had confirmed it while Neil stepped away to answer nature's call.

Taylor saw Tom's face, that quirky lopsided smile and the way his eyes brightened whenever he looked at Taylor. He liked Taylor, just as Gen had said. But what would it take for him to acknowledge and accept that to himself? Neil liked him, too. Did he deserve a chance?

As he pulled into town, Taylor groaned to himself. The last few weeks had been virtually perfect. He'd been able to forget about Ryan, focus on his interest in Tom, and share a relaxing time with Gen. Neil was going to make his life complicated—that much was certain. How would Tom feel to know there was someone else around? How would Neil feel about Tom? On that one, Taylor felt fairly sure Neil wouldn't be worried. His self confidence was clearly not an issue—he was more self-assured even than Taylor, and certainly more so than Tom.

Taylor glanced up at Tom's windows involuntarily. They were dark, as he expected they would be. Tom was no doubt catching a few hours of sleep before having to get up and bake. Taylor considered that—Tom was certainly worthy of his respect and admiration. He worked hard and still managed to be a part of the community. Neil had said his family was from New England and, from his descriptions of their activities, clearly had money. He was a nice guy, but he hadn't had to work for what he had the way Tom did.

He parked the Jag expertly in the garage, closing it behind him. The kitchen light was on, as expected, and Gen was in bed. For once, the table had no note waiting for him. He would see Tom tomorrow, so there was no need for him to leave a message, and he'd spent the evening with the other people who would most likely call. He noticed Molly was stretched out in the living room, but she made no effort to greet him.

Shaking his head, he turned off the light and took the back stairs to his room. His night vision intact from the drive, he took off his suit and put it with the one from the night before, where he would remember to take it to be cleaned on Monday. As an afterthought, he moved it back to the other end of the closet, realizing it was still clean after having only been to John and Sandy's.

He sighed, falling onto the bed. It was warm enough that he didn't need the covers and he bunched a pillow under his head. Tom or Neil? Neil or Tom? Their faces both appeared before him. Really, he hadn't known either of them very long. He felt a loyalty to Tom, but Neil's pull was strong. Resist the Dark Side, he heard the voice from the childhood space opera call. Neil wasn't the dark side. He was just someone other than Tom. Taylor knew a good, balanced decision was one where the reasons for the choice were clear and well thought out. If he really was to choose Tom, Neil's presence would cause him to better understand and validate his choice. Likewise, if he was to be interested in Neil, he would do it with the understanding of the differences between him and Tom.

Taylor sighed, rolling onto his stomach and closing his eyes. He hated conflict, especially when it involved him. Fortunately, he was tired. As he drifted off to sleep, he realized he almost wished he hadn't gone after all. Almost. Choices were a mixed blessing...and for the first time in weeks, there was a face other than Tom's in his thoughts as the darkness overtook him.

CHAPTER SEVEN

A Quandary of Faith

Monday morning traffic was always slow—a fact that consistently irritated Taylor, even as he told himself he was powerless to do anything about it. It was the same story every Monday—about fifteen miles from the city, traffic slowed from its reasonable speed of about sixty-five to seventy to about forty. He reminded himself, as he always did, that he should be thankful it was at least moving.

He thought over the events of the previous night and a smile crept onto his face. He had arrived at Tom's promptly at seven o'clock, as promised. Tom was waiting for him at the top of the stairs, his Taylor Smile on his face. Taylor had felt a pang of guilt when he thought about the previous evening spent getting to know Neil, but set it aside in favor of enjoying his time with Tom.

Tom had invited him in, quickly showing him the small apartment. One bedroom had a computer and some bookshelves covered in a wide variety of literature. Taylor was reminded that Tom's undergrad degree was in English. Tom just didn't have the haughty academic quality to him and it was easy to forget his background.

The next room was Tom's actual bedroom, consisting of a small double bed, night stand, dresser, and TV stand. A small bathroom separated the two rooms. The kitchen opened into the living room area, facing a small table, then a sofa and two chairs faced a reasonably sized television set.

Everything was in light muted earth tones, giving a sense of space to an otherwise small room. Even on a fixed budget, Tom had managed to decorate well, with pictures of various people and places on the walls of the hall and living room.

He had stood in the middle of the room with a waiting expression on his face as Taylor surveyed the space. "What do you think?" he asked.

"Very nice," Taylor had said, genuinely impressed. "Did you take the pictures? They're fantastic!"

Tom smiled broadly then, proud both of their quality and that Taylor had noticed them. "I've always taken pictures as a hobby. I used to travel more and had a lot of opportunities to get good shots."

As he moved back into the left lane to pass a semi, Taylor smiled, too. Tom's enthusiasm was contagious and he appreciated the humble pride Tom had in his work. They had shared a couple Diet Pepsis before going down to the field.

Several of the other players failed to show so that there were just three and Taylor. Realizing an actual game wasn't going to be possible, they talked Taylor into joining them for some basic practice. Tom warned them that he was deceptively good, and while he didn't think he'd really been able to live up to the billing, he at least managed not to embarrass himself. They had played until just after dark, then retired to Alberto's for pizza and beer.

Taylor begged off at ten, feeling tired even though Gen had taken care to let him sleep in again after his return from John and Sandy's. She had barely asked any questions about the evening, either. Taylor figured she'd just call up Sandy and get the skinny from her.

So it was that Taylor Connolly, twenty-nine year old Jaguar driver, found himself traveling along the interstate at forty miles per hour in a seventy mile per hour zone and still managed to find something to smile about. Gen was right—living in "the Sticks" was addictive and he was hooked.

He and Gen had agreed that his residency in her house was a short term fix. It would give him the opportunity to sell the flat and adjust to being on his own again. Gen was sure he wouldn't want to move back to the city once he'd been away…and he didn't. The town was warm, friendly, and inviting. They'd even more or less stopped referring to him as "the Jag Guy," as word got around about who he was and what he did. Gen had spent enough time introducing him to people the people greeted him by name when he walked down the street. Where else would he find that?

Traffic slowed another five to ten miles per hour and he reclined lower in his seat with a yawn. Even though he had left at ten, Tom had walked him back to his car and they spent another forty-five minutes talking, just standing in the parking lot next to his car. Tom had finally reluctantly admitted that he needed to get to sleep too, as he had to bake in the morning and it was finals week, so he would be spending a lot of time studying. Taylor promised they would talk later in the week, then said good night and drove away, again feeling the longing for physical closeness that couldn't be requited.

He sighed. He didn't know what to do to make Tom more comfortable. He'd stopped by at Gen's a couple times, but Taylor got the distinct impression he was repressed by her presence. He knew Gen had sensed it, too, as she tended to stay around just long enough to be polite, then she would go upstairs or find a reason to leave the house. He appreciated her efforts, but knew that it was hard for either of them to have a relationship with the other one there.

An idea sparked in his head and he unclipped the small cell phone from his belt. As traffic slowed to a virtual crawl, he plugged the phone into the car audio system and dialed information.

"What listing?" the person on the other end said.

"Faith Roberts," Taylor said.

"I have two listings for a Faith Roberts. One appears to be a business."

"That one, please," Taylor said. The operator connected him to the number and he heard the phone ring.

"Good morning, Faith Roberts," the voice on the other end replied.

"Good morning, Faith," he greeted. "This is Taylor Connolly."

"Taylor!" she exclaimed, clearly remembering *exactly* who he was. "Great to hear from you!"

Taylor rolled his eyes, braking as traffic stopped. "Good to talk to you," he said politely. "I didn't expect you to be in so early."

"The business phone forwards to my cell phone," Faith explained. "Anytime is a good time to sell a house, you know."

Taylor shook his head, glad that he didn't have to pretend to be amused even as he played along over the phone. "I know it," he said. "That's what I'm calling about. I hear you're the woman to talk to for a house in town."

"Really?" she replied gleefully. "That's wonderful! Did Gen refer you?"

"Gen and about a half dozen other people," Taylor said. He hated playing games, but recognized that Faith was the kind of person who responded well to unsolicited praise.

"Wow! That's great," she said. "Well, I am *definitely* here for you. Would you like to just get together and we can go over what you're looking for?"

No, Taylor thought. "That would be great. When is a good time for you?"

He heard paper rustling in the background as Faith tried to keep the receiver and consult a calendar at the same time.

"I have a closing tonight at five, then I'm free. How 'bout we meet at Alberto's around seven and I'll buy you dinner?"

Inside, Taylor groaned. He knew she wanted more than just a home sale. Being thin, blond, and attractive had made him the target of women for years, but he could handle it.

"You don't have to buy me dinner," Taylor said, the truth far more real than the politeness Faith would take it for.

"It's the least I can do for you letting me help you find a house," she said. "Seven p.m. at Alberto's?"

Taylor let out a quiet sigh, hoping the road noise would mask it. "Seven is great. Thanks, Faith."

"Thank *you*, Taylor," she said. "I'm looking forward to it. Is there anything else I can do for you?"

"Nope, that'll do it," Taylor said, meaning it. "You have a great day."

"You, too. See you tonight," she said. He punched the phone key on the steering wheel before it could go on any further.

The city loomed ahead, traffic once again crawling along. He wondered if he wanted to live within twenty miles of Faith Roberts, but the image of Tom returned the smile to his face. He thought of Saturday and meeting Neil, but it just didn't have the same effect—he hoped it stayed that way.

As though sensing his thoughts, the phone rang. Hoping it wasn't Faith, he waited while the caller ID displayed the info on the screen in the dash. "McEwan, Tho" Tom! He hit the phone key without a second thought.

"Hey there!" he greeted informally.

"Mornin'," Tom said, equally informally. "I didn't wake you?"

"Only from falling asleep in this blasted traffic," Taylor said, smiling unabashedly.

"Careful with the car," he said. "Remember, next weekend I have visitation."

"Thanks for the concern."

"Oh, and we don't want to have to scrape you off the road, either."

Taylor laughed. "Was there a point to this call, or are you just harassing me?"

"I would never harass you—you're a harassment attorney!"

"Right," Taylor said, shaking his head.

Tom continued. "Actually, I was calling to see if you wanted to come help with the kids tomorrow."

Yes! Taylor thought, but then Neil's face swam into his vision. "I'd love to, but I can't," he said. "I am meeting a friend for dinner."

"Oh," Tom said. Taylor could hear the disappointment in his voice, even as he tried to masque it. "Cool—another time, then."

"Definitely," Taylor said, feeling bad. He wondered if he ought to just cancel the dinner plans with Neil. Of course, he had no idea how to get in touch with Neil and didn't want to be rude. As Gen had said, he didn't want to put all his eggs in one basket.

"So, what else is new?" Tom asked conversationally, trying to get past Taylor's decline.

"Actually, I just got off the phone with Faith Roberts before you called. I'm going to talk to her about buying a house tonight."

"Really?" Tom's voice sounded as though it brightened, but Taylor heard something else he couldn't quite place. "Where?"

"In town," Taylor confirmed. "I wouldn't mind finding something in the same neighborhood as Gen."

"So you're staying out here?" Tom said.

"I think so. I like it there. Think you can put up with me?"

"We'll try," Tom answered, smile back in his voice. Taylor felt a little bad, knowing his dinner with Neil was probably more than just dinner with a friend, at least as far as Neil was concerned, but he didn't want to push things right then.

"That's good. I'd hate to have my chocolate supply cut off."

"Ah, the power of the baker," Tom said, voice pretending to be evil. "Muwahahaha."

"I know *I'm* scared," Taylor said, laughing.

"You're safe for now," Tom said. "And, I need to get back to work. I'll be stuck getting ready for finals the rest of the week. Tomorrow with the kids is the only break I get. I probably won't see you until next week. I'm going home Thursday night."

"Busy week," Taylor observed. "We'll catch up when you get back, okay?"

"I'll be here," Tom said. Taylor heard the same little disappointment in his voice and again felt a twinge of guilt. He really would rather get together with Tom, but as the old saying went, absence makes the heart grow fonder.

"You have a good week and good luck with your exams. I'll be around if you need a study break," Taylor said, finally navigating in toward the office.

"Thanks, bud," Tom said. "I'll catch you later."

"Have a good one," Taylor said. This time, he waited for Tom to disconnect, not wanting to be the first. He watched as the connection went dead and he thumbed the phone off.

Tom had given him the list of stuff for the camping trip while they were in his apartment last night. Taylor made a mental note to start collecting it this week so he could report he was ready to go the next time they talked. He knew it would go a long way to making Tom feel better about not having gotten to see him before finals.

Taylor was convinced Tom was interested in him—the only question remaining was what they would do about it?

For a Monday night, Alberto's was fairly busy. Taylor had to park across the street to get a spot anywhere near the door. He had hoped Gen might be able to go to the meeting with him, acting as a balance to Faith's apparent interest, but she was meeting a guy she knew for dinner. Taylor was glad she was trying to get out a little herself, as he felt his presence had slowed her social life, too. Buying a house was probably the best decision for everybody.

He pushed open the door and the proprietor, Alberto, greeted him warmly. Alberto was a first generation immigrant from Italy. He had come to the US as a child in the fifties, during a tough economic depression. His father had worked in the steel mills in Pennsylvania and his mother had worked in a restaurant. She had often taken him to work, where he had nothing to do and so stayed in the kitchen. By the time he was twelve, he could cook with the best of the chefs and his vocation was a natural choice. He had cooked in some of the best restaurants in the country, ultimately choosing the small comfortable town as a sort of semi-retirement.

"Taylor, my friend, how are you tonight?" he said, a smile so big it nearly overtook his face, his eyes bright with life.

"Wonderful, Alberto," Taylor said, typically subdued, but happy to be recognized. "How are you?"

"Fantastico," he said. "You are here to meet Ms. Roberts?"

"I am," Taylor confirmed. "Is she here?"

"Just arrived," Alberto said, letting him know he wasn't too late. "Right this way."

He led Taylor to a comfortable table at the back of the restaurant and pulled out a chair for him to sit. Taylor would have preferred to sit across from Faith, but Alberto pulled out a chair next to her at the square table.

"Can I get you anything?" he asked.

Taylor noticed Faith had a mixed drink of some clear liquid, but decided he didn't want anything that might impair his judgment, not that he felt there was a great danger of that with Faith Roberts.

"I'll just have a diet coke," he said.

"Right away, sir," Alberto said, shuffling back to the small bar. Taylor had first thought he was a very formal person, but later realized it was just the way he talked and he was one of the most warm and friendly people in the town.

"Isn't he just great?" Faith said, watching Alberto jump from table to table to see how his guests were doing.

"Definitely," Taylor confirmed.

Her attention turned from Alberto to him and Taylor immediately felt as though he was under a microscope. Faith watched him closely, her eyes scanning every aspect of his features. Taylor wondered if it might have been a good idea to select a different realtor, but everyone, including Gen, had said Faith was the best in town.

"So, how are you?" she asked.

Taylor felt himself tighten up a bit, his back going a little more rigid, his demeanor more business-like and professional. "I'm great thanks. I really appreciate you making time to meet with me," he said, politely avoiding asking how she was doing. He wasn't sure he wanted to know.

"Not a problem at all, Taylor. Part of my job is to meet with people on their schedules."

Taylor waited politely, hoping she would start getting down to business, but she just continued to stare at his face. So, he cleared his throat and picked up the menu.

"I think I've had pizza almost every time I've eaten here," he said. "Any favorites?"

"Pizza!?" Faith exclaimed. "You have missed out. Go for the lamb. It's superb."

"And expensive!" Taylor said, looking at the price.

"You're not buying tonight, remember?" she said, again looking into his eyes.

"I do remember something about that," he said, feeling himself be charming against his will. Gen had told him it was impossible for him not to flirt, try as he might not to. He just couldn't be rude to people and tended to treat them as they treated him.

Lamb did sound good, though, and he was interested to see how Alberto's would stand up to Sandy's grandmother's recipe from Saturday. He suspected it would be good. Closing the menu, he set it to one side and sampled the bread Alberto had apparently left on the table earlier.

"So, what kind of house are you looking for?"

Finally, Taylor thought, down to business. "That's a good question," he said. "I've been trying to figure that out."

Faith smiled, taking out a notepad. "Well, let's start with the things that are important to you."

"Okay," Taylor said, listing things off. "I want a big porch, sort of like Gen's, a two car garage, at least two bedrooms, maybe three, enough property for my dog to run around, and in a good neighborhood."

"Not too tough," Faith said. They went through and named a few other features that would help her narrow the selections and she took notes on her pad. "What's your price range?"

Taylor shrugged. "Money shouldn't be a problem. My caseload is way up and they just made me a junior partner at the firm. I made about sixty thousand on the flat after I paid off my roommate's interest, so I should have a good sized down payment."

"You and your roommate owned your flat?" Faith asked, seizing on the bit of personal information.

"Yeah, we thought it was a smarter investment than renting. It didn't really occur to us that it would be a problem if one of us had to move away." Taylor always neglected to point out that Ryan had to move away because Taylor told him to. He didn't figure it was anyone else's business.

"Where did he move to?" she asked, going two for two. She was making Taylor confirm his roommate was a guy and testing what he knew about his status.

"California," he lied. "He's been staying with an aunt." In truth, he had no idea where Ryan was, nor did he care. He'd paid Ryan the money he was due from the flat, which was almost nothing after he took all the contents, and hadn't heard from him since.

"I've always wanted to live near the coast," Faith said. Taylor smiled politely, but said nothing, hoping she would move on. "If you're looking for a house like Gen's, you're in luck. They're fairly common in the town and most are priced comparably. With your income and down payment, you'll afford one easily."

Alberto picked that instant to walk up and take their order. As he left, Taylor quickly leapt on the opportunity to keep Faith on task.

"Do you have any listings we can review?" he asked.

She nodded. "I guessed you might be looking for something like Gen's. As I said, it's one of the more common styles in town." She laid out a variety of pages and Taylor flipped through them, thankful for the diversion, praying Alberto would be quick with their meals.

As the plates were cleared away, Taylor felt like the lamp over the table should be swinging ominously. Faith had practically interrogated him, asking about his childhood, schools he'd attended, marital plans, places he'd traveled, and more things that he couldn't even remember. Whenever she managed to get close to questions about his social life, he answered vaguely and steered the conversation in another direction. He didn't care if people knew his sexual orientation, but found it annoying when they tried to find out by being coy. If asked directly, he would answer directly, but the twenty questions routine just smacked of being nosey.

For her part, Faith didn't seem put off at all. Several times throughout the meal, she got a dreamy expression on her face as Taylor described his exploits in college and law school and some of the early cases he argued in court.

At one point, he smartly asked about Faith's background, noting that she didn't wear any rings. He'd made the comment before he could retract it, meaning only to push back on her incessant questions about his personal life, but it came out as though he was interested and wanted to make sure she was available. He had mentally kicked himself and made a note to kick himself for real later.

"My husband and I split six years ago," Faith said. "He wanted a house wife and I wanted a career. We couldn't find a way to make it work."

Taylor had nodded politely, noting, "It's hard to have a social life and a career at the same time. One of them always seems to lose."

Faith had smiled and nodded. "That's why a great guy like you is single, huh?"

Taylor had nearly gagged, but managed to contain himself, answering with a simple, "mmm-hmm," as he sipped his diet coke.

With the meal over and the plates gone, Alberto returned to the table, holding the dessert tray. Taylor eyed the chocolate specialties, but wanted nothing more than to retire to the comforting confines of Gen's house. He shook his head and held his stomach, saying, "none for me, thanks." Faith looked disappointed, but clearly didn't want to be the only one to order dessert.

Alberto took the desserts away and Taylor prayed he would be quick with the check. Faith took the napkin from her lap and gently folded it to lay it on the table in front of her.

"Well, this has certainly been a pleasure," she said, again gazing at Taylor.

"Yes, it has," he said politely, thinking exactly the opposite. *Note to self,* he thought, *Next time, straight male realtor.* He nearly laughed, but managed to contain himself.

"We shouldn't have any problem finding you a house. I know of a couple that are just down the street from me," Faith said, smiling.

On a cold day! "That would be nice, wouldn't it?" he said, then continued on without giving her a chance to answer, "I'd really like something near Gen, though. We've always spent a lot of time together and it would be really great to be able to walk home rather than drive."

"That should be possible, too," Faith said, carefully trying to conceal the disappointment in her voice.

Alberto returned with the bill and she quickly tossed down her MasterCard. He took it away and Taylor made a mental note to double his tip next time if it came back in less than two minutes.

"If you'd like, we can get together tomorrow night and visit a few houses to help narrow down your requirements," Faith offered.

Taylor shook his head. "I'm meeting a friend for dinner tomorrow," he said, for once glad to be getting together with Neil. "How about later in the week?"

Again, disappointment showed on her face, but she hid it behind happiness to get together later. "Wednesday night?"

Taylor knew he would have to do it sooner or later. "That'll work just fine. Let's see what we can find around Gen's and work from there."

"Sounds good," Faith said, interrupted from any further commentary by Alberto's return. *Double tip next time*, Taylor thought. Faith signed the slip, then put the pen back in the vinyl folder and slipped her glasses into their case.

"Well, sounds like you need to be going," she observed. Taylor wasn't sure what he'd said to give that impression, but decided to just go with it.

"'Fraid so," he said. "It's been a very long day and I'm exhausted. I really appreciate dinner, though," he said, rising and pushing his chair back in. Faith followed suit, reaching down to collect her sport coat, purse and briefcase.

"Anytime," she said. "With any luck, we'll be back here in a few days celebrating your new house." She smiled up at him, the dreamy eyes returning.

"That would be nice, wouldn't it?" Taylor agreed, leading the way to the door. He held it for her, waiting while she made her way through. Her car was parked right in front of the restaurant and he waited while she filled the back seat.

"I'll call you tomorrow and fax over some listings for you to review. Once you know what you're interested in, I'll make the appointments for Wednesday," she said. Taylor agreed and they bid good night, then she pulled out and headed down the street.

As she drove away, Taylor looked to see if Tom was home. The lights were on in the front of his apartment. He sighed, wanting to stop by, but knowing he should leave Tom to study. Still, he had seemed so disappointed when Taylor had been busy earlier. He looked back in time to see Faith's lights disappear up the hill on the other side of the river, down the street by the ball diamond. Taylor's eyes narrowed and he went back in the restaurant.

"Back again?" Alberto asked, face happy as always.

"Changed my mind about dessert," Taylor said. "I'd like one of those chocolate devil's food slices to go."

"Right away, sir," Alberto said. He returned with a Styrofoam container and a check for three dollars. Taylor handed him a five.

"Keep it," he said. "Have a good night, Alberto."

"You too, Taylor," he said, patting him on the back in a fatherly way.

Taylor took the cake and walked down the alley to Tom's. He climbed the stairs and knocked on the door. Seconds later, he heard someone coming to answer it. The door swung open and a young girl in her early twenties stood there.

"Yes?" she said politely as Taylor stood speechless.

"Uh, hi," he managed. "Is Tom home?"

"Sure," she said, turning back to the apartment. He saw Tom in the shadows of the darkened hall, coming toward them.

"Who is it?" he asked.

"I don't know," the girl said, walking back inside.

As Tom got closer, he recognized the form in the darkness outside and his face brightened. "Hi there!" he said.

"Hi," Taylor said, feeling a little stupid that other people were over.

"Dinner over?" Tom asked, looking at the package in Taylor's hand.

"Yeah, just finished. I saw the light on and thought I'd stop by."

"Cool," Tom said. "We're just having a study group, but you're welcome to come on in."

Taylor shook his head. "No, that's okay. I shouldn't have bothered you—I know you have exams this week."

Tom smiled reassuringly. "It's no bother."

Taylor nodded, as much to himself as to Tom. "I should go," he said, then held out the container. "Chocolate cake from Alberto's. I figured you could use a little caffeine at your next study break."

Tom took the container, opening it to look inside. "I love this stuff," he said. "Crazy for someone who works in a bakery, huh?"

Taylor shrugged. "It's an addiction," he said. "Anyway, I'll take off so you guys can keep at it."

"Sure you won't come in?" Tom said.

"Yeah, we'll catch up later. Have a good week and keep those grades up!"

"Sure, Dad," he said, laughing. Taylor waved a goodbye, then walked back down the stairs. Tom went back inside and closed the door behind him.

He walked quickly back to the car parked just up the street on the other side. Of course they were studying. What did he think they would be doing? Taylor felt really dumb—Tom didn't seem upset, but what kind of message had he sent to that girl? And who was the girl? Just a study partner? Probably—at least, he hoped so. What if she'd been a girlfriend?

Taylor shook his head at himself, climbing into the driver's seat. What was wrong with him today? He was dancing with the devil for dinner and making himself look ridiculous for dessert. *Way to go, idiot,* he said to himself, making the single turn to get back to Gen's. *Could I possibly find another way to screw up?* he thought.

As had become ritual, the kitchen light was on and Gen was upstairs. Taylor remembered she had been going out on a "sort-of" date. If she was already home by nine-thirty, it must not have gone well. He noticed a note on the table.

Neil called. Will meet you here at seven tomorrow. Sounds cute. G

Oh yeah, Taylor thought, *Neil. There's the icing on the cake.* So, he had flirted with Faith, made a fool of himself in front of Tom and his friend, and still had to go out on a date with Neil. *Note to self, don't ask self stupid questions.*

He made his way upstairs and found Gen's door open and the light of the TV casting a blue glow in her room. He quietly walked to her door and gently knocked as he peered inside.

"Hey, you," she said. Molly lay on the bed next to her.

"Hi. How'd it go?"

"Not bad. I mean, I'm home early, but it wasn't a disaster." Her eyes said something else.

"See him again?"

"Maybe," she sighed. "I'm in no hurry. How was Faith?"

"Hot to trot," Taylor said, laughing.

"Yep, that's Faith. Can she help you?"

"Looks like it. We're going out Wednesday to look at houses."

Gen nodded, yawning. "Cool. I'm free. Want me to tag along?"

Taylor smiled. "Definitely!"

"I'll be there. You saw the note from Neil?"

"Yeah."

"Good," she said. "Well, I think I'm going to sleep."

"Have a good night," Taylor said, walking back to his own room.

As he lay atop his covers in the warm air, he thought, *what a day*. Faith, Tom, Neil, Gen. His life definitely wasn't ordinary by any definition. Maybe it would be one day, but he had no idea when. Ever one to think on the positive side, he saw Tom's face as he handed him the cake—if he was bothered by the visit, he hadn't shown it in the slightest. Tom's smile was the last thing in his mind's eye, just as it had been virtually every night since they met. Taylor could only hope it would stay that way for a long time.

CHAPTER EIGHT

What Are You Doing this Weekend?

Neil arrived promptly at seven, just as Gen's note had promised he would. Taylor decided to stick with his original plan of not trying very hard, opting for a comfortable summer sweater and jeans with sandals. Some unseasonably cool weather had set in, so he grabbed a jacket, too, just in case.

As he saw Neil's black BMW pull up to the curb, he walked to the door. For once, Molly just turned and went upstairs, uninterested in whoever was coming to the door. Taylor watched her leave, surprised by implicit snub. When he looked back, he saw Neil walking up, dressed in an almost identical outfit, tossing his keys around his right index finger. *Damn!*

"Hi there," he greeted. "So, this is the place?"

"This is it," Taylor said, holding open the door. Neil leaned in to give him a kiss, Taylor held out his hand. "Find it okay?" he said, covering the less familiar greeting.

For his part, Neil recovered well, shaking Taylor's hand firmly. "No problem at all. Gen's directions were right on."

"Great! What do you want to do first, see the town or get some food?"

"Why don't we take a drive around, then we'll catch dinner—you know, use the sunlight while we can."

"Okay," Taylor said, reaching back to close the door behind him. He led Neil around the side of the house, to where he had left the Jag parked in front of its garage door.

"So this is what those new Jags look like," Neil said, examining Taylor's car closely. What was it about that car?

"Yeah, I've had it for about six months," Taylor said, backing out of the driveway. He headed off in the direction of the newer part of town, figuring he'd make a long loop and wind up back in the old section.

"How long have you known Sandy and John?" Neil asked.

"About four years," Taylor said. "I met John when I started with the firm—he had only been there a couple months longer than me. He does corporate law and I do employment law, so the two overlap pretty often."

"Sounds like you probably wind up sharing cases?"

"Sometimes. Most of the stuff I've been doing lately has been pretty cut and dry. I just bring John in when I get backed up more than anything. He does the same with me if an employee issue crops up in one of his cases."

Neil nodded, watching the neighborhood pass by. "They seem like really great people. I've only known Sandy for about a month, but we've had lunch together a few times and she's kept me under her wing."

Taylor gestured to the newer part of town as they emerged from the neighborhood. "So, you think you want to live all the way out here?"

"It's working for you, isn't it?" Neil asked. Taylor realized he was quite charming, but also wondered if the charm was more forced—like he knew he was charming and meant to be. He felt a coolness come over him.

"True," Taylor admitted, knowing that he also worked in the city and opted for the more rural life. Well, not *rural*, exactly, but certainly not the city.

"What's the community like out here?" Neil asked, looking at the storefronts and fast food restaurants as they passed.

"Very friendly. People are always saying hello as you pass them on the street."

"Not the *people*, Taylor, the Community. You know, are there a lot of people like us?"

The question snapped him around. Taylor was so used to avoiding the topic with Tom he had forgotten Neil was out. He didn't want to know if it was a nice town, he wanted to know if it was a town with other gay people.

"Uh, Gen says there are some. Honestly, I haven't really met any." *At least, not any who are admitting it.*

"Oh," Neil said, something more in his voice. "I assumed you'd already be connecting with them."

"I figure I will in time," Taylor said. "I've never been overly active. My last boyfriend was—you know, stickers, T-shirts, activities. I went along on a lot of it, but it was never a big deal to me."

Neil smiled. "That's okay. I've never been real active, either, but I've thought it would be a good idea to live somewhere where I wasn't the only gay guy."

Taylor laughed. "You'd at least know you were one of two in this town. Gen tells me there are more, but, as you said, they're not that active. The town accepts them, though. They find other reasons to apply titles. When I first moved here, I was the Jag Guy."

"The Jag Guy? Because of your car?"

"Yep. Almost everybody drives a nice conservative American car. My little cat stood out like a sore thumb to them. Everywhere I went, if I didn't know someone, I heard them whispering about 'the Jag Guy'. It's let up a lot, but it still happens once in a while."

"Do they know you're gay?"

Taylor shook his head. "Not as far as I know. I mean, Gen does, but I think she's the only one."

"Doesn't that bother you?"

"Why should it? Who I spend my time with is no one else's business. I think it's more fun to keep 'em guessing."

Neil considered Taylor's words, uncertain. "I guess that's true, but I like to feel like I can be who I am."

"Oh, it doesn't keep me from being who I am, I just don't put out a billboard, you know?"

"Yeah," Neil said, but Taylor could tell it bothered him.

They circled around past the new part of town and the chain stores lining both sides of the street. Taylor turned back for "down town."

"How long is the drive to work in the morning?" Neil asked, shifting the topic back to more neutral territory. Taylor watched him in his peripheral vision, trying to gauge his reaction to their previous discussion.

"Not bad," he answered. "It takes about a half hour on a good day, forty five minutes on Mondays."

"Only on Mondays?" Neil asked, looking to Taylor.

Taylor laughed. "Well, usually on Mondays. I just notice it's always bad on Mondays."

"Okay, stay at home on Monday," Neil said, laughing back.

They came down the road toward the river and Taylor looked up in time to see Tom talking to a couple of the kids on the ball diamond. He felt immediately guilty, even though he had told Tom he was having dinner with a friend. He knew it was, at best, a half-truth and he didn't like that. As he passed by, he thought he saw Tom look up, but then he was over the bridge and heading for downtown.

"Even kids playing baseball," Neil observed. Taylor waited for him to make another comment, but if there was one, he kept it to himself.

"Yep," Taylor said. "Well, that's about it. This is what everyone refers to as downtown, though you can see it's only about four blocks."

"I like it. They've been talking about moving me to the New York office," Neil said. "I won't know for sure for a couple days, but I can see where I could call a place like this home." He looked at Taylor. "It seems to have the right kind of people."

Taylor realized he was doing the whole dreamy eyed thing like Faith was doing last night. He nearly jumped, but kept his cool as he pulled into a spot just past Alberto's. The last thing he wanted to do was parade Neil past the bakery, or anywhere near the bakery, for that matter.

"This is the best Italian food around," he explained, unconsciously holding the door for Neil. Taylor had been raised to be a very polite young man by his parents and it left him always looking out for the people he was with.

"Taylor!" Alberto called as he came in. "Two nights in a row?"

Taylor smiled warmly as the host walked up. "Can you think of anywhere else I should take someone interested in the town?" he asked.

"Good point. Come right this way and we'll give you such a dinner that you'll never want to leave," Alberto said, leading them to a small table by the window. Taylor would have preferred something more secluded, but their late arrival during the dinner hour had left few options.

As they sat, Alberto held out menus. "You can look at the menus if you like, but I will tell you the veal is absolutely fantastic. Try the veal."

Neil looked to Taylor, his dark eyebrows raised. Clearly, he had not expected someone of Alberto's large personality. They shared a quick, silent conversation and Taylor handed back the menus. "Veal it is," he said.

"You won't be disappointed. Something to drink?" Alberto automatically looked to Neil first. Taylor wondered if he had a clue from his regular visits with Tom, but appreciated the propriety of him saying nothing.

"The house red?" Neil asked.

"Excellent," Alberto said. "And Mister Connolly?"

"I'll have the same. Thanks, Alberto."

"Two glasses of the house red, coming right up," Alberto said cheerfully, then bustled off to the bar.

"Wow," Neil said.

"He's great," Taylor replied. "And it really is the best food I've had."

"I guess, if you were just here last night."

"Oh, that. I was here with a real estate agent. I'm thinking about buying a house."

Neil looked surprised. "Really? I guess you do like this town."

"That I do," Taylor agreed as Alberto returned with the glasses. He turned and walked away as quickly and they each sipped their wine.

Taylor heard the door open and close, glancing over the edge of his glass at the person walking by. He nearly choked as he saw Tom in his little league uniform, obviously just up from the ball diamond. Alberto waited on him, handing him a pizza and breadsticks. Taylor hoped he might blend into the bright light coming in from outside enough to avoid notice, but then he saw Alberto gesture in his direction and Tom looked over. *Shit*, was the only thought that ran through his head.

Box in hand, Tom came over smiling, but not as broadly as usual. For his part, Taylor tried to act casual, waving in a friendly manner as though to call him over. Neil turned to look and see who had caught Taylor's eye and followed Tom as he walked to stand next to the table.

Taylor quickly pulled the greeting together in his head as Tom stood next to them. "Tom McEwan, Neil Gardener," he said, gesturing to each.

"Hi, nice to meet you," Tom said.

"Same here," Neil answered, shaking hands.

"I didn't realize you were coming here," Tom said to Taylor.

"Yeah," Taylor said, realizing it wasn't the best idea. "Neil is new around here and was interested in seeing the town."

"Good place to start," Tom said. Taylor noticed he was more subdued and felt the guilt grow in his gut. "Anyway, I was just picking up pizza for the group again tonight. You guys have a good evening."

"You too, Tom," Taylor said. *Take me with you.*

Tom and Neil exchanged a round of "nice to meet you's" and Tom headed out the door. Through the window on his left, Taylor could see him make his way back up to the apartment.

"Nice guy," Neil said. "Gay?"

Taylor nearly snarfed his wine, glancing to see if anyone had noticed. No one had. "I don't know," he said honestly. He also realized he *didn't* want the people around him to hear the conversation. He wasn't embarrassed to be gay, he just didn't want to be stereotyped in a place he felt comfortable. Not yet. Not ever.

"So, they're thinking about moving you to New York?" Taylor asked, changing the subject and moving the topic of conversation back to Neil. As Neil talked, he barely listened, thinking about Tom. He had looked bothered and maybe a little hurt. Taylor couldn't be expected to just wait around for him forever, but maybe he needed a little help. Of course, Taylor wasn't the poster child for relationship experience himself, so he could scarcely be a good choice to offer it to someone else, but he remained confident that Tom liked him and he knew he needed to try to help him express that…somehow.

Rainy Wednesdays were really no better than sunny Mondays in Taylor's humble opinion, at least insofar as driving from town to the city was concerned. Traffic was at a virtual crawl, leaving him time yet again to ponder the previous night.

He wouldn't go so far as to say dinner had gone smoothly, but it wasn't a total disaster. He sensed that Neil was frustrated with him for not being more open and aggressive. Much of the conversation had carried a fairly "Faith Roberts" tone, only this time coming from someone Taylor actually found physically attractive.

There was no question Neil was hot—he could easily have foregone a business career in favor of being a model. In truth, Taylor wondered what it was about himself that Neil liked. Certainly, he wasn't ugly—he maintained a good waistline, well-defined abs, and a nice butt. His blond hair was in a somewhat conservative though trendy enough style. His contacts let his natural blue eyes sparkle from his tan complexion…but there was nothing distinctive about him, nothing to attract a fashion model like Neil to want to date him.

Yet dating was exactly what Neil wanted, he was sure of it. He had asked what Taylor was doing for the weekend, forcing him to admit he had no plans. With Tom out of town, he really didn't know anyone else in town and hadn't focused much of late on his other friends. Neil said they would have to get together in the city and go to a club.

While Taylor didn't *hate* clubs, they'd never held a huge allure for him. He just felt like a slab of meat parading around hoping someone would take interest and haul him home to be grilled. He preferred relationships and friendships of some depth. Reluctantly, he'd agreed to Neil's advances, and Neil said he would talk to him once he knew what the company was going to want him to do about moving.

Secretly, Taylor hoped he *would* move. Then he would have an excuse to only focus on Tom. Egg basket be damned, Tom was the one he wanted. In fact, to prove it, Taylor decided he would stop by the sporting goods supply store on the way home tonight and pick up all that stuff Tom thought he needed for the camping trip. Then he would stop by and tell Tom.

Crap! No, he had to go out with Faith tonight, looking at houses. Taylor's eyes narrowed in thought as he pondered Faith. He determined he wasn't ready to deal with her again. Tom was the priority, or at least finding another excuse to talk to him.

He dropped his cell phone into the cradle, then hit the button on the steering wheel. "Faith Roberts," he said and the phone dialed her number from memory.

"Good Morning, Faith Roberts."

"Hi, Faith, it's Taylor. How are you?"

"Taylor! I'm great, how are you?"

"Fine, thanks. Listen, I need to reschedule tonight. I forgot that I have to go do some shopping that can't wait. How about next Wednesday?"

There was a pause on the other end. Taylor wondered what scheme she had cooked up for him, but her voice interrupted his thoughts. "Sure, Taylor, that'll work. I hate to have you miss out on some of those listings though. Were there any you really wanted to see? I'm sure we could work out something sooner."

Taylor shook his head. "Sorry, that's the next day I have available. There were a couple I'd like to see, but if they go, something else will come in."

"That's probably true," Faith agreed, but her voice clearly belied her disappointment. "Okay, next Wednesday it is. Say five-thirty at Gen's? I'll pick you up?"

He wasn't sure he wanted to ride with her, but said okay. They said their goodbyes and he hung up, smile returning as he thought of Tom. The phone rang seconds later and he half expected to see Tom's name show up. Instead, he saw, "Gardener, Neil".

"Taylor Connolly," he answered formally, nose wrinkled in disappointment.

"Taylor, it's Neil. How are you this morning?"

"Hey, Neil. I'm good. What's new with you?" Taylor said, being friendly, but not too much so.

"Well, as it happens, I just found out about New York. They're transferring me for sure. I have two weeks to find a place and make arrangements."

Yes! "That's wonderful, Neil," Taylor said, playing on his true enthusiasm to have the distraction gone. "I'm happy for you."

"Thanks," Neil said. "I was calling to see if you felt like going apartment hunting in New York for the weekend."

Taylor wasn't expecting that. He sat for a minute, trying to decide what the right answer was. He liked Neil as a friend and knew how hard it was to look for a place. And he *had* only asked him to help look. *And* he hadn't been to New York City in years. And Tom was going to be gone for the weekend.

"How long will you be gone?" Taylor asked.

"I was thinking of just going for the day Saturday."

A day trip—kind of a lot of driving for a few hours, but he could do it. "Sure, that'll work."

"Great! Pack a light bag just in case. My parents have a place in Manhattan if we decide we don't want to drive home Saturday night."

"Got it. What time Saturday?"

"Seven a.m. We'll get an early start to make the most of the day."

"I'll be ready," Taylor said.

"Cool—I'll see you then."

Neil disconnected and Taylor hung up his phone. *Good*, he thought. *Neil will move to New York and I can focus on Tom.* With renewed confidence, he exited the freeway, bound for work.

Traffic home was light at five-thirty and Taylor navigated with his usual agility. The day had flown by as he prepared to argue a case the following week. One of the benefits of his newfound fame was that he was able to get more clerks to do the dirty work for him, leaving him free to do more enjoyable things, like buy sporting goods.

He laughed, catching the thought as it rolled through his mind. Taylor had never been a particularly athletic person, gifted as he was with a naturally fast metabolism and good build. Athletics were for the jocks, a category in which he did not count himself.

Passing the exit he usually took to go downtown, he headed for the ramp to the new section of town, one exit farther down the freeway. He knew one of the strips of chain stores had a place that should have the items Tom had told him to get.

When he had finished, Tom's list had grown lengthy as he asked Taylor to buy virtually everything they needed for the trip. Taylor remembered how he'd look at it and realized how much it would cost. He'd brought out his checkbook and started to write a check.

"What are you doing?" Taylor had asked.

"I'm going to give you a couple hundred dollars to make up for some of this stuff. You won't use it again, so it's not fair to expect you to buy it."

"Why won't I use it again?" Taylor asked.

Tom had looked up, meeting his gaze. "Uh, I just didn't think…"

"That I'd go camping again? It can't be that bad." Taylor laughed and told him to put away his checkbook.

"Taylor, you can't foot the bill."

"Yes, I can. Call it a graduation gift."

Tom had grumbled a bit further, but ultimately relented.

Taylor pulled into the lot and parked his car near the front. He hopped out, still wearing a pressed white shirt, maroon patterned tie and khaki colored dress slacks. Several store clerks turned to watch him as he walked in.

"Can I help you?" one of the clerks said, watching Taylor's lost expression.

"Actually, yes," he said, pulling the list from his shirt pocket. "I need to pick up this stuff."

The young man's eyes bulged as he saw the list. "We'd better get you a cart," he said, grabbing a shopping cart. Tom had explained that he had a lot of the items on the list, but many of them were in sad shape from years of use. He'd crossed off a couple items as things he would bring back from his parents' house, but left many things they would still need.

The clerk zigzagged Taylor through the store, collecting the items—tent, inflatable mattress, mattress inflator, sleeping bag, camping stove with gas tank, bug repellant, and a variety of other odds and ends.

After everything had been tallied, it was Taylor's turn to be surprised—two hundred fifty dollars. And they still had to buy food. Ugh. The clerk offered to help him unload everything into his car. They walked outside and Taylor hit the trunk button, swinging it open. The clerk gasped in surprise.

"A Jag X-type!" he exclaimed.

Taylor rolled his eyes, but said nothing, tossing the items into the trunk.

"Nice car," the clerk offered.

"Thanks, uh, Steve," Taylor said, observing his name tag. "Steve" had to be all of sixteen if he was a day.

"No problem, man. Have a safe trip." He pushed the cart back to the store and Taylor hopped into the front seat, satisfied that he had successfully completed his mission.

His phone, which he had forgot he left in the car, said "1 Missed Call." He brought up the caller ID menu and saw Tom's name. He tapped redial and dropped it in the cradle while he backed out of the parking spot.

"Hello?"

"Hi there," Taylor said informally, heading home.

"Hi!" Tom greeted happily. "I tried calling you about ten minutes ago."

"I know. I saw it on caller ID—that's why I'm calling you back."

"Oh. Cool!"

"Guess where I was," Taylor said, smiling.

"Uh…bathroom?"

Taylor laughed. "Good try. Sports Authority."

"You got the stuff!"

Taylor smiled proudly. "Everything on the list. We're good to go."

"Great! Did you talk to Gen about the boat?"

Tom had offered to bring his parents' boat back if Gen wouldn't mind if he parked it in her back yard for a couple weeks.

"All set. She said you can just park it next to the garage."

"Excellent! Taylor, you're going to have a blast."

"I'm looking forward to it."

"Great! Hey, weren't you supposed to be looking at houses tonight?"

Taylor turned into the neighborhood, heading for Gen's. "I put it off until next week," he explained. "I wanted to be sure I picked up the stuff for our trip."

"Couldn't you have done that this weekend?"

Taylor shook his head. "I just wanted to get it done so there wouldn't be any problems. Turns out it's for the best, too. I'm going to spend the weekend in New York City with my friend, Neil."

There was a pause at the other end of the phone. "New York City? What are you doing there?"

Taylor realized too late it probably would have been better to bring that topic up later as he sensed apprehension from Tom. "Neil has just been transferred there. He asked me to come along and help him look for an apartment."

"He's moving away?" Tom asked. Taylor would swear he could hear Tom's mood brighten.

"Yeah—he has to be there full time in two weeks."

"How long will you be gone?"

Taylor didn't want to say much about Neil. He didn't want to upset Tom before his big final. "Just during the day Saturday. We're going to leave early in the morning and come back that night." Technically, that was true. The fact that they might stay over that night would just make Tom feel bad.

"Sounds like fun," Tom said. "Not as much fun as camping, but fun."

Taylor laughed, relieved Tom was okay. "Nothing is as much fun as camping...or so I'm told."

"You're told right," Tom said.

"Aren't you supposed to be studying?"

"I was just taking a break. But you're right, I should get back to it. This is the last big night before tomorrow's final."

"Then you're off to your parents'?"

"Yep."

"Good deal. I'll let you get back to it and catch you when you get back next week."

"Sounds good. Have a good time in New York—try not to get mugged."

"Thanks, I'll work on that. Good luck on your test."

The alarm clock went off, pulling Taylor from a happy slumber. He pushed himself up and saw the red numbers on the clock—6:30. He fell back to the pillow, face first. How had he managed to let someone convince him to get up this early. Oh yeah, that's right, Neil is beautiful. Damn him!

He rolled off the bed and stumbled to the shower. Molly was nowhere to be found—she had virtually lived in Gen's room the last few weeks. Fickle dog.

Minutes later, the mirror was covered in steam as Taylor toweled himself off. He went back into his bedroom and pulled on casual clothes. A sweatshirt and jeans seemed like enough for apartment hunting in New York. In front of his bed lay the bag he had packed the night before. Somehow, he had a feeling they'd be staying.

He pulled on a pair of running shoes, deciding they would be better for walking than his sandals. The clock read 6:57, so he headed downstairs, not wanting Neil to ring the doorbell.

His timing was perfect—as he came down the stairs, he saw Neil through the door, walking up from the curb. He opened the door and Neil smiled broadly, holding out a hand. Taylor smiled thinly as he remembered Neil trying to kiss him before.

"Good morning," Taylor greeted.

"Morning," Neil said. "Ready to go?"

"Yep." He closed and locked the door behind him. They walked to the BMW and put Taylor's bag in the back seat. As they took off down the street, Taylor realized they were headed in the wrong direction.

"It's faster if you go through the new part of town to get to the freeway."

"We're not going that way," Neil said. "You didn't think we were going to *drive* all the way to New York, did you?"

Taylor looked over to him confused. "There's another option?"

"My Dad's plane is waiting at the regional airport for us."

To say that Taylor was surprised would be an understatement. It didn't hold a candle to the surprise he felt as they pulled up to the hangar, though. When Neil said, "my Dad's plane," Taylor assumed a little Cessna. Instead, they pulled up next to a Gulfstream jet.

"*This* is your Dad's plane?"

"It's the little one," Neil said as the pilot loaded their bags into the storage area. "He has the big one in the Bahamas right now."

Taylor laughed nervously and wondered just what he had gotten himself into.

It was quiet in the house, and for once, Gen knew rattling pots and pans wasn't going to pull Taylor out of bed. It amused her the way he would come stumbling downstairs, hair askew, eyes puffy. She had wondered how long it would work and was surprised it still did.

She had heard him leave just before seven the day before and wondered what had happened last night. She thought he needed to get out and date a little more. She knew he liked Tom, but Tom was going to have some issues of his own to deal with and it wasn't fair to either of them to try to have a relationship right now. Of course, that was her opinion and she kept it to herself, but the thought remained.

Molly sat looking at her expectantly. Taylor's dog had all but adopted her since they'd moved in a couple months ago and she wondered how Molly would handle it if Taylor found a house. He'd even commented to her that Molly hardly paid any attention to him anymore.

As she pulled the box of Molly's favorite treats from the top of the refrigerator, Gen wondered what she may have done to curry such favor. Molly ate the bones and Gen pulled her leash from the wall, attaching it to her collar.

"Come on, Mol, let's go for a walk. I want chocolate."

Molly leapt to her feet and they went out the front door. It was still early, so most of the neighbors were in bed. Gen greeted the few who she recognized, but didn't stop on her quest to go to the bakery. Taylor had said Tom was going to be out of town, so she could only hope her chocolate croissants would be there and of any quality.

Together, she and Molly made their way across the street, stopping in front of Downey's. Gen took Molly to the light pole and tied off her leash. From Molly's level of disinterest, she was sure it wasn't the first time she had experienced the activity.

Gen walked through the door and stopped in surprise as she looked behind the counter.

"Tom!" she exclaimed. "I thought you were going to your parents'."

He smiled warmly as he saw her. "Hey, Pussycat," he said, safe because no one else was around. "I did go home for a couple days, but I got back late last night."

Gen smiled. "All the better for me, I'd say."

"Probably so," he said, going automatically to the case with the croissants. "Talk to Taylor?"

Gen shook her head. "Not yet. He said he might not get back until today. They weren't sure how long it would take to find something his friend was interested in."

Tom gave her a funny sort of look, but just folded over the bag and walked to the register. "I didn't get to talk to him much this week with finals and all," he said, ringing the sale. "I thought he said he and Neil were just going yesterday."

An alarm went off in Gen's head and she realized what the look on Tom's face was. "Yeah, that was the plan, but Taylor said they might stay at Neil's parents' place in the city if it got too late. It was going to be a lot of driving, you know, and they didn't want to push it." She handed Tom a ten and he made change.

"Better safe than sorry," he said, but she could see his smile was forced.

She tried to appear reassuring. "You never have to worry about Taylor. He's good at keeping himself out of trouble." *Almost as good as I am at getting him into it*, she thought.

"Maybe we'll catch up later," Tom said. "Let him know there's no baseball tonight. Everyone had to be somewhere else, so we just called it off."

"Will do," Gen said, feeling pretty low. "Will you be around? I can have him call you."

"Whatever is convenient," Tom said. "See 'ya round."

"Have a good one," Gen said and went back out to get Molly. In all the time she'd known him, he'd been happy and cheerful. This was the first time she'd ever seen him remotely moody and she found herself wondering if maybe there was something more there than just Taylor being infatuated. *And I just told him Taylor spent the night away with another guy...ohhh, what have I done?*

CHAPTER NINE

Weekend Retreat

Taylor's eyes snapped open like they were spring-loaded. It was still dark and he rolled over to see the time. 6:15. Perfect. He tossed aside the covers and stood up, giving himself a moment for a good stretch.

He'd talked to Tom Tuesday morning on the way to work. Taylor smiled as he realized it was becoming a fairly regular event—yet another good sign that Tom was interested in him. Tom had invited him to come to another of the little league practices, to which Taylor again had to decline because Neil had beat Tom to the punch. Taylor had promised himself that he would break things off with Neil—he wanted to give Tom his undivided attention. In truth, there wasn't anything to break off except Neil's interest, which would shortly be separated by several hundred miles.

Tom's disappointment was a little more pronounced then, though. Taylor knew he needed to reassure Tom that he wanted to spend time with him, so he'd quickly segued them to discussing the details of their weekend camping. Tom had brightened, but Taylor sensed a distance in him that he knew he needed to repair. Tom had said they should plan to leave around seven o'clock, as it would take about three hours to get to the small lake where he planned to camp. As much as he wanted to take the Jag, he wanted to take his parents' boat so they could cruise up and down the river that fed the lake, so he told Taylor he'd pick him up at Gen's.

Taylor hadn't heard from him for the rest of the week. He'd gone to dinner with Neil at a fancy predominantly gay restaurant in the city and mentioned he was going to be pretty tied up between house hunting and the camping trip. Neil had been disappointed, but said he would call Taylor the following week before he made the final trip to New York. Taylor agreed, thinking one last phone call wouldn't be a big deal.

He finally stopped by Tom's last night, hoping he would be in a better mood. Taylor had been at his most charming, even hauling him off to Alberto's for dinner, but the distance was there. He was conversational, but barely. Taylor avoided any mention of Neil or his recent absences. He realized in retrospect that was exactly the wrong choice. *He needs to know nothing happened,* Taylor thought. He decided he would tell Tom all about the trip to New York City in the car—start the weekend off right and release the tension.

Taylor made a quick trip through the shower and messed his hair to let it air dry. They were going to be in the woods for the next three days—he wasn't going to be looking or smelling too good anyway, so he figured he'd start it off right.

Opting for a T-shirt, sweatshirt, and shorts, he pulled on an old pair of hiking boots and grabbed the bag of stuff he'd packed. He'd already loaded the camping gear in the boat under the tarp and everything else waited at the back door for Tom's arrival. Another glance at the clock indicated it was only 6:40. He went down the back stairs and dropped the bag next to the other equipment.

A dull blue light illuminated the living room and he poked his head around to see Gen sitting in one of the easy chairs, Molly at her feet.

"Morning," she greeted, smiling over a steaming cup of coffee.

"Hi there," Taylor said, taking a seat on the couch.

"'Bout ready to go?" Gen asked.

"All set. Just need Tom," Taylor replied.

Taylor realized Gen looked bothered and he knew of very few things that ever bothered her. His gaze held hers briefly, then she looked down and took a sip from her cup.

"Did you talk to Tom about your New York trip?"

Taylor shook his head. "Not yet. I was planning to tell him about it this morning."

"Does he know you spent the night with Neil?"

Taylor frowned. "I wouldn't say I spent the night with him. We stayed at his parents' house, but that was all."

Gen nodded and took another sip. "I talked to Tom on Sunday and he was surprised you weren't back yet. He said he thought you were only going to be gone for the day. I think he was a little upset."

Taylor's eyes narrowed. "You told him I stayed with Neil in New York?"

Gen sighed. "We were just having a conversation. I didn't realize you hadn't told him. I didn't realize he would react so strongly."

Taylor looked at her sharply. "What do you mean, 'react so strongly'?"

She shook her head. "He just seemed a little agitated. Taylor, I'm sorry, I had no idea. I feel like an idiot."

Taylor stood, pacing toward the TV. "He thinks I spent the night with Neil. That's why he's been so moody all week."

"Have you two talked?" Gen asked.

"*No*, we haven't talked," Taylor said, a little shorter than he really meant to be.

Gen winced slightly, as though his irritation had a physical manifestation. "I'm really sorry. I wouldn't have said anything if I'd known. I'm sure he'll understand when you tell him about the weekend."

He looked back at her, feeling bad for his tone before. "It'll be okay. At least I know now. Why didn't you say something sooner?"

"I haven't had much of a chance to talk to you," Gen explained. "I knew I had to tell you before you left, though, so you didn't get ambushed."

"Thanks for that," Taylor said. He heard the sound of a key tap at the back door and turned to see Tom staring in at him. Thankfully, he was wearing his Taylor Smile, so they were starting off on the right foot. He went and opened the door and Gen waited at the door to the kitchen.

"Hi!" Tom greeted, sounding every bit his usual self. "Ready to go?"

"As soon as we load this stuff," Taylor said, trying to be jovial in return after Gen's revelation.

"Won't take a minute," Tom said, then looked at Gen. "Mornin', Pussycat," he said and produced a bag to hand her. "I'll bring him back in one piece. Promise."

Gen took the bag, thankful Tom wasn't mad at her, either. "Just remember, he's breakable."

"Speak for yourself!" Taylor defended, then picked up several of the bags.

They loaded the Jeep in a matter of two trips, then Tom backed it up to connect to the boat he had left after his return the previous weekend. Minutes later, they were on the road, bound for their weekend together.

Taylor decided to go for it before he lost his nerve or Tom shifted them to a different topic.

"Hey, sorry again about Tuesday," he said, referring to his most recent failure to be available to help with the little league team. "Neil—the guy you met the other night? He's moving to New York and just felt like getting together for dinner. He called right before you did."

Tom's knuckles took on a slightly whiter tone by the thin light of dawn and Taylor watched his jaw clench and unclench a couple times as he spoke. The smile was pretty much gone.

"It's okay, I know you're busy. Don't worry about it."

Taylor sighed, knowing his only choice was to press on. "I do worry about it because I don't like turning people down."

Tom smiled a little. "There's only so much Taylor to go around."

Taylor returned the smile and laughed, but more from nervousness than at the implied joke. "I do not have any plans for this Tuesday, though," he said, leading.

"Sorry, all our guest invitations are used up," Tom said, eyes on the road.

"Well, hell. I guess I'll have to go find some other little league team to embarrass myself in front of."

This time Tom did laugh. "Good point. Okay, we'll give you one more chance."

"Thank you," Taylor said with a small bow of his head. He fell back into his seat, letting the conversation lull for a minute. Tom continued to grip the steering wheel tightly and stared straight ahead as he navigated them down the freeway, lost in his own thoughts. Taylor sat straight up again, turning to face him.

"Hey, speaking of Neil moving, I have to tell you about last weekend. You're not going to believe this!"

Tom glanced over briefly, knuckles whitening again. "Oh? What happened?"

"Let me tell you!" Taylor said, hoping his own upbeat approach would carry over to Tom. "Neil called me Wednesday morning after our dinner to tell me that he had been transferred. He'd only been in town for a couple months, so he didn't know very many people around here—that's why he came out to see our town. He was looking for places to live. Anyway, instead of being here, he's getting transferred to New York."

Tom relaxed a little and Taylor knew he was on the right track. He needed Tom to understand, without actually saying it, that he really didn't have competition.

"Anyway, he called and asked what I was doing for the weekend. Since *you* were out of town, my own weekend was shaping up to be pretty light." He made the statement pointedly, again wanting Tom to understand he would rather have been with him. Tom shot him a sidelong glance, but kept his eyes on the road, the corners of his lips upturning ever so slightly.

"He asked me to go to New York City with him. He said we'd only be gone for the day Saturday, so I said that would be cool. A few hours in the car, hang out in the city for the day, and then back home."

"Yeah, I remember you said you'd be gone for the day," Tom said, message: but you spent the night with him. Taylor knew he had Tom's attention.

"Right. Then Neil said I should pack a light bag in case things ran late and we didn't want to have to come back right away. His parents have a place in Manhattan."

Tom glanced over again, meeting Taylor's eyes briefly. "A place in Manhattan? Neil's family must be doing fairly well."

Taylor rolled his eyes. "You haven't heard the half of it! Just wait! Anyway, I said I'd go, so we agreed we'd leave Saturday morning, bright and early." Taylor nearly went on to describe how he had tried to make himself look less desirable through plain clothing, be remembered Tom wasn't quite ready for that. He pressed on. "Neil showed up right on time and we headed off in his car. Thing is, we didn't head off in the direction of New York City."

Tom looked over, frowning. "Where'd you head?"

Taylor's eyes narrowed. "The regional airport about ten miles from Gen's house."

Tom continued to glance back and forth between the road and Taylor. "The airport? He has a plane?"

"His *Dad* has a plane."

Tom nodded. "Of course—daddy's money."

Taylor laughed. "Right. Neil had arranged for us to use the *small plane.*"

"Small plane?"

"A Gulfstream 10 jet."

"No shit!" Tom exclaimed, staring wide-eyed at Taylor. It was the first time Taylor could remember hearing him swear.

"No shit," Taylor replied in kind, nodding.

"You *flew* to New York in a *private jet?*"

"All told, it took us about forty-five minutes. We landed in New Jersey and picked up Neil's spare car—a Porsche Boxster—then he drove us into the city. We parked at his parents' and made it to a nice little French pastry shop in Forty-Second Street in time to still have breakfast."

"Holy crap, Taylor! Way to spend the weekend," Tom said. Taylor saw him tensing up again, no doubt considering how he would compare against someone like Neil. He kept talking, trying to keep Tom going in the right direction.

"No kidding," Taylor agreed. "After breakfast, we went to a few apartments. Let me tell you, these were not 'just getting my career started' type places. Most of them were two stories, all had designated parking, security, and all kinds of amenities like gyms, pools, cleaning services, et cetera. He finally decided on one near Central Park, not far from his parents, signed the papers, and that was that."

Tom glanced over. "So then what?"

"Then," Taylor said, continuing the tale, "He told me he his parents had tickets for an opera playing that night at the Metropolitan Opera House. He said if I didn't mind staying, we could catch dinner at Tavern on the Green and then move on to the show."

"You went," Tom said, not so much a confirmation as an order, as though he would stop the car and flog Taylor if he had even thought of coming back early.

"Do I look stupid?" Taylor said laughing.

"Wow—you must have had a *blast*!" Tom said. "I'd have *loved* to do something like that. I haven't been to the theatre in years."

Taylor was again reminded that Tom had a very literate, cultural side to his otherwise easy-going personality. He made a note to set something up for another weekend soon.

"It was a blast," Taylor affirmed. "Dinner was great, the opera was incredible, and then we went to some club Neil had frequented when he lived in the city before and met up with some of his friends. I think we rolled in around three a.m. His parents' place is a virtual mansion sitting twenty stories above Central Park. I was in one of the *three* guest rooms, facing the Park directly."

"Must have been hard to come back," Tom said, glancing peripherally at Taylor.

"Nah," Taylor said, a hint of a smile dancing on his lips. "New York City is a nice place to visit, but not somewhere I would want to live. There is a lot to do, but that is sort of the magic of going there—you go, have some good times, then go home."

"Did you go by the site?"

"No," Taylor said. "Neil had visited there a few months before, but I didn't really want to. I've seen it on TV and it would have made me feel like a gawker. I don't have a problem with people needing to see it themselves, but it's not for me."

Tom nodded. "I'd like to see it, but I can understand why you wouldn't."

They sat for a minute and Taylor let Tom process what he had told him. He'd laid it all out in his head over the last couple days, making sure to catch every major point in a linear format to allow Tom to be sure nothing had happened. Taylor realized he really had no doubt about Tom anymore, so it was only a matter of waiting him out…until he came out.

Taylor did choose to omit a couple of semi-relevant facts—among them, that Neil had seemed disappointed when he accepted the offer of the guest room, that the club they had gone to was one of the nicer gay clubs in the city, and that Neil had spent the entire evening flirting with him. Neil was a nice guy, charming, and flattering, but Taylor had unfinished business with Tom—business that he hoped could last a lifetime.

"So, after a stunning weekend of wealth, prosperity, and culture," Tom said, breaking the silence, "You had to return from Neverland to the Sticks and go even farther from the highlife to spend a long weekend in a tent. I feel honored."

It was Taylor's turn to shoot Tom a look. *I'd rather spend the weekend with you,* he thought. "I'd rather spend the weekend with you." Taylor realized the words had come out before he'd even consciously realized he was going to say them. Tom's knuckles had gone white again. Crap! Recover!

"When I was with Neil, I felt like the pauper boy who was being shown what the world could be like. When I'm with you, I feel like I'm enjoying the company of a friend, sharing something he likes." *Not bad*, Taylor thought.

Tom considered his words and he nodded. "In that case," he said, voice sincere, "I really do feel honored."

There it was—the Taylor Smile. Taylor felt himself relax.

"So," Tom said, "That was some weekend, but I've got a few surprises in store for you, too. It may not be the Metropolitan Opera House, but there's nothing like cleaning and filleting your own fish dinner." Taylor looked at him sharply and Tom laughed. "Or, I've got some nice T-bones, hamburgers and hot dogs."

"Whew!" Taylor said. "A weekend of cheese and crackers wasn't sounding so appetizing."

"No fish, huh?"

"Not a big fish fan, but don't let me rain on your parade."

Tom smiled. "Don't worry, I won't make you eat them...but I'm still gonna make you catch them."

Taylor smiled back and knew he was going to be in for quite a weekend.

The fire crackled from the damp logs mixed in with the dry twigs and leaves. The golden glow pushed away at the darkness, warming and illuminating the two men sitting a few feet from it.

It was almost summer and the days had been comfortably warm, allowing Tom and Taylor to get away with shorts and T-shirts, or jeans and boots for hiking. The evenings still cooled off fast, though, and they quickly switched to long pants and jackets.

As Taylor felt the chill on his back, he wished they could start a fire *behind* them as well. He had to admit, though, that he was thoroughly enjoying himself. Over the past two days, Tom had given him quite a workout. They spent the morning hiking the rocky outcroppings surrounding the almost completely vacant lake. They would then come back and make something for lunch, followed by boating for the afternoon. Taylor spent the time soaking up sun while Tom fished for his dinner.

There were only two other campsites with people on them around the lake. One site was a father and son who had also spent the weekend fishing. The other was a party of four or five guys who seemed to spend most of the weekend drinking. Taylor was thankful that they hadn't been a problem—everyone seemed content to keep to himself.

Taylor felt his muscles ache from exertion, his skin itch with slight sunburn, and his eyes grow heavy in the waning hours of the night. It was wonderful—he felt as though he would never stop smiling.

Beside him, Tom sat in a low-slung folding chair, roasting a marshmallow over the fire. Taylor watched as he slipped the marshmallow onto the end of a twig and held it over the flame, letting it get a dark golden brown color without burning black. He brought it back and gently blew on it to cool it off, then pulled it from the stick in one swift bite. He promptly replaced it with a new hapless victim and plunged the stick back into the flame.

"You are going to be *so* sick," Taylor observed.

"Am not," Tom said, slowly turning the twig to allow even heating. "We used to eat whole bags of them when I was little."

"Ugh," Taylor groaned, laughing.

"There's still a good half a bag left. Sure you don't want more?"

"No, thanks."

Tom had settled into his chair after their dinner of hot dogs and potato chips, smiling broadly as he held the bag of marshmallows and two sticks he had selected from the woodpile they'd collected on the first day. He had insisted that they roast marshmallows and make s'mores. Taylor ate a couple, then begged off, the rich sweetness being more than he was used to. Tom had then steadily worked his way through the bag, abandoning the other ingredients in favor of just eating warm, gooey marshmallows.

Tom realized he was being watched and looked over, flashing a relaxed smile and returning Taylor's gaze from under his dark navy blue baseball cap.

"Still having fun?"

"Time of my life," Taylor said, meaning it.

"Better than New York?"

"How could Tavern on the Green hope to compete with hot dogs and s'mores?" Taylor answered, grinning broadly.

"I could take a shot at singing Tosca for you if you'd like," Tom said.

Taylor laughed loudly, but said, "Thanks, I'll pass."

"Your loss."

Taylor lay back in his chair, legs stretched out in front of him, crossed at the ankles. High above, in the broad opening between the trees, the stars looked down upon them. The sheer beauty of it amazed Taylor, having always been around city lights. Even at Gen's, there was enough ambient light to block many, if not most, of the stars. In the distant woods of the foothills, however, the stars were bright and numerous. Taylor wondered if, in orbit of one of those distant lights, another person, alien to him, looked back, wondering if he was there.

"You're awfully quiet," Tom observed.

"Just enjoying the serenity of silence," Taylor said.

"How poetic."

"Must be the company."

They had talked about many things throughout their time together, yet somehow the issue of the burgeoning relationship between them never came up. Taylor wondered about that, knowing he played at least a fifty-percent hand in it. He was supposed to be out of the closet, had been for years, yet somehow he was content not to say anything to this man. Why? He wasn't embarrassed about his lifestyle—he'd gotten over that years ago. He didn't fear rejection, either. If it was one thing he was sure of, it was that Tom was not the kind of person to condemn another person for being who he was.

Maybe he was just content with the way things were, at least for the time being. It was easy to just be friends—no demands, no responsibilities, no commitments. Taylor had spent much of his 'out" life with Ryan and had put up with a lot of the demands Ryan placed on him for behavior. Now he was free to do whatever he wanted, to be whomever he wanted—most importantly, to be himself.

He also didn't want to pressure Tom. Whatever his reasons, if he was gay as Taylor had come to assume, he wasn't out. Taylor had gently probed several times, trying to find out if Tom had been in any long term relationships. Each time, Tom would give partial answers that evaded more than they answered and allowed him to change the subject. Taylor knew he could have pushed at any one of those times, but also knew that it would have forced the issue in a way he didn't think was fair.

Perhaps most importantly, he really *was* enjoying himself, in a way he wouldn't have thought possible. While he didn't have anything against nature, "being one with nature" had never been an important part of his life. The weekend had taught him that was probably an error on his part. The peace and tranquility brought by the absence of people and technology was unique in his experience and he welcomed it.

Beside him, Tom stood, folded over the bag of marshmallows and clipped them. He set both atop the cooler next to him and turned to Taylor.

"Well, if you're just going to sit there and stare off into space, then I'm going to write."

"Write?" Taylor asked, refocusing on him after his eyes had adjusted to the darkness above.

"It's this thing we English majors do," he said over his shoulder as he went in the tent. He returned with a leather-bound book and a pen.

"Thank you, I know what writing is," Taylor deadpanned. "What are you writing?"

"It's just a journal. I've kept one for years—just personal thoughts I like to write down from time to time. I wrote a little the other day before you woke up."

Taylor was fascinated. "Anything about me? Can I read it?"

Tom looked stricken, but recovered. "Uh, it's personal. Seriously, I don't mean to be rude—you just seemed to be enjoying the quiet, so I thought it was a good time to write. I can write later if you want to talk."

Taylor had to admit, he was very curious, but he knew better than not to respect his friend's privacy. He shook his head. "It's okay. We're not keeping a schedule here and I'm not going anywhere. Enjoy yourself."

Tom smiled and nodded, then turned his chair so he could write in the fire's light. He propped his feet up and touched pen to paper. Taylor's gaze returned to the sky overhead and he felt contentment on his face.

Tom watched as Taylor resumed staring at the heavens, his boots resting on a large log acting as a footrest. His dark denim jeans were loose on his thin frame and he had pulled on a sweatshirt under his navy blue jacket. His hair parted naturally off center to the right, a mix of light and dark blond over his rapidly darkening skin, still messy from having been under the baseball cap Tom had given him.

They had spent the later afternoon in the still chilly waters of the lake, taking a quick camping shower in their bathing suits, then knocked a volleyball over an imaginary net.

Taylor looked the most relaxed Tom had ever seen him. He remembered the first time he had laid eyes upon him, when he tied Molly's leash to the lamppost outside the bakery. He was one of the most beautiful guys Tom had ever seen. Somehow, he'd brought himself to be witty enough to talk to him while taking his order. Even more miraculously, Taylor had seemed to like finding reasons to keep the conversation going.

Over the last few weeks, he realized he had truly grown to like, and perhaps love, this Taylor Connolly…and it was scary. He'd rejected romantic relationships, telling himself he would worry about them once he took care of the more pressing issues in his life—finishing college, establishing his career. In truth, it hadn't been that hard because he'd rarely come across anyone he was attracted to—certainly never anyone who seemed to be attracted back.

Taylor was unusual. Tom felt he liked him, but he never seemed to put on any pressure. Tom figured he would say something sooner or later, ask about his past relationships. Yet every time the opportunity came up, he would let Tom's defensive deflections move them off to another topic. He seemed to care as much about Tom as Tom did about him.

He browsed through his last few entries. Taylor had asked if any were about him. Tom smiled as he saw they were exclusively about him. He was nervous about the situation with this guy Neil. He may not have had a lot of experience, but he'd seen people like Neil before and it grinded him to think Taylor could fall for someone like that. Even if Taylor wasn't interested in him, Tom wanted him to be with someone better than Neil. Neil just wanted another trophy.

In the night darkness, under the firelight, Tom reached into his heart, seeking the emotions that he had long pushed back, asking for their help in a way he had never sought help before. Taylor stared straight up, into the endless field of stars, eyes wide. Tom doubted he even realized he was looking at him. He wanted nothing more than to take those beautiful tan hands and ask Taylor to spend his life with him.

Tom felt something stir within him and turned his attention back to his journal, letting his pen touch the paper...

If only the winds had the strength
To push me to you and you to me
I could be complete, I could be whole
We are two halves of one person
I long to be joined with you,
To be one with you
Come to me, Taylor—
Let me feel your strong arms around me
Your warm soft breath against my cheek

Let me know my love for you is real
And that your love for me is eternal
Let us never again be apart
As we go hand in hand to the end of time
Come to me, Taylor,
And be one with me, forever...
I Love You

CHAPTER TEN

Crisis of Faith

As they pulled up to the house, Taylor felt his nose wrinkle involuntarily. Immediately, he knew there wasn't anything specifically *wrong* with the house. He just wasn't interested. It had been the same at the other three houses they had already stopped at. He could sense aggravation from Gen, but Faith kept her cheery face as she hopped out of the forest green Bonneville to lead them up the steps to the front porch.

Taylor had known he was in trouble from the moment he saw Faith pull in the driveway. She had worn a black suit with a skirt cut well above the knee and a white blouse with a neckline that dipped low enough to offer quite a view when she leaned to pick her pen up off the floor after "accidentally" dropping it there.

Gen, ever helpful, had simply smirked behind her hand as she offered Faith something to drink. Faith had politely declined, commenting that they had a full schedule of houses to visit that night. Taylor would have paid money to have a picture of her face as Gen said, "Then you're right, we should get going." Clearly, Faith had not anticipated Gen's presence on their evening ride-along.

Three houses later, Taylor stood before yet another house that was probably perfectly fine, yet he couldn't get excited about it. He wasn't sure what the problem was. The house was on a street about two blocks from Gen's, nearly the same distance from downtown, just as easy to access from the freeway. As Faith studiously made the sales pitch, it had three bedrooms, a spacious kitchen, a small den, and a nice-sized living room. The garage was only a one car, but there was plenty of room to expand if he decided to get married. The yard had plenty of room for Molly, probably just a little more than Gen's own house had.

As the two women chattered back and forth about various amenities, Taylor strolled around the house again by himself, trying to put a finger on the root of his discontent. He was committed to living in the town, just as he had been before. The weekend with Tom had only further cemented his feeling that this was the place he wanted to live.

Standing in the second floor master bedroom, Taylor thought about Tom. Their weekend had gone very well, except for the nagging fact that they had not had "the talk." It had been too perfect—too idyllic—to risk messing it up. On the one hand, he felt a little guilty for continuing the deception, but on the other, he hadn't felt any sense of curiosity from Tom. If he suspected, or was even interested, he'd kept it to himself, all the while being very attentive to Taylor's comfort and needs, ensuring he enjoyed his first official camping experience.

Tom had said, in no uncertain terms, that he planned to seek a teaching job in the area. There were a number of them open for which he would be qualified and he knew several of the people making the hiring decisions. Technically, he could make more money at some of the districts nearer the city, but he was comfortable where he was and that said a lot. Taylor had caught the subtle message that part of the comfort had to do with his presence in the town. Tom was friends with a number of other people in town, many of whom played Sunday Night Baseball, but Taylor had noticed his attention was uniquely focused on him lately.

Taylor realized he had been unconsciously rating each house for whether or not Tom would like it and he realized that was part of his problem—he wanted Tom to be with him looking at the houses, not Gen. It wasn't that he didn't appreciate Gen's help or input, but that he felt like Tom should have a say in selecting the place in case he wound up living there.

Taylor stopped cold. The situation was getting out of hand and he knew it. He had to do something before it got any worse. He couldn't let it continue to affect his life without something more definite.

"Checking out the view?" Faith's voice called from the doorway. Taylor jumped, not expecting anyone behind him.

"Uh, yeah," he said. He hadn't realized it, but he was sitting at the foot of the bed. Unconsciously, he reached down and straightened the covers.

"Sorry to startle you," Faith said. "You seem to like this one a little more."

"It's nice," Taylor said, getting his wits about him. "I'm still figuring out what I'm looking for."

"Gen thought this one fit your requirements a lot better than the previous ones. What do you think?" Her blue eyes watched him intently, as though reading his mind to determine what he was really thinking.

"It looks good. I'm still not one hundred percent sure what I want, but Gen's right that this is a lot closer to the mental image I've had."

Faith frowned. "Not a perfect fit, though?"

Not unless Tom likes it, Taylor thought, but caught himself. "It's not bad, but I think it's a good idea to evaluate all my options," he evaded.

Faith smiled. "Very smart indeed," she agreed. "There are two more I wanted to show you tonight. Ready to go?"

"Yeah, I'm ready," Taylor said, following her out and down the stairs. Gen waited at the bottom of the stairs, her dark eyes following his every move. As Faith locked up, she got in the car behind Taylor.

"You're not ready yet, are you?" she asked.

"I don't know," Taylor said honestly.

Gen placed a calming hand on his shoulder. "Honey, there's no hurry. You know I'm not kicking you out."

"I know," Taylor said, his head hanging a bit. "I just need to figure out what's going on."

"It'll work itself out with time," Gen said. She pulled her hand away as Faith came up to the car and got in the driver's side.

"Okay, that was a little closer," she said, as much to herself as them. "Good. The next one may be closer yet." She backed out and headed down the street, turning to Taylor as she drove.

"So, are you planning to go to the dance Friday?" she asked, an expectant smile on her face.

"Friday?" Taylor asked, again lost in thought.

"Yeah, the Spring Dance. Surely you know about it?"

Taylor blinked, a deer in the headlights. There could only be one reason Faith would bring up such a thing and he had no idea what she was talking about.

"I, uh, wasn't sure I'd be in town," he stumbled, searching for a way to get out of the discussion.

"Really? You sure do have busy weekends, don't you?"

"Sometimes," Taylor answered, trying to think of a way to deviate the discussion.

Faith nodded, glancing briefly at the road to make sure she wasn't going to hit anything. "I haven't decided if I'm going yet, either. I'm not really seeing anyone this year and I couldn't make up my mind if I want to go stag."

Her attention focused back on Taylor, her eyes big and expectant. He felt beads of sweat pop out on his brow.

"You know, Faith, I have been having that same problem," Gen said. "Of course, I was lucky enough to talk Taylor into promising to take me if he was going to be here,"

Taylor made a mental note to buy Gen a really big birthday present this year. Faith's expression drooped and she turned her attention back to the road, saying, "Oh." She then turned back to Taylor, eyes bright again.

"What about your friend, Tom? He seems nice. Is he taking anyone?"

"He mentioned taking a girl from the college," Taylor lied. He hated lying, but he'd be damned if he was going to have Faith going after Tom.

"Oh. Naturally. You know, that's the problem with this town—not enough eligible bachelors."

"No kidding," Taylor said before he even thought about it. His breath caught as he waited for Faith to realize what he'd said.

"No, really," she said, missing the meaning of his comment. "I've lived here for years and spent very little time actually *in* the town, except for work. If I want to meet people, I always have to go hang out in the bars in the city. It's just kind of depressing for someone my age."

"They say there's someone out there for everyone," Gen prophesized from the back seat.

"With my luck, he lives on the other side of the earth," Faith said.

Hopefully, his luck with hold out, Taylor thought, then mentally smacked himself for such an unkind comment. Wasn't it possible to just shop for a house without the "personal" angle?

Faith slowed, then pulled into another drive. The sun was setting and it was hard to see much of the exterior, but Taylor could see it was a virtual copy of Gen's house. The lights were on inside, but there was no car in the drive nor the two car garage, so Taylor assumed the owners had just left the lights on to make the home seem more inviting.

She led them inside, then on the usual tour, pointing out rooms, closets, bathrooms, and other features meant to make Taylor want to move in that very instant. The biggest thing the house had going for it, in his opinion, was that the floor plan truly was almost identical to Gen's. He had to admit, he liked Gen's house, but he felt the same hesitation he had before.

Again, he left the girls chattering on the main floor and made his way upstairs. He realized another problem he had as he shopped—these houses were all too big for one person. He didn't need this much space. The flat had consisted of two bedrooms, two bathrooms, a living room and a kitchen. That was it. He didn't need three bedrooms, a den, et cetera, if it was to be just him.

Hopefully, it won't be just me, Taylor thought, looking out the window into the near darkness of the back yard. It was almost pointless to look at houses in the dark—it was too easy to miss something important. Still, he could see that the yard had a couple good-sized trees and plenty of room for Molly to move around. If he looked carefully, he could just make out the roofline of Gen's house, a couple blocks in the other direction.

He felt his waist vibrate and reached down to pull the phone from its clip. As he flipped it open, he saw the characters display, "Tom," as he had programmed it a few weeks before.

"Hi there," he greeted in a warm, casual voice.

"Hey, buddy, how are you?" Tom asked.

"Good, thanks. What's up?"

"Just checking to make sure you're not going to stand me up tomorrow afternoon."

"Tomorrow? What's tomorrow?" Taylor asked, smiling in spite of himself.

"Little league practice!" Tom said, taking the bait.

"That was *this* week?"

"Taylor!"

He laughed. "Relax, I'm just pulling your chain. Of course I'll be there."

"I knew that," Tom said, then changed the subject. "Whatcha doin'?"

"House shopping. This is number five, I think."

"That good, huh?"

Taylor shrugged. "I'm just not really in the mood tonight."

"You need ice cream."

"What?"

"You need ice cream. When you're done, come by here and we'll go get ice cream. Bring Gen along."

Taylor felt his mood brighten, but he suspected it had nothing to do with the ice cream. "Okay. I'm about shopped out for tonight anyway. We'll see you in about fifteen minutes."

"Sounds good. See you then."

Tom hung up and Taylor closed the phone and returned it to his belt. He turned and found Faith giving him a quizzical look in the door. He jumped, then took a breath.

"I keep sneaking up on you, don't I?" she asked.

"Yeah, I guess so," he said.

"Ready to move on?" she asked. He could hear in her voice that she already knew the answer and he wondered how much of the conversation she'd caught.

"Actually, I think I'm ready to call it a night. A friend just called and wants me to swing by this evening. Let's postpone for now and pick it up again in a couple days."

Faith nodded, looking down. "Okay," she said. For once, she didn't try to persuade him. Taylor felt bad for her, but reminded himself it wasn't a situation he'd asked for—his only wish was to look at houses and that was the sole reason they were together.

Faith led the way back downstairs and Gen again eyed Taylor. They repeated their pattern, getting into the car while Faith locked up.

"What's up?" she asked.

"I told Faith we're done for tonight," Taylor said. "Tom called and invited us to join him for ice cream."

"Sounds good," Gen said. "I think you've got the idea of what's available anyway."

"True enough," Taylor said. Faith got in and got them back on the road, her mood perceptibly altered. She was all business.

"There is still one more whenever you'd like to see it and I can setup second visits if you decide you're interested in anything you saw tonight," she said, navigating them swiftly back to Gen's house.

"That's cool," Taylor said. "Sorry I'm not more into it tonight. I'll try to be more prepared the next time."

"That's okay," Faith said, still maintaining her professional demeanor. "I'll be ready when you are." She pulled into Gen's driveway and waited while they got out, never turning off her car.

"I'll call you later this week," Taylor confirmed.

"I'll look forward to that," Faith said, smiling thinly. He closed the door and she backed out, driving swiftly away. Gen stood with Taylor, watching her departure.

"She seemed miffed," Gen observed.

"I think she heard my call with Tom. I don't think she appreciated someone taking us away."

"Or at least someone taking *you* away."

"Yeah. Thanks for saving me."

Gen smiled broadly. "What are friends for, baby?"

Taylor looked up the street at the lights of the downtown area. "You want to just walk? It's a nice night."

Gen nodded. "Sure. Let me dump these heels and grab Molly."

Taylor was again drawn to the realization that Molly spent more time with Gen than him, but he realized he was just thankful they were there for each other. He had enough on his mind without worrying about Molly or, for that matter, Gen. He knew he was *really* going to owe her when everything settled down.

Gen reappeared at the front door, Molly trotting along behind her. She locked up and joined Taylor at the sidewalk.

"Ready?" she asked.

"Yep, let's go," he said and they headed "downtown."

"Is it my imagination or have they improved since the last time I saw them?"

Taylor relaxed on Tom's deeply padded sofa, the TV tuned to that show about neighbors who each went into the others' house and remodeled a room. He watched it absently, observing as he had so many times that *he* wouldn't be letting his neighbors redecorate for him anytime soon—he'd seen their taste and it was frankly frightening.

"They'd better be improving or I'll get fired," Tom said from the kitchen. He had invited Taylor to join him for "a homecooked mystery meal" while they lapped away at their ice cream cones the night before. Taylor felt guilty discussing their plans in front of Gen, but she graciously declined Tom's offer to join them. *A very* big *birthday present*, Taylor thought again, remembering his promise to himself the night before.

"How long do they get to stay co-ed?" Taylor asked. The people on the screen were painting the walls in alternating red and white color sections. He moaned in spite of himself.

In the kitchen, Tom had something sizzling in a frying pan, but he had forbidden Taylor from looking at the meal before it was presented. "They group them by skill level for the co-ed teams. There are still strictly male and female teams, too. They can go all the way as a co-ed team, but they're less competitive teams, generally. God, that's awful!"

Taylor turned sharply, not following Tom's segue in the conversation. He found him looking over his shoulder at the TV.

"I would not be happy to come home to *that*," he observed, continuing to prepare the meal behind the bar separating the two rooms.

Taylor suppressed a grin at his friend's indignity over the bad decorating, considering his own thoughts.

"You just have to be careful who you let through the door," he said.

"I suppose that's why it's best to leave the wild color schemes to the professionals," Tom said, turning back to the stove.

"Aren't these the professionals?"

"No comment," Tom said, again creating sizzling noises as he cooked.

Taylor craned his head to see over the counter. "Come on, how 'bout a hint?"

"Down, you," Tom said over his shoulder. "All good things come to those who wait."

Taylor bit back a more pointed comment, falling back onto the couch. "Fine," he mock pouted, turning back to the TV. It was nearly time for the unveiling. The other couple hadn't been nearly so wild with their color and decorating choices, so he was eager to see both couples' reactions.

"What kind of rice?" Tom asked, standing at the cupboard.

"I'm being given a choice?"

"Take it while you can get it."

"What are my choices?" The show was coming out of commercial.

"White, brown, or yellow." The owners were being shown their new room. The wife's reaction was about how Taylor would have felt, if a little more dramatic. She held her hands to her face.

"Oooh, I don't think the wife is too thrilled," Tom said from over his shoulder.

"Can you blame her?" Taylor asked.

"Not a bit," he said, then tapped Taylor on the shoulder. "Rice?"

"Brown," he said. When all else fails, go healthy, that was his philosophy.

"Got it," Tom said, returning to the kitchen.

Taylor again relaxed into the couch, watching the other couple as they saw their room. In their case, the wife was thrilled, but the husband thought it was a little too wild for his taste. In Taylor's opinion, the only wild thing was a bright color, but who was he to judge?

He lay back into the couch again, closing his eyes. Onions, green pepper, garlic, oregano, chicken, and a couple other things he couldn't quite place. He was glad Tom liked to cook real food—eating out was okay for a time, but it was nice to be able to relax once in a while, and he had no patience for boxed food. For someone skilled in the kitchen, it really didn't take that much longer to prepare "real" food that was more nutritious, tastier, and generally healthier.

"Beverage choice?" Tom called, drawing him back to consciousness.

"You pick. I don't know what I'm eating, remember?"

"Wine it is." Taylor glanced back in time to see him pull a bottle of white wine from the rack. "Dinner table or coffee table?"

"Casual's fine," Taylor answered. Tom came around the counter and set two glasses on the coffee table. He then returned with two plates of salad, setting one in front of Taylor and one for himself.

"Gotta get your greens," he said, then handed Taylor a linen napkin.

He looked at the salad, again feeling impressed. It was big enough to offer a good taste, small enough not to overpower and spoil the rest of the meal. Tom sat down next to him at a discrete distance on the other end of the couch.

"Nice presentation," Taylor said, taking a good-sized bite of salad.

"I'll bet you thought all I could do was bake," Tom said, forking a mouthful himself.

Taylor shrugged. "Nah, I knew better. You kept us well fed last weekend."

"Hot dogs and hamburgers? Even my *dad* can't screw those up."

"Thereby implying your gourmet skills aren't inherited from your father?" Taylor observed.

"Neither of my parents, actually," Tom admitted. "Mom overcooked everything and Dad was fine as long as it involved a grill. I learned to *really* cook when I was an undergrad. I had two roommates who were both fairly good…and then there was Emeril."

"Emeril!" Taylor exclaimed. "I thought I smelled garlic."

Tom laughed. "Maybe a *little*. I make a killer béchamel."

"Yeah, well my alfredo would stop your arteries."

"There's a selling point," Tom said. Both their plates were empty, so he took them away, returning to the kitchen.

"Sure I can't help?" Taylor asked.

"You're not very good at being served, are you?"

Taylor laughed. "Always the host, never the guest."

Tom returned with two plates. "Well, tonight you're the guest." He set one plate in front of Taylor, taking the other for himself, as before.

"Yes, sir," Taylor said, eyes widening in surprise as he observed the meal before him. His assumptions on the content were way off base. Clearly, his nose needed a tune-up.

"Surprised?" Tom asked, watching his reaction.

"A little," Taylor admitted grudgingly.

Tom laughed delightedly, patting him on the back. "Now for the truth—I cheated."

"Huh?" Taylor said.

"I had some diced onions and green peppers from the other night, so I left them on the counter while I cooked up the other stuff. You know, to throw you off the trail."

"Not fair."

"All the better to keep you guessing, Watson," Tom said, picking up his fork. "Dig in!"

Taylor picked up his own fork, admittedly eager to try the spread. Instead of his initial thoughts, he found a plate of sautéed breaded veal chops drenched in a rich garlic butter sauce with capers and steamed mushrooms over a bed of brown rice with a side of steamed veggies including carrots, broccoli, asparagus and water chestnuts. He cut the veal with a fork, eagerly devouring a hefty bite.

"Wow!" he exclaimed between bites. He chased the bite with a sip of wine, then turned to Tom. "Is this yours?"

Tom nodded proudly. "We ate *well* in college."

As Taylor took another bite, he felt the phone on his hip vibrate. He set down his fork, then pulled the phone free to see who it was. Without a second thought, he flipped it open.

"Hi, Pete," he greeted, wiping his mouth with his napkin. "Having dinner with my friend, Tom. No, that's okay, what's up?"

He gestured with one finger to Tom. Generally, he hated taking phone calls in front of people, but Pete had called a couple times recently with a lot on his mind and he felt like he needed to be there for him.

"Really!?" Taylor exclaimed. Pete's voice continued dully on the phone. "That's great! Tomorrow? Sure, no problem. Where? Yeah, here is fine. I'll take you to Alberto's. Yeah, Italian, you'll love it. Great, see you then. Have a good night and congratulations!" He hit "end" and clipped the phone back to his belt.

Tom's attention turned back, eyebrows arched in the natural question. "Sorry, that was my friend Pete."

"I caught that," Tom said, reaching for his fork. "Congratulations?"

"Yeah, he just called to let me know he asked Anita to marry him." He took a bite, watching Tom's reaction. He visibly relaxed, resuming his own meal.

"That is good news. So they're coming out here?"

Taylor nodded. "They want Gen and me to be in the wedding party, so they're coming out to discuss plans."

"Sounds like fun," Tom said. "I did that once for a friend from school It kept me fairly busy for a few weeks, but we had a great time."

"I'm looking forward to it," Taylor admitted. "You should come by tomorrow night. Gen and I have known Pete and Anita for a while. They're great people."

Tom shook his head and made a dismissive gesture. "That's okay, I don't want to be a fifth wheel. You guys will have a lot to go over."

"If you've already done it, you can offer valuable suggestions," Taylor pointed out.

Tom shot him a look. "I've been in *one* wedding."

Taylor nodded. "See? That's one more than any of us have been in."

Tom's face took on a quizzical expression, then morphed to resignation. With a sigh, he asked, "What time?"

"Seven o'clock."

"Okay."

"Tommy! How are you?" Gen asked, still keenly aware of the bomb she had dropped the last time she'd seen him. Tom's smile immediately set her conscience at ease as he accepted her hug.

Gen had quietly taken the seat next to Pete, leaving two empty chairs together at the round table. Taylor sat next to her, leaving Tom to sit between himself and Anita.

"Hi, buddy," Taylor greeted. Before he thought to stop himself, he pulled Tom into a friendly hug as Gen had. To his surprise, Tom didn't pull back. Quickly, Taylor turned to Pete and Anita.

"This is my friend, Tom. He and Gen have been friends for a while. He lives here in town."

Tom shook hands with the other two, then took a seat. Pete turned to him with an expectant gaze.

"So, Tom, what do you do?" he asked.

He ducked his head a little self-consciously. "Right now, I run the bakery up the street, but I'm starting out as a teacher this fall."

"Really? Taylor mentioned you were just finishing college. Now you're going right back to school, huh?"

Tom shook his head. "Actually, I finished my bachelor's degree a couple years ago. The business scene wasn't for me, though. So, I went back to school to get my teaching certificate and now I'm just waiting to hear how my interviews went."

"That's great," Anita interjected. "We need more good teachers. Pete and I have talked about me switching careers down the road. I've always wanted to teach and the schedule would make having kids a lot easier."

"What do you do now?" Tom asked.

"I'm a chemist."

"And you're marrying a lawyer?"

Pete laughed. "Actually, she's helped on a couple cases. A regular Angela Landsbury."

"I'm not sure that's a compliment," Taylor said.

"Yeah, everyone around her kept coming up dead," Gen added.

"Okay, here's to me not being Angela Landsbury," Anita said, raising her water glass. The sound of the toast brought Alberto back and he quickly took their drink and dinner orders.

A short time, and five full stomachs later, Pete and Gen switched seats so Gen could look over some of the planning materials Anita had brought while Pete, Tom, and Taylor discussed important things like where to have the bachelor party and what kind of beer would be the most popular. Tom excused himself to go answer nature's call and Pete turned sharply to Taylor as soon as he was out of sight.

"Okay, so what's the scoop?"

Taylor pulled back, not expecting the direct question. "Scoop about what?"

Pete rolled his eyes. "Come on, Connolly, we've known each other too long. He's cute and he obviously likes you. Have you done it?"

"Pete!" Taylor exclaimed, face reddening.

"Well?"

"No!"

"What are you waiting for?"

Anita and Gen had looked up and were following the conversation. Gen put a hand on Pete's arm. "Tom's not out," she said.

"You should be able to fix *that*," Pete said, still looking directly at Taylor.

Taylor was about to retort as the door opened. His eyes went wide as he saw who walked in. "Oh, shit," he said under his breath.

Gen followed his gaze and winced as she saw who was looking back at them.

"Hi, guys!" Faith said. She walked over and stood next to Taylor, a casual hand on his shoulder.

"Hi, Faith," Gen greeted, ever graceful. Tom returned at just that moment, standing to one side as Faith stood in front of his chair.

"I just stopped in to pick up a sub on my way home," Faith explained, though no one had asked.

"We're just finishing dinner," Taylor said, stating the obvious. "These are our friends Pete and Anita. They just got engaged," he explained. "And, of course, you know Tom."

"Congratulations!" Faith said to the couple. "I'm always glad to see happy couples—happy couples buy happy homes."

"Faith is our resident realtor," Taylor explained to the out of towners.

Faith eyed Tom as she moved out of his way. "I guess this is your seat, huh?" she observed.

"That's okay," he said, remaining standing so as not to be rude.

"Anyway, I just wanted to say hi. I'll let you get back to your evening." Again, she eyed Tom, glancing between him and Taylor. "I'll see you at the dance on Friday?"

"Dance?" Tom asked.

Taylor pulled back the growl that threatened to escape from his throat. "The Spring Dance," he prompted. "Remember, you said you're bringing your friend Mandy." He deliberately used Tom's sister's name, hoping he'd catch that something was up.

"Oh right. I forgot that was *this* Friday," he said, playing along.

Faith shook her finger at him. "You'd better not forget—there's nothing worse than being stood up."

"That's true," Tom agreed.

She turned toward the counter. "Anyway, have a good evening," she said and walked away.

"See ya, Faith," Taylor called, turning back to Pete.

"She seemed nice," Pete said.

Taylor just blinked at him and said nothing.

"So, Taylor, I'm going to a dance with Mandy?" Tom said from the other side.

Taylor turned to him. "She asked me if you were going the other night. Gen had already said she was going with me, so I wanted to get you off the hook. I assumed you would rather not spend the evening having Faith chase you all over."

"But now I'm going to a dance with my sister who lives five hours away."

"Just say she stood you up," Gen said. "After all, there's nothing worse than being stood up."

"Good point," he observed again. "And that way, I don't have to go."

Gen shook her head. "Oh no, if we have to go, you have to go. You can go with Taylor and me."

"That should be fun," Pete observed with a pointed look in Taylor's direction.

Again, Taylor just glared at him as Gen came to the rescue. "It will be a lot of fun. We can just go, hang out for a while, and not have any expectations."

"We might even be able to get you tickets," Taylor said, eyes never leaving Pete.

Pete smirked at their inside joke. "While that would be tempting, we're going to Anita's folk's on Friday to share the news with them."

"Bummer."

Gen turned her attention from the two sparring friends back to Tom. "So, will you join us?" she asked expectantly.

"How could I say no?"

CHAPTER ELEVEN

The Spring Dance

Taylor stood in front of his closet, arms crossed over his bare chest, a scowl on his face. What to wear? It was a gay man's nightmare—night out with his best friend, who was supposed to be his date, and the guy he was in love with, who he really wanted as his date, and no idea what to wear. He knew he shouldn't push it—it was just a casual dance, but wardrobe was important as a means to continue to send a message to Tom.

"Genevieve, what are you wearing?" Taylor called, still staring into the double-wide track of clothes.

"I was thinking about a nice little black dress, cut short, and lots of cleavage," she called from her room.

Taylor stuck his head out the door, looking down the hall to her door at the opposite end. As usual, Molly was lying in front of it looking back at him. "You'd better be kidding!"

Gen appeared at the door, clad in a light strapless summer dress covered in small green flowers. "Of course I am. Relax, stud-boy," she said laughing. "Besides, I don't think the flowered summer dress is quite the look you're going for...at least, not tonight."

Taylor shook his head, a thin smile grudging its way onto his lips. "Thanks," he said, too nervous to come up with a better quip in return. "Care to offer more useful advice?"

"Nice button-down, khaki's, sandals," she said. "The polka-dots are a nice touch," she observed, looking directly at his boxers.

Taylor immediately became self-conscious and went back into his room. He tended to think of Gen as a sister and wasn't particularly worried about what he wore in front of her, as long as the main concerns were covered.

"What are you and Tom doing later?" Gen asked.

He pulled a shirt with a muted green pattern and looked it over. Satisfied, he turned to the waiting ironing board to press out the few wrinkles and hangar pulls. "No plans," he called out the door.

"Don't you think you should come up with something?"

"I figured I'd see how the evening went," Taylor said, pulling the shirt over his shoulders. "It's to the point where we really need to start talking about the reality of where we're going. If it goes well, we'll talk. If not, then we'll probably just go home."

Gen appeared at the door, her black hair pulled back and arranged in little ringlets that danced between her shoulder blades and down her back. She generally opted for subdued makeup, but had gone for a darker eye shadow and a subdued mauve blush that accentuated her cheekbones, making her almost regal.

"Wow," Taylor breathed.

"Think you can be seen with me?"

"And how," he said.

"Good, then put your pants on," Gen laughed, leaning against the doorjamb.

"That's not the reaction I'm supposed to get from a girl, is it?" he asked, reaching for a pair of sand-colored khaki's.

Gen nodded. "It's the reaction *you're* supposed to get. Now you just need to get off your butt and get the reaction you want from Tom. I've never seen you so nervous."

Taylor tucked in his shirttails. "I don't think I ever cared so much."

Gen smiled knowingly. "I don't think you ever did, either."

He stopped, staring her straight in the eye. "Really?"

Gen reached into the closet and retrieved a belt to hand him. "Honey, you liked Ryan, maybe even loved him for a time, but you were never like you are when you're with Tom. You love him completely and I think you have from the moment you met him. That's why you're trying so hard not to do anything wrong."

"Am I succeeding?"

She smiled and put a loving hand on his shoulder. "You seem to be. I've known Tom for a few years now and I've never seen him like he is when he's with you, either. The only thing that scares me is that he's not out. You're going to have to be gentle with him about that—he has to come out in his own way and in his own time."

Taylor sighed. "I've been trying to be patient."

Gen laughed. "You've had the patience of kings…or queens. But trust me, sweetie, nobody is going to fault you for being patient. And I think Tom knows that, too, in his own way. Camping went well, remember?"

Taylor remembered their couple of nights around the campfire. "I kept thinking he was going to say something, but it was like he could never quite work up the courage."

"Maybe he's afraid you'll reject him," Gen analyzed.

"I can't imagine what I would have done to make him think that," Taylor worried, pulling the belt through the loops.

Gen shook her head. "You probably haven't done anything. He's not out, remember.; he has no frame of reference to judge whether or not someone will accept him."

"How do I tell him I will?"

She smiled again. "By accepting him. You've already done it and you're continuing to do it. You're showing that you like being a part of his life and having him be a part of yours. Slowly, it'll just happen. Come on, *you're* not the novice. You know how it goes."

"I'm not exactly that experienced, either. A couple short relationships and one long-term failure don't make for much of a resume."

Gen shrugged. "Look at it from the positive side—you don't have that much of a lead over him, either. You've been out for a few years longer and have a little more life experience, but that's it. That should be less intimidating for both of you and leave you a lot of space to explore your own relationship together."

Taylor watched her through narrowed eyes. "Why don't you do this professionally again?"

"My friends already wear me out," she said. "You look fantastic. I need to finish getting ready. I'll meet you downstairs in a couple minutes."

"Sounds good," Taylor said. She walked back to her room and he heard his phone buzz from where he had dropped it on the dresser. Picking it up, he expected to see Tom's name, but instead saw something else. With a groan, he opened the phone.

"Taylor Connolly," he answered.

"Taylor! It's Neil. How are you?"

"Hey, Neil. I'm doing good, how are you?" Taylor asked.

"I'm good, thanks. I was wondering what you're doing tonight. This is my last night in town and I wanted to see you before I take off for the big city."

Taylor shook his head, though Neil couldn't see the action. "There's a dance in town, tonight," he explained. "I'm taking Gen."

"Oh," Neil said, disappointment obvious. "A girl?"

Taylor sighed. "Long story. But, yeah, Gen and I will be at the dance."

"What about later? Is it an all-evening thing?"

He wasn't sure how to answer that. He wanted it to be an all-evening thing with Tom, but had no idea what would happen. "I don't know," he said honestly. "All I can do is let you know if plans change."

"I understand," Neil said. "Listen, I'll check in with you later. If you're free, great. If not, maybe you can come up to the city some weekend. I'd like to get together, though."

Taylor shrugged. "Yeah, that would be great. Listen, I need to go right now, but we can catch up soon and work something out, okay?"

"Sure. I'll talk to you later."

"Okay. If I don't talk to you before, have a safe trip."

"Thanks. Take care, Taylor."

"You, too," Taylor said, then folded the phone closed. He reached down to pull on a pair of sandals, then walked downstairs.

Gen sat in one of the chairs, watching the evening news.

"Was that Tommy?" she asked.

Taylor shook his head. "No, it was Neil."

"Neil?" she repeated. "I thought you told him you were done."

Taylor squirmed. "Not exactly. I just told him I was going to be tied up with a friend."

"Taylor!"

He sank into the other chair. "I didn't know what was happening. At that point, we'd just spent an incredible day in the city and I didn't want to just shut him down."

"So you built up false expectations?"

"I just didn't shut him down."

Gen shook her head, unexpected anger in her eyes. "Taylor Connolly, that is a cop-out and you know it."

Taylor looked at her pleadingly. "He's just so...aggressive. He went after me all night, but never crossed the line. I've never felt anything like that. I liked it. I'm so confused."

She sat back, though never turned her attention away. "I can under-stand how that would be something you would enjoy. But if you're going to pursue Tom as you seem to be, it's not fair to leave Neil on the hook."

Taylor nodded. "You're right." The doorbell rang. He saw Tom's dark form in the small window beside the door. "I'll take care of it when I talk to him later."

They rose and she put a reassuring hand on his arm. "I know you'll do the right thing." She turned and opened the door.

As soon as Tom's eyes met Taylor's, the Smile appeared. Taylor did his best to meet it as Tom pulled Gen into a hug. He stepped forward to shake hands and was surprised when Tom hugged him, too.

"Hi there," Taylor said, letting the surprise leak into his voice.

"Howdy," Tom greeted. He wore a simple navy blue polo, khaki's, and medium-brown brushed leather shoes. Comfortably conservative, Taylor observed.

"Shall we?" Gen asked.

"Lead the way," Taylor said, gesturing to Tom. He took Gen's arm and they followed Tom out the door. He had left the Jag parked in the drive-way and showed them both to the car. In seconds, they were off.

The neighborhood was bustling. Gen had promised that much of the town would turn out for the dance. What had started as just a chance for people to get out and enjoy the spring had turned into a virtual town fair, though there weren't rides.

As they drove, many people waved from their own driveways, all recog-nizing the infamous car. Gen had insisted Tom sit in front with Taylor and that made him a little self-conscious, but none of the people who were waving seemed the least concerned. *Maybe they've already figured it out, too,* Taylor thought to himself.

He made the turn at Main Street, heading in the direction of the park. In the waning sunlight, he could already see the light of candles and holiday lights that had been woven through the trees. Thankfully, the bright neon lights of the ball diamond weren't on, leaving more intimate surroundings for the dance.

Several people turned and watched their arrival, waiting while Taylor parked the car. The trio headed for the growing crowd, following the sound of music and the smell of barbeque.

"Taylor! Gen!"

They turned and promptly wished they hadn't. Faith bustled toward them, pulling some unhappy looking guy along behind her. The unintended butt of Gen's earlier joke, she wore a low-cut black dress that stopped well north of her knees.

"Hi, guys," she greeted, as though they were best friends.

"Evening, Faith," Taylor said, allowing just the tiniest hint of a drawl to slip into his otherwise unaccented speech.

She looked over Taylor's left shoulder with a curious expression. He glanced back and realized Tom was standing right behind him—closer, in fact, than Gen was standing. Gen realized it, too, taking Taylor's right arm with a warm smile to Faith.

"So, Faith, you must introduce us," she prodded.

To Taylor's disappointment, the neighbors who had waited when they pulled up just waved and continued on, recognizing that they had been stopped. He returned his attention to Faith and her guest, suspecting the information might come in handy later.

"This is Mick. He's a friend from the office," she explained. Turning to Mick, she continued, "This is Taylor, one of my clients, and his roommate Gen. Lurking there behind him is Tom, the town baker." As she said Tom's name, Taylor knew there was nothing he could do to avert her attention from him. "What happened to your friend, Tom?" she asked sweetly

"I got stood up." He did his best to look despondent, and Taylor suppressed a smile, both at the act and at Tom's country bumpkin accent. "But, Taylor and Gen wouldn't let me be by myself, so they dragged me along with them."

"What are friends for?" Taylor asked, pulling the attention back to himself. "And, if I'm not mistaken, the dancing is that way," he said, pointing to the music. Without waiting for further commentary from Faith, he turned and led the way, Gen on his arm, Tom shoulder to shoulder with him.

Faith rushed to keep up, but they made no effort to wait for her. Taylor hated to be rude, but Faith was not who he had come to spend the evening with and he had every intention of enjoying himself.

As the neared the dance floor, Taylor recognized the sound of "Wish You Were Here." He smiled, but decided he wanted to deflect any further thoughts Faith might have of "looking after" Tom.

"It's a slow dance," he said. "Why don't you two start and I'll get us something to drink?"

"Hey, I don't want to steal the first dance," Tom said.

Gen grabbed his arm, astutely grasping Taylor's intent, as always. "It's okay, Tommy. We're all just here as friends. Taylor will get his chance to dance later."

"Okay by me," Tom said and held out an arm. Gen took it and they were off. Taylor watched them go, a happy smile slipping onto his face. He had never thought of himself as tall, being just under six feet, but he realized he had a couple inches on Tom, who was between him and Gen's five four. He watched them dance, as casual and comfortable with each other as he would be and his smile grew. It would be a good night, of that he was confident.

Turning from the music, he headed in the direction of the beer tent. The town had gone all out, he saw, from a pig roast to burgers and dogs, to barbeque chicken. Gen had bought their tickets weeks before—ten dollars a person seemed cheap as he saw all the work that had gone into the event.

He reached into his pocket and pulled a wad of bills he had gotten that day just to be sure they would have enough to be well fed and watered. A young girl stood behind a folding table with large coolers of beer on either side of her.

"I'll take three Lites, please," he said, pulling out a twenty.

"Hi, Taylor," the girl said.

He looked up, noticing her as more than the person selling the beer for the first time. He'd always found it funny that he so often failed to notice girls—it had been one of his first clues about his sexual identity when he was younger.

"Hi, Suzy," he said, digging into his memory. The checkout girl from Safeway. He'd seen her around a few times since the first morning he'd met her—the same morning he'd met Faith, he remembered. Maybe Suzy wasn't so nice after all…

"Who'd you come with?" she asked.

His eyes shot up, but he let the question process through his brain a second time and shook his head at his own crudeness. *Get your mind out of the gutter, Connolly*, he thought.

"I'm here with Gen," he answered, hoping the darkness of the tent kept the redness from showing on his cheeks.

Suzy was looking at him a little more closely than he felt comfortable with, and he wondered if maybe he really had blushed more than he thought. "Who's the third wheel?" she inquired.

"Third wheel?" Taylor asked, confused. Couldn't he just buy a beer?

She pushed three bottles toward him, holding up the third one.

"Oh! Tom McEwan got stood up, so he came with us."

Suzy's face changed a bit at the mention of Tom's name. "I didn't think he got out much," she said. "Kind of an introverted jock."

Taylor frowned at the unexpected analysis of his friend. "What do you mean?"

She shrugged. "Nothing, really. I mean, he's a nice guy and all, but he never does much other than the coaching thing and baseball on Sundays."

Taylor felt himself grow defensive for Tom's sake. "He was in school full time and working full time," he clarified.

"School?" she asked.

"Yeah, he's going to be teaching high school this fall. He's been going to college full time in addition to running the bakery."

"Hmm," she said. "Never took him for being real smart." She eyed Taylor. "You guys know each other before you moved here?"

He shook his head. "No, I met him the first weekend I was here."

She nodded. "Must've hit it off well. I've seen you two together a lot since you've been here."

Taylor felt himself grow nervous at the rather obvious cross-examination and he pulled the three bottles toward him. "How much?" he asked.

"Four fifty," she said.

He handed her the twenty and waited while she pulled a five and ten from the small lock box. He took them as she handed them across the table, saying, "Keep the change."

"Have a good evening," Suzy said, acting as though the whole discussion had never taken place.

"You, too," Taylor answered politely, heading off in the direction of the music. John Fogerty's Centerfield had replaced Floyd. At least he had to give them credit for a broad musical selection.

"Hey, what took so long?" Tom asked as he found them near where they had come in.

"Sorry, I got caught by Safeway Suzy."

"Ugh, Joe's girlfriend," Gen said, looking at Tom.

"Oh, Miss Personality," Tom remembered. To Taylor, "She's always milking people for information about everyone in town by telling people what she's heard other people say. She's one of the biggest gossips around, but she always maintains a low profile."

"Nice," Taylor said, choosing to keep the contents of his discussion with her to himself. No need to tell Tom things she'd said that weren't so nice.

"Hey, there you guys are," a voice called from behind. Taylor turned to see Rob and his wife, Mel, walking up to join them. They shook hands and exchanged greetings.

"We saw you pull up, but then Faith came along and ambushed you, so we figured we'd wait until you got inside," Rob explained.

"She has a way of doing that," Gen agreed.

Rob turned to Tom. "Emily has been looking for you. She and Amanda have determined that they're going to get to dance with you tonight, if either one of them can work up the courage to ask you."

Tom smiled his same broad, easy smile. "I think I can take care of that. Where are they?"

"Come on, I'll show you," Rob said, leading the way.

"That beer looks good," Mel said. "If you guys don't mind me running off on you, I'm going to go get one."

"Don't blame you at all," Taylor said and an instant later, she was gone. He sighed, turning to Gen. "This is quite a shin-dig," he observed.

"Yeah, it's fun. I've come for the last three or four years and it's always been a good time. Hey, I saw a couple of the couples I wanted to introduce you to, too."

Taylor frowned. "I'm not sure that's a good idea. These people watch each other like vultures. Suzy was going on about Tom being nothing more than a jock who doesn't get out much. Then she commented that she's noticed us together a lot. I don't want to do anything that will cause trouble for him."

Gen gave him a look. "Taylor, you can *talk* to people. I promise, you don't have to sleep with them."

He shook his head. "That's not the point. If people see us talking, they may infer things about me. I don't care what they know about me, but I would feel bad if it extended to Tom."

Gen laughed. "Well, you're too late. Here comes one of them now." Taylor further soured and she slapped his shoulder. "Behave yourself, mister."

Two men approached them casually, as though they were just strolling by. As they got closer, Taylor was able to see them more clearly in the twilight. Both were in good physical shape from what he could see. One was slightly taller, with wispy brown hair and medium brown eyes. The other was a little shorter than Taylor, with curly blond hair kept short. Both wore light linen shirts and khakis. The taller one wore boat shoes and the shorter one had sandals similar to Taylor's. They smiled as they stopped in front of Gen.

"Hi there, how are you?" the shorter one greeted.

"I'm good. Glad to see you," Gen said.

"Nice night," the taller said.

"Yep," she agreed. "Rick and Steve, this is the friend I've been wanting to introduce to you. Taylor, this is Rick and Steve Johnson-Hayes."

"Nice to meet you," Taylor said, shaking hands with both. From Gen's gesture, he surmised Rick was the taller, darker one, while Steve was the shorter, blond one.

"Gen tells us you're an attorney," Rick said.

"That's true."

"Great! Our town could use a good attorney."

"What do you guys do?" Taylor asked.

"I'm a chiropractor," Rick answered, "and Steve is a Psychiatrist."

"And you both work here in town?"

Steve nodded. "Our office is in the new section, just before the first strip mall on the right. We've been here for about five years."

"Operating on the theory that you can cure their stress one way or the other, right?" Taylor joked.

"Exactly!" Steve said, laughing along with him. "It's nice to see you out meeting people from the town. It's a great place to live. Of course, we've been hearing about you from our respective clients for weeks."

Taylor eyed Gen. "Really?"

"You're the Jag Guy," Steve explained. "I must have heard about your from at least a half dozen of my customers."

Taylor winced and Steve laughed.

"Don't worry, it was nothing bad. You were just the new thing to talk about around here. The town is growing, but sometimes not fast enough. A little change is good for them."

Taylor turned back to Rick. "At this rate, I'll be needing your services all too soon."

He shrugged. "As you noted, people who don't go to one of us usually go to the other."

"People accept your relationship?"

"Most of them. Things were tense at first," Rick admitted. "We were one of the first couples they had ever met. But, as they got to know us, things picked up and everything was okay. We're in fields that let us help people, so they tend to warm up once their pain is taken away."

Taylor smiled. "I'm not sure they would see an attorney as a help."

Steve shook his head. "You never know. Gen said you're an employment attorney—that's a form of helping people deal with pain, too."

Taylor noticed Faith standing with her date—what was his name again—near the beer tent. She was watching them more closely than he was comfortable with, but there wasn't much he could do about it. She sipped a bottle, looking in the other direction as she noticed his gaze.

Steve spoke up again. "Taylor, I have to admit, Gen has told us a bit about your situation. If there is anything we can do to help, either professionally or just as friends, let us know. If you guys are right, and you probably are, I just want you to know we're here if you want to talk."

Taylor realized his offer to support was genuine and not just an attempt to pull in a new client. He returned the smile with a nod and realized he was glad Gen had introduced them. Since moving from the city, his interaction with other people like himself had dropped off dramatically and he didn't realize he missed it until then.

Tom returned, a broad smile and the slightest sheen of sweat from his exertion with the two players from his team. He greeted the two men standing with them without hesitation.

"Hi, docs, how are you tonight?"

"Good, Tom. Keeping busy?" Rick asked.

He nodded. "A couple of the girls from the team decided it was time to give the Coach a workout."

"Two at once?" Steve asked.

"Yeah. They thought it was the funniest thing they'd ever seen."

"I'll bet they were right," Taylor interjected.

Tom gave him a wrinkled nose in return. "Meanwhile," he said, "these two, who came together, have been standing around like bumps on the proverbial log."

"It's our fault," Steve said. "We've held them up."

"Wouldn't hurt for you two to cut a rug, either," Gen said.

Taylor felt Faith's gaze again and saw she had gotten a fresh bottle. He was about to beg off as Gen took his arm and pulled him to the dance floor. Tom, Rick, and Steve followed along behind and the five of them danced to some modern song Taylor didn't recognize.

The song changed to something faster and louder and they all moved to keep up. Taylor had never been particularly gifted on the dance floor, but he was impressed to see Tom and Gen keeping up with each other very well. They both turned and surrounded him, helping him find the beat. Rick and Steve moved off to the side, leaving them to entertain themselves.

"How 'ya doin'?" Gen asked, shouting into his ear over the beat of the music.

"I'm doing okay," Taylor said.

"Having fun?"

'Yeah."

"I told you it would work out okay."

From out of nowhere, Faith appeared, dancing up close to Taylor against the beat of the music.

"Long time, no see," she said. "I saw you from the tent."

Gen moved back over to where Tom was and they both kept an eye on Faith as they continued to dance.

"You met the docs, huh?" she said, hugging herself to Taylor to yell into his ear over the music.

"Seem like nice enough guys," Taylor said, nerves on edge.

"You know, they're *married*," she said, nearly whispering the last word, her mouth against his ear.

"They can't be married," Taylor pointed out.

"Yeah, but they had their names changed and everything," she said. She stared deeply into his eyes, searching.

"People have a right to be happy," Taylor said, wishing very much he could be happy right at that moment.

"You really believe that, don't you?" she asked.

"Yeah, I do."

They danced for a few seconds more, then she pulled him close again. "Taylor, I really like you."

He felt a bomb in the pit of his stomach. Wasn't he supposed to be over there with Tom? What was he doing here, dancing with Faith Roberts, who had obviously had a bit too much to drink.

"I think you like me, too," she said, her lips on his ear.

Taylor pushed back, no longer amused. He could be polite, but it was time to nip this in the bud, come what may.

"Faith, we spend time together because you're my real estate agent," he said over the noise. "I'm sorry if I've led you to think that it's anything more than that."

She stopped dancing, staring directly at Taylor. A few feet away, Tom and Gen also watched what was happening. Fortunately, everyone else was still moving.

"You mean you're not interested in me?"

Taylor shook his head. "Look, I'm sorry, Faith. I only called you because I needed someone to help me find a house."

She took a step back. "But you always act like you're interested."

"I was trying to be polite."

She looked down and he could see she was upset. He reached out to try to get her off the dance floor, but she tossed his arm away.

"You were trying to be *polite*," she repeated. "Is that what you're doing with Gen and Tom? Trying to be *polite*?"

Taylor sighed. "Faith, they're my friends."

"You've barely known Tom longer than me. Why can't I be your friend?"

"Faith—" Taylor struggled.

She looked back at the two of them and saw they were both looking directly at her now. Beyond, Rick and Steve were also looking in their direction, along with some of the other people from around town. She looked back at Taylor.

"I get it now," she said. "I should have seen it before."

Taylor again tried to get her off the floor. The song was coming to a close and people were beginning to watch them. She pushed him away.

"So that's your game. You just play with women."

"Faith, it's not like that."

"But you're like that, aren't you? You're like them—*Rick* and *Steve*. That's what it is, isn't it, Taylor?"

The music stopped and just about everyone who wasn't already watching turned to see what the commotion was.

"You're gay," she said finally, through a silence where the drop of a pin would have been a clap of thunder. "God, that's it. All this time, I've been chasing a fairy."

Taylor took a step backward, and then another. He looked and saw Gen and Tom frozen in place. Gen looked concerned, but Tom just looked confused and scared, unsure of what to do. Neither of them moved toward him as Faith continued to face him, defiant and angry, ready for a fight. Taylor turned wordlessly, pushing his way through the crowd, who parted readily to let him pass. In short order, he reached the parking lot, heading directly for his car. Inside, he started the engine, backed out, and roared from the parking lot, never looking back.

CHAPTER TWELVE

The Choice

Taylor stormed off, edging his way through the crowd that had gathered to watch the altercation. For a moment, it looked as though Faith was going to pursue him, but she seemed to loose her nerve as she felt the weight of dozens of eyes staring at her. She looked a bit lost as she turned, finally finding the man who had accompanied her to the dance, a couple rows back in the throng that encircled her. He looked ready to bolt himself.

Gen turned, looking to see how Tom was doing. Beads of sweat had broken out on his forehead and there was fire in his eyes, but she wasn't sure at whom it was directed.

"Come on," she said finally. "We'd better go after him."

Tom didn't move, still frozen in shock. He half glanced at her, but she could see he was still looking after where Taylor had gone and watching Faith. She took his arm.

"Come on, Tom. Let's go."

His attention finally settled on her, his gray eyes a dark violet. "What is going on, Gen? What the hell is wrong with her?"

"A little too much beer and a little too much frustration, I'd say," Gen said, pushing him along.

They made their way through the waning crowd and the music resumed. Gen was thankful for that—the last thing they needed was an audience following them all the way to the car, and that was the direction she was certain Taylor had gone.

Tom stopped, causing Gen to run into his back. They were through the crowd and no one was around. "Is it true?" he asked, simple and to the point.

Gen sighed. "Look, it's really not my place to say, but it seems kind of pointless not to say so at this point. Yes, it's true."

Tom looked away, the bottoms of his eyes clouding over with a sheen of water, whether from frustration, joy, or sadness, Gen couldn't tell.

"Why didn't he just say something? Why didn't he tell me?"

"That's something you should discuss with him," Gen said. She walked slowly around Tom and started back in the direction of the parking lot.

Tom jogged to catch up. "I wish you'd said something," he breathed.

Gen shook her head. "It's not my place, Tommy. Who Taylor tells or doesn't tell is his decision. It's his life. I'm just his friend."

They walked in silence out to the parking lot, looking for the conspicuous red Jag. They got to the row where Gen was certain they had parked, but all they found was an empty spot.

"Wow, he really freaked," she said.

"He left?" Tom asked, realizing it was more of a rhetorical question.

"He's gone," a voice called from behind them. They turned and saw Rob, the neighbor from down the street, standing behind them.

"I saw him leave a couple minutes ago. He was in quite a hurry. I guess there was some commotion with Faith Roberts back on the dance floor, huh?"

Gen shook her head. "Word does travel fast here, doesn't it?"

Rob walked over to stand with them. "Small town, small park," he said, a warm smile on his lips.

"Will he go home?" Tom asked Gen.

"I don't know, probably," she said. "Let's head back. If he's not there, we'll go look for him."

"Want me to drive you?" Rob offered.

Gen considered his offer, then shook her head. "No, that's okay. It'll probably be best if we give him a few minutes to catch his breath. It's a nice night to walk."

"He wouldn't do anything rash, would he?" Tom worried.

Gen shook her head again. "No, Taylor's not like that. Actually, he usually doesn't care who knows, but I think he was just trying to avoid the stigma while the town got to know him."

"Then he *is* gay," Rob said.

Gen rolled her eyes, realizing she was going to be hearing about that as much as she had his car. "Damn it, Rob, I don't want to be the one outing him."

Rob smiled with understanding and nodded. "Don't worry, I won't say anything. Unlike most people around here, I don't feel the need to talk about everyone. I had already pretty much figured him out anyway. My brother is gay, so I understand it and it's okay with me. When you find him, tell him I said not to judge all of us based on Faith."

Gen looked into Rob's eyes, surprised by his simple statement. She'd known him for a few years, but had never done more than make small talk. She realized he was someone who might be worth knowing better.

"I will, Rob, thanks," she said.

Rob turned to Tom. "Look, Tom, I don't know what your situation is, but I just want you to know if you and Taylor are more than just friends, Mel and I are there if you need anything."

"I, uh…thanks," Tom stumbled.

"Okay, now get moving," Rob prompted.

Gen and Tom headed back in the direction of the road. All things being equal, it should only take them a few minutes to walk back to the house, but they didn't want to leave Taylor on his own too long.

They walked in silence, the warm spring air giving them a taste of the still warmer air of summer that was only a few weeks away. To Gen, it felt wonderful, almost idyllic, and she hated that it had to be tainted with unpleasantness.

Damn Faith anyway. Gen had always hoped she was wrong about her, that she was really just a misguided unhappy woman who had been dealt some unfair emotional blows in her life. And, that may still be true, but there was no excuse, no justification, for what she had done. Taylor had resisted all of her advances, all the while maintaining a professional persona. He had only contacted her to make use of her real estate services, not to have her make advances toward him or try to coerce him into a relationship.

Gen was not a big drinker—the beer Taylor had bought them was the only thing she'd had all evening, but it struck her again what a bad idea it was to mix alcohol into an already tense situation. She was sure Faith would never have worked up the courage to confront him on her own, and certainly never so publicly. She wondered if Faith realized the damage she had done her already tenuous reputation. Gen knew the town would accept Taylor—she had no doubt of that. That was why she had wanted Taylor to meet Steve and Rick. Faith, on the other hand, already had a reputation for being a bit of a motor mouth and Gen was certain that reputation would only be bolstered. *Serves her right,* Gen thought.

Tom walked silently beside her, his hands stuffed deep into his pockets. She knew it was definitely *not* the way Taylor had wanted to tell him, but at the same time, she felt a sense of relief that it was finally done. Now they could move forward whichever way they both thought best—either together or apart. Gen was fairly sure it would be together, and she hoped she was right. The fact that Tom hadn't bolted off in the other direction told her their chances were pretty good.

He looked as worried, if not more so, as Gen felt. She realized the expression he had at the dance had been not concern over what the town would think, but concern for Taylor. And there was something else—Tom almost seemed relieved, too. Gen ached to ask him his feelings, but thought it best not to compound the situation. Tom and Taylor would work it out for themselves—her only role was to be there to support both of them. Certainly, she was closer to Taylor, but she liked Tom and considered him a good friend, too.

They turned the corner, literally and figuratively, from Main Street to Gen's house. A couple blocks and they'd be there. She hoped Taylor was there, both for Tom's sake and her own. Taylor tended to be very level headed when confronted with adversity, but she knew he also had a habit of physically running from it while he tried to deal with it. His breakup with Ryan of only a couple months ago was a perfect example—he'd confronted Ryan, then promptly gotten in his car and headed for her house. She hoped his departure from the park was just another example of that same instinct.

"How are you doing?" Gen asked Tom. He remained stooped over, staring at the ground, hands in pockets.

"I'm fine," he said, voice distant.

"Not quite the way you expected the night to go, huh?"

"Not exactly," Tom agreed. "I mean, I'm not exactly surprised," he admitted. "I'm not so naïve that the thought never occurred to me, but I didn't expect it to come out like this."

She put a hand on his shoulder. "It will be okay," she said.

Tom nodded. "I know. I just want to be sure he's okay right now," he said. Gen heard the admission in his voice and said nothing more.

Meanwhile, as they walked...

Taylor pulled his car into the garage, slamming the door shut behind him as he trudged into the house. Damn Faith! How could she do that? In front of the whole town, no less.

Tom's face swam in front of his vision. He had looked horrified, utterly furious and hurt. It was an expression Taylor had never really seen on him and hoped he would never see again. What Tom must think, he didn't even want to imagine.

He closed the back door to find Molly waiting by her dish. It had food in it, so he supposed Molly was just really waiting for their return. As she continued to lie there without moving, he realized she was really waiting for Gen's return. Whatever.

The door bell rang at the front and Taylor stopped cold. Could they already have followed him back from the dance? Information traveled fast in the small town, but would it really travel that fast?

He decided it was probably best to confront the situation head-on and quit hiding like he had something to be embarrassed about. It was probably a bad idea to have done it that long anyway, but he'd think about that later.

Passing through the living room, he reached down to turn on one of Gen's Tiffany-style lamps, then unlocked the front door and swung it open. He nearly jumped as he betook the face before him.

"Neil!" he said.

"Taylor," he greeted, a subdued smile on his face. "I just thought I'd take a shot and see if you were home on my way to the airport."

"I just walked in the back door," Taylor said. He held the screen door open so Neil could come in.

"Everything okay?" Neil asked. "You seem a little flustered."

Taylor gave Neil the thirty-second short form of what had just transpired with Faith, omitting references to Tom. The last thing he needed was to further complicate things with someone else knowing about his feelings for Tom right then.

"Wow," Neil said. "That's a pretty bad deal." He still stood in the doorway and Taylor realized it would be better to invite him inside.

Neil shook his head. "I was serious when I said I just wanted to drop by on my way to the airport. I decided to head up to New York tonight and spend a couple days getting my apartment situated and catch up with some friends there."

"Oh, okay," Taylor said.

"You're welcome to come up for the weekend, though. I can just have Skip fly you home whenever you want. It won't be too exciting, but I'll be getting together with some friends and working on my apartment. It would give you a couple days to let things calm down here."

Taylor considered the offer. Tom's face was still there, the look of shock and anger. Tom hadn't moved an inch to help him as Faith attacked. He was sure he wouldn't want anything to do with him after having been deceived for so long. Neil was right—he just needed to get away for a couple days.

"You know, that sounds like a pretty good plan," Taylor said. "Let me run up and grab a bag."

"No problem," Neil said.

Taylor bounded up the stairs. He returned a scant couple of minutes later, having traded the khaki's for a comfortable pair of jeans and a T-shirt. He dropped a large duffle bag at the door.

"I'm going to leave Gen a quick note and then we can go."

"Okay," Neil said. "I'll put your bag in the car—just come on out when you're ready."

"Thanks," Taylor called as he went to the pad on the refrigerator. He pulled off the pen and wrote a note: *G—need a break. Can't take the scrutiny right now. Going to NYC with Neil for the weekend. Please look after Molly—I'll call later. Sorry about the dance. TC*

He clipped the paper under the Lucille Ball magnet and reached down to give Molly at pat on the head.

"I'll just be gone a couple days, kiddo," he said.

She never moved. He realized she had pretty much become Gen's dog anyway and neither one of them seemed to mind the arrangement.

Taylor went back to the front door and locked it behind him. Neil stood next to his car, arms crossed over his well-defined chest, feet crossed casually at the ankles. His face brightened as Taylor approached.

"Ready?" he asked.

"Yeah, let's go."

"We're gone," Neil said, getting in the car behind him. He started it and they roared off into the darkness.

They were on the second to last block as they got closer to the house. Gen saw that a light was on in the window, so she was sure Taylor had come back and she was glad for that. She knew they would get through it and the whole thing would be nothing but a memory in a matter of weeks.

"Isn't that your house?" Tom asked.

"Yeah," Gen said.

"Who is parked in front of it?"

She looked. In the darkness, it was hard to make out much of anything, but she could see the dark shape of a car next to the old oak tree by the sidewalk.

"I don't know," she said. "Maybe they're visiting someone else."

"Everyone else is at the dance," Tom pointed out.

They walked along in silence. Seconds later, a shape moved toward the car and Gen thought it looked a whole lot like Taylor. She could barely make out the sound of voices as they got into the car. It started, the tail light showed briefly, and it shot off down the road.

"I think that was Taylor," Tom said, voice filled with dread.

"I thought it might have been him, too," Gen admitted.

Tom's head hung low. "And that was Neil's car."

"Neil's car?" Gen asked, remembering her conversation with Taylor earlier in the evening.

"Yeah. He drives a black BMW. I saw it when I ran into them at Alberto's. The license plate was from New York and read 'NHG.' Neil H. Gardener."

"I wonder where he'd be going with Neil?" Gen queried, confused.

"Maybe back to New York," Tom said. They reached the driveway and headed for the back door. Sure enough, there was a light on and Taylor's car sat in the garage.

Gen opened the back door and Molly rose to greet them. She patted Molly's head, then saw the note on the fridge. She read it, then looked to Tom with sorrow in her eyes. He took the note, read it, then dropped it to the table, shaking his head.

"He just needed to get away, Tommy," Gen consoled. "He does this when he's upset. It's okay."

"It's probably for the best anyway," Tom said. "I think he likes Neil. They went away together a couple weekends ago, too."

Gen sighed. "Tom, he doesn't like Neil. I mean, he doesn't like him as anything more than a friend."

"He told you that?"

"Just tonight, as a matter of fact. And remember, he went away last weekend with *you*, so what does that tell you?"

"I took him camping, Neil took him to the Met."

"But he told me about his trip with you," Gen said.

Tom looked her in the eye. "He did?"

"He did." She shook her head. "Look, I promised myself I wasn't going to get in the middle of this, but I guess there's not much I can do about it. I'm a meddling best friend, and that's the only way I know how to be."

Tom looked at her, uncertain about her point.

"Taylor's in love with you," she admitted. It was like a weight had been lifted from her shoulders. Tom looked like he was ready to cry. She pressed on, pulling out a chair for him to sit with her at the table.

"I've known him for a long time and I have *never* seen him like he has been since he met you. I don't know your situation, but I can pretty well guess from the way you've reacted tonight. It has been killing him because he wanted to talk to you about it, but didn't want to pressure you."

Tom stared at the table, saying nothing, face awash in uncertainty. Gen took his hand in hers. "I don't know what you're feeling," she said, "and I don't want to pressure you, either. But if you're wondering how Taylor feels about you, that's how he feels. Now you just have to figure out how you feel about him and then you guys can reach an understanding." She rose and turned to the cupboard. "I don't know about you, but I need something to drink. Can I get you anything?"

Tom shook his head. "No, thanks. I think I'm going to go."

"Are you sure?" she asked.

"Yeah. I need to get a little air and be alone myself for a bit."

Gen nodded. "I understand. You want a ride?"

"No, thanks. I'm just going to walk." He stood, heading for the door.

"Call me if you need me, okay?" Gen said.

"Yeah, I will," Tom said. "Have a good night."

"Tom," she called. He stopped, door open, and looked at her. "He'll be back. Don't worry."

"Thanks, Pussycat," he said, and was gone.

Gen drew a glass of water from the tap, then turned to give Molly a can of food.

Taylor, he loves you, too, she thought. There was no doubt now—the concern Tom had felt was the only thing she had seen on his face. No revulsion, no betrayal, only the sincere wish to see his friend again. She practically beamed as she thought about that—she had been worried that Tom wouldn't be able to express his feelings to Taylor. Technically, he still hadn't, but she was sure that now that he knew they would be accepted, it would happen. Of the two of them, she'd always thought of Taylor as the more fragile, but she realized they were both very fragile in their own ways.

Molly slopped down her food and Gen turned off the light to go upstairs. She passed through the living room, taking the main stairs up. As she headed for her room, she heard a strange buzzing sound coming from Taylor's room. Curious, she walked over and waited for the sound to come again. It did and drew her attention to the bed. There his khaki's lay in a heap, having been quickly discarded after the dance. As she looked, she realized the sound was his phone, which he typically kept on vibrate.

"You forgot your phone, genius," she said, reaching down to pick it up. The caller ID read, "Tom." Gen smiled. "Good boy," she said, flipping the phone open.

"Tom, it's Gen."

"Gen?"

"Taylor forgot his phone. I heard your call when I came upstairs."

"Oh," he said. "Well, sorry to bother you, then."

"I'll let him know you called."

"Thanks, Gen," he said, then hung up.

She closed the phone and dropped it back on the bed, pulling the belt from the slacks and hanging them in the closet. Taylor was generally tidy unless distracted, and she couldn't imagine a much bigger distraction for him.

Molly came up the back stairs and they met at her door. Gen unzipped her dress and slipped it off, reaching for her pajamas. She could hardly believe the way the night had gone. That Faith had been a pain was no surprise, but that she had created such a spectacle certainly was.

She stretched out on her bed, not bothering with the covers. The night was warm, even as the dry breeze blew over her. Molly stretched out on the rug next to the bed, ready for another night of sleep. *He loves you, Taylor*, she thought as she drifted off to sleep. *Try not to be gone too long...*

The next morning, Taylor sat before a floor to ceiling window facing Central Park. He had only awakened a few minutes before, but he knew he was the first one up. He'd pulled on a pair of sweat pants and a T-shirt, then quietly made his way from the guest room to the kitchen, where a pot of coffee waited.

He wasn't quite sure what Neil thought he was going to have to do to the apartment. It was completely furnished and, as near as Taylor could tell, everything was already put away. The only thing he could think to do would be move a couple things here or there to suit Neil's personal tastes. He had commented on how organized everything was when they arrived the night before and Neil made some passing comment about hiring his father's moving company. Taylor marveled at the casually dismissive way he thought about the process—it was clear money had never been an issue in his upbringing.

The night before remained forefront in his thoughts as he sipped the coffee and watched the interplay of light and shadow in the land and sky-line below. Tom had been clearly distraught and Taylor could only assume that meant he was unhappy about the revelation Faith had forced from him.

Bitch, Taylor thought. Not one given to negative emotions, the thought surprised him, but he didn't feel too bad. To assault someone like that was unconscionable, especially in an enlightened society. She hadn't merely insulted him—she had pulled in Rick and Steve, who he'd just met, tacitly drawn in Tom and Gen, as well as any other homosexual people who may have been in the community. He wondered who in the community would be willing to trust her with their home needs now. It was small consolation that she had shown her true colors in front of everyone—she'd shown his, too, and he didn't appreciate that.

He had noticed too late that his cell phone remained clipped to his belt on his khaki's. They were already in the air and bound for New York. He checked the clock, but it was still too early to call either Gen or Tom this morning. He'd catch up with them in a little while to make sure every-thing was okay.

"Mornin'," Neil said, walking in from the bedrooms.

"Good morning," Taylor answered, glancing back toward the kitchen. Neil was clad in a pair of plaid pajama bottoms, bare-chested, with a seri-ous case of bed head. Taylor had never seen him with his shirt off and real-ized he looked even better that way. He groaned inwardly, sinking farther into his chair. Beauty or character, he thought. It was an age-old problem. Of course, it wasn't like Tom was physically challenged, but taking a good looking normal guy and putting him next to Neil's supermodel beauty was unfair under any terms. Taylor remembered Tom's smile, the one he always reserved just for him, and felt his strength return.

"How'd you sleep?" Neil asked, taking the chair opposite Taylor, holding the cup of coffee in his hands.

"I slept well, thanks," Taylor confirmed.

"Great," Neil said, looking out over the city himself. "As you can see, the apartment turned out to be in pretty good shape. I was thinking it might be nice to take lunch and head into the mountains for the afternoon. We could do a little driving, maybe a little hiking, and just relax and enjoy the nice weather."

"That sounds nice," Taylor said. Being outdoors made him think of Tom and he felt the conflict well in him again.

"Great," Neil said again. "I haven't gotten any groceries yet. I'll call my parents' cook and have her prepare something for us—we can swing by and pick it up on the way out of town."

Taylor nodded and Neil pressed on. "Tonight, some friends have invited me to a new club in the Village. It's not far from here. You are, of course, welcome to join us. I think we're going to go out afterward to a place down near Broadway. Again, you can come with us, come back here, or whatever you'd like to do in between."

Taylor nodded. He wasn't really into the club scene, but there wasn't much else to do as he really didn't know anyone else in the city. "Sounds good to me," he said.

"Great," Neil said again, smiling broadly. He got up from the chair, standing in front of Taylor. "I'm going to catch a quick shower. Whenever you're ready, go ahead and get ready and we'll go when you're done. Towels and such are in the closet in your bathroom."

"I'll be ready in no time," Taylor confirmed.

Neil nodded and padded back to his room, closing the door behind him. Taylor was never sure if Neil's statements were meant as information or invitation. He suspected Neil would be okay with either way, but he was only ready to take them as information. He wouldn't have minded a little physical interaction, but he didn't want to cheapen what he hoped existed between him and Tom by "cheating" while he was away. They would work out their situation first. If it didn't work out, then he would just hope that Neil was still as interested later as he appeared to be then.

In the shower, with the warm water cascading down his back, he wondered what to do next. Normally, he would have gone to Gen. In a sense, that was what he had started to do—Neil had just run an interception. Now he was in New York, hundreds of miles from Gen and Tom, in limbo. He knew he tended to answer conflict by removing himself from it, but this was a little ridiculous.

He told himself the weekend was just a little time away with a friend, but he knew that wasn't true either. Neil was a nice guy, but to call him a friend, after having only been out with him a couple times, seemed a stretch. Their friendship was more based on the idea that Neil liked him. He knew that—why Neil liked him remained a mystery, but he had accepted that it was so. It was mostly amazing to him because the few times they had been out, Taylor had watched how the people around them watched Neil. He truly did look like a supermodel and he was very charming. Taylor knew, if he wasn't careful, he could easily be swept off his feet.

He also knew that Tom was charming, too, in his own less flamboyant, less forced way. Tom was a normal guy—one of the most normal guys Taylor had ever met. He came from a normal home with normal parents and a normal sister. Over the time they had spent together camping, Tom had expounded at length about his life and Taylor was amazed by how together it seemed. Not that Taylor's life was anything someone was likely to write a book about, but it had a few more twists and turns in it than Tom's had. Yet, for all that, Tom was a surprisingly interesting, caring, kind person who was very easy to be around. Taylor really never had to be anyone other than himself to be accepted by Tom and that was a trait he'd rarely found in anyone else.

He tipped his head back to let the water spray the soap from his hair. It was just one weekend. Nothing was going to happen beyond a little socializing and meeting some new people. Of that, Taylor was sure.

A short time later, refreshed and spring fresh, Taylor walked from the bedroom back to the living room. He'd opted for a light sweater, loose fitting jeans, and sandals, leaving his feet free to enjoy the grass whenever they found somewhere for the picnic. Neil had gone with a taupe turtleneck, jeans and sandals, which came as no surprise to Taylor. At least he knew how to dress the part of a supermodel, even if he wasn't one.

Neil smiled as he walked up. "All set?"

"Ready to go," Taylor confirmed.

"Great. I've called in our lunch order—we just need to stop and pick it up and we're on the road."

"Wonderful," Taylor said, following him to the door.

On the road, he sat beside Neil in the Porsche Boxter, the roof retracted to allow the warm sun to beat down on them. Taylor never minded a chance to improve his tan. He wished Tom could be with him to enjoy the view. As he thought of Tom, he remembered he needed to call him, and Gen, to let them know he was okay.

"Do you have your phone with you?" he asked Neil.

Neil reached down to his pocket and felt around, then shook his head. "I must have forgotten it in my coat from last night."

"Oh, okay."

"Who do you need to call?" he asked.

"I was going to call Gen," Taylor explained. "I wanted to let her know everything is okay."

Neil nodded. "I'll try to remind you when we get back."

"Thanks," Taylor said. He didn't like leaving them hanging, but he had remembered to leave a note and he was sure Gen would find that. As for Tom, only time would tell…

CHAPTER THIRTEEN

City Life

Saturday morning, the sunlight slipped through the window blinds. After traveling millions of miles over a span of around eight seconds, its final mission was to impose itself upon the eyelids of one Genevieve Pouissant, forcing her from the dream she was enjoying to the reality of life. Fortunately for Gen, the trip was neither long nor arduous.

As she pushed the cobwebs from her consciousness, she forced herself to remember where she was and what was happening in her world. Taylor was gone. Tom was upset. Life was insane. Molly needed to be walked. Okay, she was up to date. For once, she realized Taylor would not already be down at the bakery getting her a chocolate croissant to share over a discussion of the previous night's activities. If Gen wanted chocolate this morning, she was going to have to do it for herself. That was okay with her—she needed to check on Tom anyway.

Her feet hit the hard floor that lay under the worn oriental rug beside her bed. Molly was mere inches away, already waking herself as she knew what was coming. Gen switched from pajamas to a comfortable running suit, pulled her hair into a ponytail, and started for the door.

"Come on, goldie locks, let's go for a walk," she said. Molly trotted along behind her, ever attentive.

Gen was surprised she hadn't heard from Taylor yet. Even though he had left his phone behind, she was sure he would call. She wondered if leaving the phone was by accident or by design—maybe he really did want to get away.

She had been briefly worried that something might have happened, but a quick perusal of the news stations had confirmed that everything was okay—no planes had crashed anywhere, and most importantly, none between her general area and New York. She figured she had simply underestimated his need to get away.

The kitchen floor was cold against her bare feet. She slid on a pair of sandals, then reached up to take Molly's leash from its hook. She unlatched the door and they walked into the back yard. Molly ran over to take care of business, knowing they would only leave after she was done.

Minutes later, they walked down the sidewalk, the early morning sun already warming the air into another beautiful day. As she walked, Gen tried to remember the last time there hadn't been a sunny day on the weekend and nothing came to mind. Surely that had to be a good sign.

"Gen!" she heard someone call her name. Looking up, she saw Mel waving at her from the front door of their house. She ran down the front steps, also wearing a sweat suit and her hair pulled back.

"Hi, Mel, how are you?" Gen greeted. Molly sat on her haunches, waiting patiently while Mel walked to meet them.

"I'm good," she said, her voice going a bit lower. "How's Taylor?"

Gen sighed. "He's in New York right now."

"New York?"

She nodded. "Yeah, he left the other night. A friend of his was moving and asked him to go along for the ride. After everything that happened, he agreed."

"Have you talked to him?"

"No, he forgot his phone. I thought he would call by now, but he hasn't. He may just need some time to himself."

"Rob told me about what happened. I feel so bad. I hope he doesn't think we're all like that."

Gen smiled. "I'm sure he doesn't. He's just had a lot on his mind lately and that was the final blow."

Mel accepted that. "How's Tom?"

Gen's smile faded. "I don't know. I'm on my way to get something for breakfast now. He was a bit shaken up when he went home the other night, but he's a strong guy."

Mel eyed her closely, sizing her up. "Are they, you know, a couple?"

"Mel, even if I had an answer for that, it wouldn't be my place, you know? I don't really know what the status is between them."

She nodded. "I understand. I don't want to put you in an uncomfortable position. Rob's pretty mad—he and Tom have been friends for a while and he's liked having Taylor playing Sunday night baseball with them. He heard a couple people talking yesterday and nearly slugged one of them."

"It'll work out," Gen said, repeating the same thing she had told Tom—and herself.

"I know it will," Mel concurred. "I won't keep you—just let us know if there is anything we can do, okay?"

"I promise," Gen said. "Thanks for the support."

"Anytime," Mel said, then turned back for her house. Gen led Molly away, again taken aback and touched at the unexpected support from people she didn't know particularly well. When it did all settle down, she had every intention of inviting them over a little more often.

Molly virtually struggled against the leash, clearly understanding exactly where they were going. As they neared the door to the bakery, she promptly parked herself next to the lamppost as she had done for Taylor since their first walk into town. Gen marveled at her intelligence, reaching down to wrap the leash around the post and tied it off.

Inside the screen door, one other lady was ahead of Gen. A young girl, Emmy, helped her. Tom was nowhere to be seen.

"You're all set, Mrs. Jensen," Emmy said.

"Thank you, dear," she answered. "Have you seen Tommy?" she asked.

"He's not working out front today, ma'am," Emmy answered crisply, voice sounding rehearsed, either from actual preparation or from having answered the same question so many times.

"Terrible thing what that woman Faith did to his friend. I guess he was pretty upset."

"I wouldn't know, Mrs. Jensen," Emmy said. "I wasn't there at the time."

"Well, I was, and I can tell you it was a real shame."

"So I've heard," Emmy said, a bit exasperated. "You have a great day, Mrs. Jensen." Her voice was dismissive, as was her posture as she turned to Gen.

Mrs. Jensen seemed to take the hint and turned to leave, giving Gen the smallest hint of a smile as she passed. The screen closed behind her, leaving Gen and Emmy the only two people in the store.

"What can I get for you, Gen?" Emmy asked.

"Is Tom here, Emmy?"

"He's not really looking to see people today," she said, being more honest with Gen.

"Would you just let him know I'm here? I'd really like to see how he's doing."

"Sure," she said, turning to go back into the baking area. She returned a moment later. "Gen, he asked if you would just come on back."

She walked around the counter toward the back. Customers rarely, if ever, got to go where the food was prepared, so she felt a bit self-conscious. Emmy pointed her in the direction of the door, then went back out front.

Gen entered the baking room, immediately feeling the moist warmth of the space surround her. Tom stood in the center of the room, face long, covered in flour.

"Isn't the flour supposed to go in the baking?" Gen quipped, trying to gauge his mood.

"Most of it does," he said, unmoving.

"You've seen better days, huh, Tommy?"

"I've been an idiot, Gen," he said. "I let this happen."

Gen frowned. "You did?"

"I should have said something. We both knew what was going on and I guessed he was just waiting me out and I didn't say anything because I was too scared."

Gen moved closer to him, looking straight into his violet gray eyes. "Have you *ever* said anything?"

"To Taylor?"

"To anyone."

"No."

She smiled. "Then you shouldn't feel bad that it was hard. If you're honest with yourself, you know you're not exactly ready now, either. You just sort of got stuck."

Finally, he smiled thinly. "Yeah, that's the truth. How do I get unstuck?"

"Talk to Taylor."

He met her eyes again. "Have you heard from him?"

"Not yet, but I'm sure we will."

"You think he's okay?"

"Yeah. I'll tell you what, if we haven't heard from him by tonight, I'll call John and Sandy and get Neil's contact info from them."

Tom's gaze virtually burned into her. "You mean you know how to get in touch with him?"

Gen was surprised by Tom's intensity. "I don't know for sure. I just would suspect that Sandy will know how to get in touch with Neil."

"Do you know her number? Can you call now?"

Gen stumbled. "Uh, yeah, I guess. It's kind of early."

Tom dusted himself off, creating another cloud of flour dust. "Come on, I'll take you to the phone."

"Okay…"

He led her out front to the phone hanging on the wall behind the counter. Gen dialed Sandy's number. She felt a little self-conscious to be out in the store area, but fortunately no one else was there except Emmy.

"Hi, Sandy, it's Gen. Sorry to call so early," she said, throwing a glance at Tom. He was oblivious and she smiled in spite of herself. "Thanks. No, everything's okay. Well, sort of anyway. Listen, do you have a number to get in touch with Neil?" At the mention of Neil's name, Tom's attention returned to the conversation. "Yeah. No, Taylor's with him. Yeah, long story. I actually need to talk to Taylor, but he didn't take his phone, so I want to call Neil and see if he can get me in touch with Taylor. No? Crud. You do? Yeah, I'll take that."

Gen made a writing gesture toward Tom and mouthed the word, "paper." He quickly grabbed a pad and pencil and handed it to her. She wrote quickly, then set it down. "Thanks, Sandy. Yeah, if you do find it, I'd really appreciate it. At work? Okay. Yeah, I'll fill you in later. Great. Say hi to John. Thanks. Bye." She hung up the phone.

Tom watched her expectantly. "She left the phone number at work. She had his forwarding address in her Palm Pilot, though." She handed Tom the slip of paper. "She said this is where they're forwarding his stuff."

Tom pulled his apron off and hung it on a hook. "Emmy, everything is set. Pull the last batch out of the oven in twenty minutes," he said.

"Where are you going?"

"New York City. Call Mrs. Caillan if you have any problems."

"Tom! I've never run the store myself."

"You'll be fine," he said. "Mrs. Johnson should be here in about an hour. I have to go."

Emmy's eyes were wide, but she smiled. "Okay. Just be careful. Don't drive too fast. Tell Taylor I said hi."

"I'll definitely do that," he promised. He turned to Gen. "Are you coming?"

"Somebody has to keep you from getting too out of control."

"Okay, grab Molly and come on around back. We'll take my car."

He took off for the back door and Gen walked to the front. Emmy watched the action with a sense of amusement. "Bye, Gen," she called out.

"See ya, Emmy," Gen said through the screen. She untied Molly and headed down the alley, to whatever they might find.

Hours later, they could finally see the city skyline on the horizon. They had stopped only twice—once to let Molly have a break and once to buy a map of the city so they would know how to find their way. As they came through the Lincoln Tunnel, Gen called out directions, finally bringing them within sight of Central Park.

"According to this," she said, "It should be somewhere in here." She started reading off addresses as they drove, counting their blessings that it was only a Saturday afternoon and traffic wasn't as bad as it could have been.

"There it is!" Tom shouted, pointing to a well-appointed apartment building entrance with not one, but two doormen standing outside. He pulled up right out front and lowered Gen's window.

"Can you tell us where we can park?" Gen asked.

"Are you visiting someone here?" the man on the right asked, walking up to the car.

"The Gardeners." Gen took a chance that the name would stand out.

"Oh, fine," he said, smiling. "Parking is around the block. Follow the signs. Bring your ticket with you and we'll validate it for you."

"Thanks," Gen managed as Tom gunned the engine. "Relax, killer," she said.

"Yeah," Tom managed, pulling around the corner. A green "P" sign guided him into the structure and he reached out to pull a ticket.

Roaring into the first available spot, Tom jumped out of the Jeep.

"What about Molly?" Gen asked.

"She'll be okay here," he said. "We shouldn't be gone real long, one way or another."

Gen nodded. "We'll be back in a couple minutes, Molly. Just sit tight," she said to the dog, then closed the door.

Tom virtually ran from the garage, Gen struggling to keep up behind him. They came around the block and the man who Gen had talked to before waited to greet them.

"Are the Gardeners expecting you?" he asked, stamping the parking ticket Tom had handed to Gen.

"No," she admitted. "I don't think so. We're actually friends of a guest who is staying with them."

"The guest's name?" the man asked pleasantly.

"Taylor Connolly."

He frowned. "I wasn't aware there was a guest there. Usually they tell us so we will be sure to let them in. Let me call up for you, okay?"

"Thank you," Gen said. The man went to a phone and dialed a short number.

"Good morning, this is Vincent from downstairs. I have two people here who would like to come up. They're friends of your guest, Mr. Connolly." He waited while the person on the other end spoke. "No? Yes, one moment, I'll ask them." He turned to Gen.

"Ma'am, are you sure Mr. Connolly was staying here this weekend? Mr. Gardener's butler said he was here a couple of weeks ago, but has not been with them this weekend."

Gen frowned, then realized their mistake. "Taylor is staying with Neil Gardener," she explained. "Is this his apartment, or his parents'?"

Vincent smiled, understanding. "This is his parents home, ma'am," he confirmed.

Gen nodded. "I'm so sorry. This is the address we were given. Do you happen to know Neil's new address?"

Vincent turned back to the phone. "Yes, there was a misunderstanding. They're trying to find Neil Gardener," he explained. "Do you have Mr. Gardener's new address?"

There was more chatter at the other end, then Vincent thanked the man and hung up. He turned back to Gen and Tom.

"He lives just down the street about three blocks," Vincent confirmed, writing a number on a slip of paper. He handed the slip to Gen. "Mr. Gardener's butler indicated that Mr. Gardener just stopped by a couple of hours ago to collect a picnic lunch. He was given the impression he would be gone for the day."

Gen nodded again. "Thank you. You've been very helpful."

Vincent smiled. "It's no trouble at all, ma'am. One other thing—that parking ticket is validated until you leave. I don't know what parking is like for that building. It will probably be faster and easier for you to just walk. It's about three blocks in that direction," he said, back the way they had come.

"Thank you again," Gen said. Tom muttered a thanks, then took her hand and pulled her along in the direction Vincent had indicated.

Three blocks later, they stood before a very similar door in front of a very similar doorman. For this building, however, there was only one doorman—clearly Neil lived in the low rent district.

"Hello. May I help you?" the man greeted.

"We're here to see Neil Gardener," Tom said. They could get into the details of the fact that they were really there to see Taylor later.

"Mr. Gardener has left for the day," the man said.

Tom looked stricken and Gen stepped up. "Did he have anyone with him?"

"I believe he did. A young, blond-haired gentleman."

"Did he say when they would return?"

"No, I'm sorry, he didn't."

"I don't suppose you have a number where you can reach him?" Gen asked.

The man shook his head. "Our system only works for the building."

"Okay, thank you," Gen said and they headed back toward the car.

"Now what?" Tom asked.

"I left my phone in the car," Gen said. "When we get back, we'll try calling Sandy again and see if she can get the number for us."

"To what end?" Tom asked. "If Taylor is so all-fired upset, why is he off gallivanting with Neil?"

"Don't jump to conclusions," Gen advised. "They may just be off getting things for Neil's new place."

"With a picnic lunch?"

Gen didn't have a quick response for that. It was a good point—one she hoped would have a good explanation later. "Look, I'm just saying that you need to count on Taylor being the person you know him to be and believe that there is a good reason for everything."

"I'm not sure exactly who I know him to be, Gen," Tom said. "How do I really know what is going on?"

"I do know him," she said. "It will be okay. Here's what we're going to do. We're going to go back and ask Vincent to direct us to a decent hotel, hopefully one that will let us bring Molly. Then we're going to get something to eat—we haven't had anything since this morning. Once that's squared away, we'll go back and see if they're back. If not, we'll see if we can leave a message with my phone number."

Tom looked lost. Gen pulled him into a hug. "Don't give up on him—he hasn't given up on you, I'm sure of it."

The club was dark, smoky, and loud…just like virtually every other club Taylor had been to. There may be variations—less smoky, more light, targeted acoustics, but the mix was pretty much always the same.

He had agreed to join Neil more because he had no idea what else he would do in New York City by himself. Though he had lived in a city for a few years, it still wasn't a place he felt at home. He was reminded again how he had moved there because it was where Ryan wanted to live. He had moved to live with Gen because it was where *he* wanted to live and it was there that he found Tom.

He ached to be with Tom. He wanted to tell Neil to have Pilot take him home tonight. He chuckled to himself. They had joked about calling the various employees of his father by their positions rather than their names, like Will & Grace, and it sort of stuck because Taylor really couldn't remember what Pilot's name was. Of course, he would never be so uncouth as to do it in front of the man.

Not that Neil wasn't trying. They had shared a delightful picnic lunch in a park overlooking the Hudson River. Neil had been charming and attentive, leaving Taylor again at a loss. Why was this man so interested in him? What was it about Taylor that so intrigued him? His beauty was almost painful and the flecks of green in his brown eyes had virtually sparkled at Taylor in the brilliant sun.

In one sense, being with Neil would be easy. He was out. His friends were out. He lived in one of the most liberal cities on the planet. In New York, anything goes, and Taylor believed that. Still, there was something different. Being with Tom was so casual, so comfortable. They clicked. With Neil, things felt forced, heavy. It was as though Taylor was constantly struggling to understand who he needed to be rather than just being himself. He realized part of the reason he so readily recognized that was that it was what he had done so many times before. Tom was the first person he felt he had met as himself first and everything progressed from there.

"So, Taylor, Neil tells me you're living in some little town in the middle of nowhere and some chick just outted you to everybody."

One of Neil's apparently large circle of friends had sidled up to Taylor at the bar after giving him a once over from a few feet away. So far, Neil's friends seemed to be interested in one thing, and that was definitely not where he was at tonight. He was an unwelcome interruption in Taylor's thought process.

"Uh, yeah," Taylor said, clearing the smoke from his throat. Neil said they were going to head off to another club soon. Taylor figured that would be a good opportunity to beg off and head back to the apartment.

"How'd that work out?" Friend asked. Taylor had long since given up on trying to remember all their names.

"I ran off to New York."

Friend laughed. "Yeah, I see that. Not such a bad choice, huh?"

"Not so bad," Taylor answered, bored.

"So, you know Neil for very long?"

"A few months," Taylor said. He realized several other people were watching him, too. He felt like a slab of meat.

"You guys hook up yet?"

His attention snapped back to Friend. "What?"

"You know, did you fuck him yet?"

Taylor felt the color drain from his face and his mood worsen by an order of magnitude. He knew people tended to get crude when "out on the town," but he always hated it when it got personal. "No," he said simply, afraid he would be rude himself if he said anything more.

"Really? You're all he's been talking about. He really likes you. All you have to do is say the word and he's yours."

Taylor watched Friend. He was clearly drunk, even wobbling slightly as he stood there. He wondered if Friend had the first clue what he was saying or how Neil would feel to have his intentions broadcast for him. Of course, for Friend to know what Neil was thinking, that meant Neil had already broadcast them, and about Taylor no less. It was undeniably flattering to have someone find him attractive, but it still made him feel like an object to know he had been so openly discussed.

"Look man, don't worry about it," Friend said. "I thought you knew. Whatever. He's really good in the sack, though. Totally about you." He took a big swig from his bottle. "You shouldn't wait too long, though. Neil's a patient one, but not that patient. He'll only wait just so long. He's talked about you a lot though."

"Thanks for the info," Taylor said.

"No problem, honey," the guy said. "And if it doesn't work out, just remember there's lots more fish out here, okay?"

"I'll do that," Taylor said.

Neil walked up, ignoring the guy who had been talking to Taylor. "Hey, we're going to move on. You with us?"

"Actually," Taylor answered, "I was thinking I'd head back. I'm pretty tired."

Neil shrugged. "Sure, no problem. I understand. I'll see you in the morning."

Taylor agreed and headed toward the door, saying goodbye to a couple of the others as he went. It occurred to him that Neil didn't seem particularly disappointed by his decline. He wondered what that meant in light of what he'd just been told.

The night air was warm and smelled lightly of diesel fuel. Taylor wrinkled his nose at it, stopping at the curb. He signaled a cab and got in.

"Where to?" the cabbie asked.

Taylor called out Neil's address and they were off. New York City passed like a blur. The sheer volume of it astounded Taylor. Buildings and concrete everywhere. It was like no place else he'd ever been, and like nowhere else he'd ever go, he suspected.

Neil's friend's comments were disturbing. Was he just a conquest? And how many conquests had there been? With a face like Neil's, picking up men had to be a fairly easy task. Guys would be knocking themselves over to get to him. That wasn't the life Taylor sought—he wanted something of value, something that would last. Neil was young and gorgeous—he wanted to have fun. Taylor couldn't fault him for that, but he didn't think he fit the bill, either.

They pulled up outside the building and he hopped out, tossing a few bills at the cabbie. The sidewalk was bright with the light of the overhang at the door. The doorman greeted him and opened the door. Taylor walked straight to the elevators, waiting as a car came down to get him.

"Mr. Connolly?"

He turned to see the doorman standing beside him.

"Yes?" he answered. The man held out a slip.

"I nearly forgot, sir. A message for you."

Taylor took the slip and looked at it. In the man's handwriting was a phone number and the name, "Jen." Taylor was confused for a moment, until he realized it was a misspelling of "Gen."

"Thank you," he said and the man walked back outside. The elevator doors opened and Taylor walked in, signaling his floor. He wondered how Gen had tracked him down to the apartment—leave it to her to be that persistent. He checked his watched—twelve thirty. He'd wait until the morning to call her.

The doors parted and he found himself in the hall to Neil's apartment. He felt strange—the day had been okay, but he could definitely have done without the evening. He couldn't even imagine Tom ever putting him in a situation like that.

He walked in, dropping the key on the table by the door. His room was to the back, Neil's was to the front. He closed the door behind him, unbuttoning his shirt as he did. As an afterthought, he reached down and locked the door. He had no idea what might come home with Neil and he didn't need any surprise guests in the middle of the night.

He reeked of smoke and alcohol, most of which had been spilled on him by others. He decided to take a quick pass through the shower, then hit the sheets in his boxers. His last thoughts were of Tom. No matter what, he was going to talk to him in the morning and make sure he knew everything was okay. He would apologize for today. Hopefully his apology would be enough…

CHAPTER FOURTEEN

The Power to Forgive

The light of morning called Taylor up from sleep at seven eighteen. He blinked in the subdued light, surprised he had slept so soundly. He thought he heard Neil come in around three thirty, but if it was him, he'd gone straight to bed without so much as a test of Taylor's door.

Maybe he'd just overreacted. After all, Friend had been pretty drunk. Maybe he was making up stories to get Neil in trouble or to see how Taylor would react. If the purpose was getting a reaction, Taylor had certainly provided one last night. He felt a little guilty for ditching the party. Neil had been nothing but kind and attentive since he picked Taylor up on Friday night. To accept the words of one person—one drunk off his butt person—would be unfair to Neil.

The doorbell sounded. Taylor glanced at the clock again. Seven twenty. Who would be ringing the doorbell at twenty after seven on a Sunday morning? He tossed back the covers and reached for the sweater and jeans he'd worn yesterday afternoon. Even as he zipped his jeans, he heard Neil walk by his door and the front door was unlatched. He opened his bedroom door, curious to see who it was, too.

He opened his door in time to see the front door swinging back and hear, "Ryan?"

"Gen?"

Taylor walked to the door, seeing Gen there and Tom behind her. "Gen?" he asked.

"Taylor?"

He looked at the person holding the door—it wasn't Neil. "Ryan?"

"Taylor?"

"Taylor…" he heard Neil's voice from behind him.

"Neil?" Taylor said.

"Taylor, what's going on?" Tom asked

"What the hell?" Taylor exclaimed.

"What are you doing here?" Gen asked Ryan.

"I was going to ask you the same question," he retorted. He was covered in only boxers.

"Taylor!" Gen yelled.

"What?" he shot back. Tom turned and walked back down the hall. Taylor pushed by Ryan and Gen, running barefoot after him. "Tom, wait!" Tom pushed open the door to the stairwell and disappeared inside.

"So, Ryan, do anybody new lately?" Taylor heard Gen ask as he ran into the stairwell after Tom.

"Dammit, Tom, wait!" he called.

Tom was a flight and a half ahead of him, looking up from below. "Taylor, never mind," he said. His eyes were already red and Taylor continued down after him, trying to appear unthreatening.

"I will *not* never mind," he said, stopping at the landing just above Tom.

"Look, I know all about Ryan and Neil and everybody else. Gen told me everything last night. I understand." Tears glistened in his eyes, the gray having gone a deep purple.

"What do you understand?" Taylor asked gently, his voice calm.

"I understand that you need this life. I had hoped you really liked the town and me, but I know it's not enough."

"What makes you think that?"

Tom gestured around him. "Look where you're at?"

"A stairwell?"

Tom gasped a laugh through his tears. "No, not a stairwell. New York City!"

"I hate New York City," Taylor said simply.

Tom froze, looking straight at him from his position three steps down. Taylor was already taller than him and it made him feel like a giant. He went down the steps so he was staring directly into Tom's damp red-rimmed eyes.

"I needed to get away. I shouldn't have just left, but I flipped out. I was so scared what *you* would think. Neil was there—to say goodbye on his way to New York—and I just got in the car and left. I'm so sorry."

Tom said nothing, just watching him as the tears ran down his cheeks.

"It may go down in history as one of the dumbest things I've ever done if you forgive me," Taylor said, his own voice catching.

"Forgive you?" Tom sobbed. "Taylor, I *love* you. I've loved you since the first time I saw you."

Taylor froze. There they were—the words he had prayed to hear. This man, this perfect man, who he loved so much, loved him back. Taylor reached out, gently wiping the tears from Tom's cheeks and pulled him to him.

"I love *you*," he said and kissed Tom softly and lovingly, pulling him close and holding him like he would never let him go. Tom answered the kiss with a force borne of longing and hope requited, his hands clutching at Taylor's shirt as though to keep from falling into an abyss. He leaned into Taylor's shoulder.

"It took you long enough," he managed through sobs, his chest warm against Taylor's in the cool air of the stairwell.

"Me?" Taylor said, turning to kiss his cheek again and again as he pulled back to meet Tom's eyes. "I was waiting on you!"

"I was waiting on you."

Taylor smiled, his Tom Smile. "Okay, we agree right here and right now to not wait anymore."

"Done," Tom said, planting another long, deep kiss on him.

"Wow," Taylor said. "I'm liking the not waiting plan."

"Yeah, how 'bout that?" Tom said.

"You're okay with this?" Taylor asked.

"Taylor, as long as I'm with you, I'm okay with anything."

"All right," he said. "We should go get Gen. Let's go home."

"Home?"

"Home," Taylor said. He took Tom's hand and they walked back up the stairs to the door. He pushed the release on the handle and it didn't move.

"What?" Tom asked.

"It's locked."

Tom kissed him again. "Maybe we'll have to stay here forever."

"No food," Taylor said. "We'd only last a couple days. I plan to be with you a little longer than that."

"You'd better be," Tom said, holding him tight.

Taylor pounded the door. "Gen!" he called. "Hey, Gen, we're locked in here!"

She appeared in the window, pushing the door open for them. "I figured you might need a couple minutes," she said. They walked back into the hall and the door closed behind them. Gen regarded them skeptically.

"So, I see you two have worked everything out."

"We're ready to go home," Taylor confirmed.

"Good," she said. "I was just having a nice talk with Neil and Ryan. Would you believe Neil had no idea you dated Ryan? I filled him in on the details. Ryan had to be going, so he didn't get to hang around to say goodbye."

"Pity," Tom said, still holding on tightly to Taylor. For his part, Taylor didn't seem inclined to let go of Tom, either.

"I took the liberty of collecting your things," Gen said.

"You can't help but be a mom, can you?" Taylor asked.

"What would you do without me?" she asked. They walked back to Neil's apartment, where the door stood open.

"I should say goodbye," Taylor said.

Tom gave him one more good squeeze and kissed him on the mouth. "Don't forget about me," he said, smiling through red eyes.

"I never have," Taylor said, kissing him back. Tom picked up his bag and followed Gen back to the elevator. Taylor walked into the apartment, leaving the door open.

Neil waited by the giant windows where they had shared coffee the morning before. He wore only his pajama bottoms again, his arms crossed over his bare chest. He turned as he heard Taylor approach.

"Gen is quite a woman, isn't she?" he commented.

"Yeah, how 'bout that?" Taylor said.

"I had no idea about Ryan," Neil said.

Taylor laughed. "Actually, I'm just glad we were here for your sake. I'd hate to think how much it would have cost you to find out on your own."

"I'm really sorry it couldn't work out, Taylor," Neil said.

He smiled apologetically. "I'm sorry, too. I needed to work a lot of things out, and I probably still have a few to go, but I'm in love with Tom."

Neil nodded. "I'm glad for you. Does he have a brother?"

Taylor laughed again. "Nope, just a sister."

"Damn," Neil said, laughing as well.

"Well, I need to be going," Taylor said.

"Good luck, Taylor," Neil said, following him to the door. "If you're ever in New York, be sure to drop by."

"I will," Taylor said, shaking hands.

"Bye, Taylor," Neil said.

"Bye, Neil," Taylor said. He walked away and the door closed behind him.

And he smiled.

Taylor wambled through the small lobby to the door and the doorman pulled it aside for him. Taylor offered a silent thank you, not even breaking stride as he headed for Tom's Grand Cherokee. Gen was in the back seat and he saw Molly stretched out next to her. He pulled open the passenger door and climbed in.

Planting a quick kiss on Tom, he looked back to Gen. "So, the whole family's here, huh?"

"Nobody wanted to miss the action," she said.

Taylor sat back, taking Tom's right hand in his left, watching the city pass them by again. It didn't seem nearly so imposing as it had the night before and he smiled.

"I know it's no *jet*, but I hope you don't mind us coming to get you," Tom said.

Taylor smiled. "I've never been happier about anything in my life," he said.

"Are you two going to be gushing all over each other all the way home?"

"Probably," Taylor admitted. "Isn't that what you wanted?"

"Yeah, I guess it is," she said.

"When did you get here?" Taylor asked.

"Yesterday afternoon," Tom said. "Gen tried everything she could think of to track you down, but we couldn't find you. We left a note with the doorman, but he must not have given it to you."

Taylor tried to hide the guilt from his face. "Uh…well…"

"Why didn't you call?" Gen said, smacking him in the back of the head.

"I got it at twelve thirty last night. It just had your name and number. I figured you just wanted me to call you back. I was going to call first thing this morning."

"Damn right—I was worried!" she said, smacking him again.

"Ow! Stop that."

"If you ever run off again like that, I won't be so nice," she said.

"He'll never run off again like that," Tom said. "Will you?"

Taylor looked at him, a longing in his eyes. "Never," he said with finality.

Gen watched the city recede. "So, Central Park is fairly nice."

"Spent some time there?" Taylor asked.

"Spent quite a bit of time there. We couldn't think of anywhere else to walk Molly. We couldn't think of anywhere else to stay, so we spent the night in the car."

Taylor turned to face her, shocked. "What? Please tell me you're kidding."

"She's not kidding," Tom said, his grip on Taylor's hand firm.

"It's really not that bad," Gen said. "We each put one of the front seats back and Molly sprawled out in the back end. We listened to the radio, told stories, sang songs. It was like a camp out, only no fire and we were in a parking garage under Neil's parents place."

Taylor sighed, looking into Gen's bemused face. "I don't even know how much I owe you, do I?"

A wicked smile appeared and her eyes brightened. "Honey, you don't know the half of it. Am I right, my man T?"

"You go, girl," Tom shot back, a pathetic attempt at jive.

Taylor smiled, realizing they really were his family. He loved his brother and his parents, but they were part of a different life. These people were the ones he cared about, the ones he would spend the rest of his days with. For the first time, the value of that became truly clear to him. Now, as to *where* they would spend those days...

"So, how are things in town?" Taylor asked. Tom had successfully navigated them out of the city and they were bound for home.

Gen's eyes livened with excitement. "You are not going to *believe* this. Remember, I told you the town was pretty supportive? When we went to go after you, Rob, from down the street, stopped us and told us we had his complete support. I talked to his wife Mel yesterday morning and she said he nearly boxed a couple people for making fun of the situation. Then, Trudy called me last night to tell me some people nearly ran Faith out of the Safeway yesterday morning. Rick called and said, after we left, a bunch of people started in on Faith at the dance, too. I guess people are pretty hot."

"That's incredible," Taylor said. "I never would have expected a reaction like that."

Tom nodded, eyes on the road. "A bunch of people came into the bakery, too. Most of them were nice. There were a couple who were kind of rude, but Emmy lit into them pretty good. She says hello, by the way."

Taylor turned his attention back to Tom. He could hardly believe this was the same guy who had so steadfastly avoided any discussion of sexuality for the last few months. "Tom, are you sure you're okay about all of this?"

He smiled a little hesitantly, still staring straight ahead. "I won't say I'm thrilled, but it was bound to happen sooner or later. After all, we can't go through life alone." His grip on Taylor's hand tightened.

"Speak for yourself," Gen said.

Tom eyed her in the rear-view mirror. "We'll find a nice guy for you, too. Remember, Taylor and I know how to shop for them."

Taylor shook his head. "There will be no shopping," he said. "We have bought all we can afford, right here. Gen is an able shopper all by herself—besides, we shop in different stores."

"Party pooper," Tom said. He realized Taylor was still watching him, examining his reactions. "I'm okay," he said glancing over and flashing the Smile.

Gen snickered from the back seat. "Well, Taylor, at least you can be fairly sure they're not talking about your car anymore."

"That's true," Taylor quipped. "Now they're talking about Tom."

"Heeey!" he whined. "At least I won't have Safeway Suzy chasing after me anymore."

"What about Safeway Steve?" Taylor asked.

"Who's Safeway Steve?"

"Kidding!"

They relaxed back into their seats, the banter continuing on. Again, as they were about halfway home, Tom stopped to let Gen walk Molly. Taylor offered to do it, but neither Gen nor Molly seemed interested in his offer.

The girls out of the car, Taylor turned to Tom. "You're really okay?"

"How long are you going to worry about this?"

Taylor smiled—his Tom Smile. "Probably for a while."

"I'm fine," he said. "I've thought about variations on this for a long time. It's okay. Yes, it's a change and there will be bumps in the road, but I have you and that makes it worthwhile."

"I've never loved anyone like I love you," Taylor said.

"My feelings exactly," Tom said.

"It's not an easy life," Taylor said, a sort of warning.

Tom smiled, a relaxed easy expression of someone who was at peace. "I'll let you in on a little secret I've learned," he said. "No life is an easy life. Doesn't matter if you're rich, poor, gay, straight, male, female, black, or white. Life is what you make of it. It's about the people around you and the relationships you create. I've wanted to find someone like you for a very long time. Once I did, I was scared because I didn't know if you felt the same way about me. Over the last few weeks, I'd become more and more sure, but it wasn't until I felt like you were slipping away that I knew I had to tell you. When you were gone, Gen told me how you felt, and I knew I was going to find you. I made her find out where you were and I came here without hesitation."

Taylor listened, only smiling at the warm hand in his own, where it had been since New York. "I will never be able to put into words how happy I am you did," he said.

"Honestly, Taylor, it's like a weight has been lifted from my shoulders," Tom admitted. "You have no idea how many things I have wanted to say to you that I couldn't without my true feelings being plainly obvious."

Taylor laughed, rolling his eyes. "Oh, I have *some* idea of how that felt," he corrected.

Tom eyed him. "You slipped once, when we went away, didn't you?"

"What do you mean?"

Tom looked him straight in the eye, his irises just slightly lavender again. "When we were driving out to go camping. I made a comment about spending the weekend with Neil and you said, 'I'd rather be with you.' Then you tried to cover it up."

Taylor remembered the exact moment—it had been the first time his mouth had gotten away from him. "Damn! I thought I did a pretty good job of covering it up."

Tom shrugged. "A fair attempt, but you don't lie well."

"Neither do you."

"How so?"

"Every time you thought I was going out with someone else, you got all crabby."

"Crabby?"

"Cranky, moody, grumpy."

The corners of Tom's eyes crinkled. "But only when I thought you were going out with someone else?"

"Yeah."

"Then I guess I won't have anything to be crabby, cranky, moody, or grumpy about anymore, will I?" he asked, leaning forward to kiss Taylor.

As he pulled away, Taylor caught his breath. "I guess not," he gasped, still taken aback by the sensation of finally being able to fully express his feelings and having Tom express them in return.

The door opened and Molly jumped in, followed by Gen. "Okay, you two, I saw that. I leave you on your own for five minutes!"

"Just imagine what it'll be like when you leave us alone for ten," Tom said, starting the car. Taylor looked at him sharply, eyebrows raised. Tom gave him a wink as he put the transmission in drive and pulled back onto the freeway, headed for home.

The weather had gotten a bit cloudy by the time they started toward Main Street. Taylor was surprised. There had been very little rain since he arrived in town, a point the weather prognosticators were always complaining about on the evening news—whenever he was home to watch it. He'd nearly forgotten what day it was, until the quietness of the town reminded him it was Sunday. He was supposed to go to work tomorrow—not likely.

Tom slowed as they moved down Main Street.

"Where do you want me to take you?" he asked, looking to Taylor.

"Home," Taylor said simply.

"Which home?"

"My home."

"Oh." Tom sped up, heading for Gen's street.

Taylor smiled thinly, trying to keep it from being something Tom could see.

"Don't give me, 'Oh.' I'd like to at least catch a shower and pack some fresh clothes before I come spend the night at your place."

"Oh!" Tom said, a little more lively. The car moved even faster.

"Tommy!" Gen called from the back seat, holding on to the front seats to steady herself. Tom slowed down, just in time to swerve into her driveway.

"What will the neighbors think?" she asked.

Taylor laughed. "Oh, I'd say we've not yet begun to give the neighbors something to think about." He held up his and Tom's hands, where they had remained since leaving New York hours before. He looked Tom directly in the eyes. "I will see you inside a half hour." He kissed Tom's hand, then leaned over and kissed Tom.

"I'll be counting the minutes."

"Oh, ghack!" Gen said, swinging open the back door. She and Molly hopped out. She grabbed Taylor's bag and headed for the house. Taylor let go Tom's hand, finally, reluctantly, and stepped out of the car himself.

"I'll be right down," he said.

"See you in a few," Tom said. He backed out, then shot off down the street.

Taylor bounded up the front steps and through the door. Gen stood waiting for him in the living room.

"I love you I love you I love you," he said, pulling her into a hug and planting kisses on her cheek.

"Save it for your boyfriend," she said pushing him back. "I'm just glad you're not mad at me for meddling."

"How could I be mad? He loves me!"

"Duh!" Gen said. "Now get your butt upstairs so you can get your butt over there. I'll pack your bag for you."

"Gen, you don't have to do that."

"Go!" she ordered. "This is the best chance I've had in weeks to not have you moping around this house."

He looked at her with puppy eyes and she shushed him up the stairs, following along with the duffle he had taken to Neil's. She tossed the clothes from the trip in a heap on the floor, nose wrinkling at the smell of clothes he'd worn to the club, then pulled some fresh stuff from the closet and dresser and refilled the bag. The shaving kit was set, so he was good to go.

Taylor came out not a minute later, the new world record holder for fastest shower. He wore only a fresh pair of boxers, hand plunging into the closet to pull out a fresh shirt and shorts. Another minute and he was ready to go.

"How do I look?"

Gen smiled proudly. "Honestly, Taylor, you could look like you just came back from running the Boston Marathon and he wouldn't care."

"Yeah, but you know, for the first official date and all?"

"Honey, it's all I can do to keep from throwing you down on the bed myself."

"That'll work," he said. He hit himself with a couple quick spritzes of cologne, then reached into his top drawer and pulled something out that he promptly dropped in his pocket.

"Protection?" Gen asked.

Taylor's face darkened. "In a manner of speaking." He picked up the bag, then gave Gen another peck on the cheek. "Thanks again."

"Don't mention it," she said.

He shot down the back stairs and out the door, landing in his car. A second later, he was pointed up the street, bound for Tom's. Rob and Mel sat in the front yard, tossing a ball with Amanda. They waved as he passed and he waved back. He reached the end of the street, turned, rounded the block, and pulled up next to Tom's Jeep.

Bag in hand, he topped the stairs like they weren't even there, then stopped at the door. Tom had left the inside door open, but he didn't know if he should just barge in. What if Tom wasn't dressed? He pulled the door open and kicked the inner door closed behind him.

"Honey, I'm home," he called.

Tom came around the corner from the kitchen, took the bag from Taylor's hand and pulled him into a deep kiss. He stepped back and the Taylor Smile appeared. "Seventeen and a half minutes," he said.

"Sorry I'm late," Taylor said.

"You're right on time," he said. "Come on in."

As they walked by, Tom reached in to drop Taylor's bag in his room, not even bothering to offer the guest room. Taylor liked that. In the living room, he had Carly Simon playing on the stereo and Taylor smelled stir-fry coming from the kitchen.

"We haven't eaten all day, except for that fast food out near New York," he reminded.

"That's okay, I can eat," Taylor said.

"Five minutes," Tom said, turning back to the kitchen. Taylor followed.

"Do I get to see what we're having tonight?"

"Chicken stir-fry and white rice. Quick, simple, easy. I haven't been to the store in a couple days, so we'll have to get more creative later in the week."

Taylor shrugged. "That sounds perfect." He danced softly behind Tom.

"Like Carly Simon?"

"One of my favorites," Taylor said.

"Carole King?"

"Yep," Taylor said.

"She's up next," Tom said, pulling two plates. "Will you set some silverware and napkins?"

"Got it," Taylor said, singing along to "As Time Goes By."

"To drink?" Tom asked.

"Water is fine with me for now."

He pulled down the glasses and filled them, then brought the dishes and glasses to the coffee table. After the day, they downed their meal in near silence, broken only by Taylor complimenting Tom's cooking skills. As they finished, Tom glanced at Taylor, something on his face Taylor didn't quite recognize. Taylor met his gaze evenly, letting him collect his thoughts.

"What do we do now?" Tom asked.

"What do you want to do now?" Taylor asked.

"I don't know," he admitted. Taylor saw what was on his face—nervousness and embarrassment.

"Tommy," he said, turning to face him directly. "We don't have to do anything right now. We can just sit here and listen to Carly and relax."

He seemed more embarrassed and looked away. Taylor took his hand and he didn't pull it back. "Tom, look at me." He did and Taylor continued. "Just relax, okay? We've been through the hard part—we've admitted our feelings. It's smooth sailing from here. There's no agenda, no hurry. We're friends, remember? Friends who care about each other."

Tom leaned into Taylor and sighed. Taylor wrapped his arms around him and held him. "I guess it's just all hitting me a little now," he admitted.

"It had to sooner or later. No matter how gallant you are—and let me tell you, you were gallant today—this is still a lot for you to take. I want you to know I do not have to stay here tonight and that's okay."

Tom shook his head. "I want you to stay."

"Then I'll stay. Just know that we're not in a hurry and you don't need to feel like you're racing against anything. You've got me, buddy, and I'm not going anywhere."

Tom took in a small sob and held Taylor's hands in his a little tighter. "Thanks, Taylor." They sat for a while in silence, he in Taylor's arms, warm and comfortable. Carly Simon crooned for them in the background, setting the tone.

After a couple more songs, Tom took in a breath and sat up. Taylor watched him quietly. "There's something I want to show you."

"Okay," Taylor said, starting to rise. Tom pushed him back.

"No, it's okay, I'll bring it here." He disappeared down the hall, returning a short time later, journal in hand.

Taylor had moved back into the corner of the couch, several pillows positioned to make sitting more comfortable. Tom sat back down, relaxing against him as he had a moment before. He paged through the journal, explaining as he went.

"When we were camping, you asked me if I had written anything in here about you. As you probably guessed, I did, but the part that I want to share with you I wrote while we sat there that last night, under the stars."

Taylor held Tom's left hand in his while Tom held the book in his other hand and read. Taylor rested his head against Tom's, eyes closed, listening to his voice as he recited the poem he had written. He felt hot tears in his eyes as Tom closed the book and set it down next to them. He kissed Tom on the cheek as he moved his arms to hold him tightly, as the words of the poem had said.

"I love you, too," Taylor said.

"I didn't mean to make you cry," Tom said, choking back a sob himself.

"It was beautiful," Taylor said. "I don't have anything to equal that."

"You're more than enough all by yourself," Tom said.

Having anticipated a gift might be appropriate, Taylor reached into his pocket.

"I brought something for you, too. It feels like a big nothing compared to your poem, but here you go."

He dropped a key in Tom's hand and he felt Tom laugh in his arms as he saw the logo of the roaring cat.

"My own key?" he asked.

"For weekend visitation," Taylor said.

"I plan to see it more than just weekends," Tom said. He reached down and slipped the key into his pocket.

"Trust me, you will see it whenever you want," Taylor said.

Tom took Taylor's other hand in his and held it to his lips, kissing his palm. Taylor sigh, leaning into him, cheek to cheek. Tom turned and kissed his cheek, leaning back into him, too.

"Show me how to love you," he said.

"Now?" Taylor asked.

"Now," Tom confirmed.

"Okay," he said, softly kissing Tom on the neck. "We'll start with Lesson One."

CHAPTER FIFTEEN

Faith's Redemption

"Here you go, Mrs. Jensen."

She took the bag of rolls and donuts—the same one she had been getting every Saturday morning since the formation of the universe—with the same smile she wore each and every Saturday morning.

"Thank you, Taylor dear," she said, patting his hand and she took the bag.

"You're welcome, ma'am. We'll see you next weekend, okay?"

"Yes, you will, dear. How's Tommy?"

"Tommy's just fine, Mrs. Jensen," Tom said, coming up behind Taylor with a tray of bagels.

"I'm so glad you boys are doing well," she said. "My granddaughter is a lesbian, you now."

"We know, Mrs. Jensen," Taylor said, still a little embarrassed when she mentioned it.

"You kids these days," she laughed, shaking her head.

"Bye, Mrs. Jensen," Tom called after her. She waved as she walked out the door.

"Every weekend," he said, turning to Taylor.

"It's better than the alternative," Taylor pointed out, wiping the glass free of fingerprints.

"How're you doing?" Tom asked.

"Fine. This part's easy. The customers just point to what they want and I toss it in a bag and try to add it all up in my head."

"Sounds right to me," he laughed.

"And," Taylor said, wiping a smudge from his face, "I don't have to get covered in flour."

Tom gave him a sly grin. "Just wait 'til later. You know what happens when you mix flour and water together."

He went back into the baking room, leaving Taylor alone up front to ponder exactly that. The door swung open and Gen appeared.

"Pussycat!" he called.

"Chocolate," she said.

He handed the croissant across the case, not even bothering to put it in a bag. Outside, Molly lounged on the sidewalk, basking in the summer sun.

"How's my dog?" he asked.

"She doesn't even miss you," Gen said.

"Feeling's mutual," he shot back.

She laughed. "You still want to go shopping?"

"Yep. Tommy said I can go in about another half hour. He'll have the baking done by then and he can hold things down 'til I get back."

"How much longer is Emmy gone for?"

Taylor sighed. "One more week. I will never be happier to have her back as I will be next Sunday."

"Hard life?"

"Not a lot of rest," he said. "Between the firm, the bakery, Pete's wedding, and, you know…"

"Yeah, I feel really bad for you," she said, taking another big bite of her croissant.

"Hey, since you're here," Taylor said, "I've been wanting to run something by you."

"Okay," she said.

"It looks like that settlement is going to be coming through finally. I'm going to get a pretty good chunk of change in the next couple of weeks."

"Does Tom know?" she asked.

"Of course," Taylor said. "Okay, not really. He knows it's coming, but he doesn't know how much. I didn't want to get his hopes up."

"Your question?"

"Do you think I could get away with starting a firm out here?"

"A law firm?"

"Yeah."

Gen considered the question. She had lived in the town long enough to know most of its ins and outs. There was one other law firm, in a less traveled area near the park. She knew little about the attorney, and as far as she knew, he didn't live in town. In the weeks since their return, the town had actually warmed to Tom and Taylor being together. She felt seeing them running the bakery together had helped significantly

"It might work," she allowed. "But I don't know that there's a big call for employment law out here."

"I can practice any law. I don't have to specialize. In the city, specializing helps because I can charge more. Out here, I can practice general law and help people with their specific needs."

"Has Tom heard about a job yet?"

Taylor shook his head. "That's the other reason I'm waiting. I don't want really want to say anything until we're sure we really can stay."

"Tell you what, I'll think about it. You let me know when Tom finds out and that'll help decide whether or not it matters, right?"

"Good plan," Taylor said.

"What's a good plan?" Tom asked, coming out to stand next to Taylor, his arm casually around his waist.

"Dinner tonight. Gen is going to come pick me up in about a half hour so we can buy food."

"Oh. Okay," Tom said. He turned to Gen. "Will you make sure he remembers to pick up some veal scaloppini? I've been wanting to make it for a week and he keeps forgetting."

"That's what happens when you let the man do the shopping," Gen said. They both gave her blank stares and she held up her hands. "Kidding!"

"Pussycat is getting frisky," Tom said.

"A little catty, perhaps?" Taylor countered.

"Reeowrrr," Tom said, holding up a clawed hand.

"All right, all right," she said. "I give!"

The door opened and Mel walked in. Tom quietly took a single step away from Taylor as they all greeted her.

"A whole party," she said.

"Normal Saturday morning," Gen said.

"And I've never been invited?"

"Sorry," she said. "I'll get you next week."

"Sounds good," Mel said. "How are the bakers this week?"

"Only one baker," Taylor said. "I'm just the counter boy."

"At least they picked a cute one."

"I'll say," Tom said, smacking Taylor on the butt as he walked back to the baking room.

Mel laughed, walking to the donut case. Gen walked to the door.

"I'll be back in about a half hour, Tay," she said, using Tom's new nickname for him. "See you tonight, Mel?"

"I'll be here," she said. "Seven o'clock, right?" she asked Taylor.

"Seven it is," he confirmed. Gen left and he started filling a bag for Mel, accidentally forgetting to add some of the things as he dropped them in.

An hour later, Gen pulled up in Taylor's Jag. They had left it at her house since he and Tom rarely needed a second car and Gen liked using it. Taylor came down the steps from Tom's apartment, then got in the passenger's side.

"I really like this car," she said, backing out of the parking lot.

Taylor shrugged. "Okay, it's yours."

She laughed. "Funny boy, be careful what you say."

"I'm an attorney, I'm always careful what I say. You can keep the car."

She looked at him uncertainly. "You're not kidding, are you?"

"Nope."

"Taylor! You can't give me a Jaguar!"

"I just got the settlement letter. Trust me, I can give you the Jaguar. It's the least I can do for what you've done for me."

Gen patted the steering wheel. "Did you tell Tom?"

"Not yet," Taylor explained. "There was a letter from the district. I left it on the counter for him. Of course, he won't open it until I get back."

"You're cruel!"

"I didn't want to know until after I shop for the party. If he didn't get it, I'd be so down I'd wind up buying cabbage or something."

Gen laughed. "I guess that means the law firm idea is more pressing, huh?"

"That'll be up to Tom. He can make or break it at his discretion. Even if he didn't get the teaching job, it's up to him. With the money I got today, even a small firm would be enough to support us. I just want him to be able to do whatever will make him happy."

Gen pulled up to the Safeway store and they headed in. They both took separate carts, shopping for their respective houses. Taylor felt a little like he had abandoned Gen, but she didn't seem to mind. She had lived alone for a while prior to his stint, so it wasn't that much of a change to have him out again. And Molly had stayed—he knew having Molly there made a big difference.

They pushed their carts down the aisles collecting food for themselves and for the party. Tom and Taylor had asked a number of their "in town" friends over for the evening, including Gen, Rob and Mel, Rick and Steve, and Pete and Anita. The latter were not yet a part of the town, but Taylor suspected that would change—he had several thoughts on how that might happen.

At the meat counter, Gen reminded Taylor to pick up veal, which he almost certainly would have forgotten again. Tom loved him dearly, but his absentmindedness was sure to be the source of one of their first fights. He tried hard to remember things, but it just wasn't in his nature to plan ahead like that. He generally went to the grocery store three or four times a week, preferring fresh food to "stocking up."

He turned the cart to head back down one of the aisles and promptly ran into another cart.

"Excuse me!" he said, looking to see who he'd hit. He gasped. "Faith!"

"Taylor," she acknowledged. He tried to maneuver around her, wanting nothing more than to be out of her presence. Gen watched from behind him.

"Taylor, please, can I talk to you for just a minute?"

"I have nothing to talk with you about, Faith," he said. Taylor was one of the most fair, even-handed people in the world, but he had nothing to say to Faith Roberts.

"Please, you don't have to talk," she said. Her expression was pleading, but then she was a master of airs, Taylor knew. "I just want to tell you how incredibly, massively sorry I am for what I did to you at the dance. It was so terribly inappropriate I can't even begin to tell you how embarrassed I am for what I did, both to you and to everyone else there that night. I was drunk and I acted like a fool. I feel so bad. I just wanted you to know that."

Taylor looked at her squarely, his usually happy expression heavy with anger and resentment. As he looked at her, though, another thought occurred to him. Though it had been unintended and awful at the moment, her actions ultimately led to him getting together with Tom. Faith had been the catalyst that finally pushed them both out of their comfort zones and to each other. He felt himself relax and, for the first time in weeks, feel something other than hatred toward Faith.

"Faith, what you did was mean and spiteful and self-centered," he said. Her head hung low. "You wanted to hurt me and those close to me because I rejected your advances. For that, you should be ashamed." He saw tears well in her eyes. Several other shoppers had stopped to watch the interchange and that was fine by him. Let the town rumor mill do its damndest now. He and Tom were together and that was all he cared about.

He continued on, "What you did had another effect, though. It brought Tom and me together and forced us to acknowledge the feelings we've always had for each other. You didn't intend for that to happen and it wasn't what you set out to do, but it did happen and I'm grateful for that. It's for that reason, and that reason alone, that I accept your apology and forgive you."

She looked up, tears in her mascara, a sob on her lips. "Thank you, Taylor. I mean that. I hope you and Tom find all the happiness you seek together."

"Thanks, Faith," he said, pulling his cart free. "Have a good day."

"You, too," she said.

Gen followed him down the next aisle, pulling up next to him. "Way to go, Tay," she said. "Tom will be so proud of you!"

He sighed. "You know, it's true what they say, you never feel better. I thought I wanted to just light into her, but in the end, I just wanted to walk away."

"It takes the bigger man to walk away, honey," Gen said, a reassuring hand on his arm. "Besides, you only told her the truth and you can't be faulted for that."

Later in the afternoon, Mrs. Caillan relieved Tom, freeing him to get a little rest before the party started. Taylor heard the door close, but didn't move from where he lay on the couch. He knew Tom was about to find the letter and he wanted to find out what it said. He heard Tom stop at the counter and heard the rustle of the envelope as he retrieved it from the counter.

"Taylor, are you here?" he asked.

"On the couch," Taylor answered. Tom appeared from behind the couch, picked up Taylor's feet and sat down next to him, resting Taylor's legs in his lap.

"So, you knew this was here?" he asked. His hair was still matted with sweat from baking all day and his clothes were covered in various hints of flour, batter, and the like.

"I have no idea what you're referring to," Taylor said. "What have you there?"

"A letter from my Mom," he said. "I'll open it later. We need to get ready for the party." He started to get up again. Taylor held him down.

"Okay, okay, I'm guilty. Just open it."

"I don't know if I want to." He stared at the unopened envelope.

Taylor sighed. "Will you just open it? I have a surprise for you, but I want to know what that says, first."

Tom glanced over. "A surprise?"

"Yeah."

An expectant smile appeared on his face. "What kind of surprise?"

Taylor glared at him. "The kind you're not going to get if you don't open that letter."

"What if it's not a surprise I'll like?"

"Tom!"

"Okay," he said. He tore off the end of the envelope and slid the folded page from it. With another glance to Taylor, he gently unfolded the sheet and read, one hand holding the letter, the other on Taylor's leg. He felt Tom's hand tense as the other hand slowly lowered the letter.

"Well?"

"I got it!" he cheered, falling over on top of Taylor to clutch him tight and kiss him deeply. Breathless, he stared into Taylor's sky blue eyes, his nose no more than an inch away. "So, what's my surprise?"

Taylor reached under the pillow behind his head and pulled out another trifolded white sheet. He handed it to Tom, who held it off to the side where he could read it without moving from his position.

"Taylor X. Connolly, *esquire*?" he observed. "Very formal."

"Yeah yeah, read on," Taylor grumbled.

"And I thought your middle initial was 'M'."

Taylor nodded. "Long story—*read*."

"Dear Mr. Connolly, this letter is to inform you that final litigation has occurred and an agreement has been reached regarding final disbursement of proceeds. The portion of the proceeds to be received directly by you will be...sweet Jesus, Taylor!" Tom's gray eyes were wide when they turned back to look upon him.

"Think we could use that?"

Tom pushed back a bit, leaning onto the cushion. "We? Well, I mean, it's your money. I—"

"Tom, it's *our* money."

He shook his head. "No, this is your money. You earned it. You made it before you even met me."

Taylor put a hand to his face, gently turning it to face him again. "Tom, are we together?"

"Well, yeah..."

"Are we going to stay that way?"

"I hope so...yes."

Taylor smiled. "Yes, we're going to stay that way. We can't get married but we're sure as hell living together. It's *our* money. We'll use it to buy things for *us*."

"I don't know what to say."

Taylor pulled him back down. "Say you'll never leave me and you'll love me forever."

Tom stared straight into his eyes, a gaze as piercing and loving as Taylor had ever known. "I'll never leave you and I'll love you forever."

"I'll never leave you, either, and I'll love you forever," Taylor said. "And that's all I need to know." He kissed Tom.

Tom sighed, his head resting on Taylor's chest. "I just don't feel like I can contribute equally," he admitted.

Taylor nodded. "I understand and I want you to feel like you're contributing equally. I'll tell you what—I have another idea for what I'd like to do with that money, but it involves you and will require your support."

Tom sat up again, his attention on Taylor.

"I think I want to start a law practice here, in town. Gen said there's an old guy who is already practicing. I want to find out what his story is— maybe I can buy him out. Otherwise, I'll just go for broke."

"All by yourself?" Tom asked.

Taylor smiled. "Not exactly. I was thinking about asking Pete to join me."

Tom considered the idea. In the weeks since their relationship had become "official," he had spent a lot of time with Taylor and Pete, working on Pete's upcoming wedding. He'd gotten to know Pete and Anita and liked them both very much. He knew Pete had mentioned moving out to be somewhere around them, but he didn't know how serious he was.

"Have you asked him?"

Taylor shook his head. "No. I just got the letter today and I wouldn't say anything without talking to you first."

"Taylor, I don't have anything to say about what you do with your life."

Taylor looked at him like he'd just said the sky was red. "Didn't we just go over this?"

Tom realized he'd been caught. "Well, yeah…"

"Would you do something like this without talking to me about it?"

"Of course not!" Taylor said nothing, simply staring at him. "Right," Tom said, laying his head back down.

Taylor laughed, hugging him close. "So?"

Tom nodded. "I think it's a great idea, as long as you're happy. I wouldn't mind having you closer to home."

"Home?" Taylor asked.

"Home," Tom confirmed, kissing him again.

"Funny you should mention that…"

The summer sun was warm, even in the early morning hours. In the leaves of the old trees, the birds were undaunted, singing their happy songs to greet the bright light of day. The loud banging of a door and the muted sound of expletives coming from inside the house interrupted their tune, however.

"Anita!"

"Sorry!" she said, pulling the door open.

Pete and John maneuvered the dresser out the door as Tom and Taylor followed along behind carrying some of the drawers.

"You know, you'd think with the kind of money this guy makes that he could afford to just hire a mover," John objected.

"Hey, it was your idea to help," Taylor defended.

"I was being polite," John griped.

"Oh, for cryin' out loud, it's just next door, you big whiner," Sandy called from inside the house.

The team carried the dresser and its contents across the driveway and between the hedge into which Tom had recently trimmed a hole. Next door, Mel held the other door open so they could move back up the stairs unimpeded.

"That's the last of it, right?" Rob asked from the top of the stairs.

"Yeah, that's it," Pete said.

Gen came around the corner, tray in hand, offering iced tea to the already sweaty, weary crew. Sandy and Anita arrived from next door, helping her bring out the other tray with baked goods from Downey's.

"It's going to be another scorcher," Gen observed. "Ah, August."

"At least we got the moving done early," Tom said. He fell back onto the couch—his couch, recently moved from the apartment. Taylor sat down next to him, his shirt stuck to his chest in the heat.

"Don't you have A/C?" John asked.

"I turned it off with the doors open," Gen admitted.

"I'll get it," Tom said.

"I've got it," Taylor said, beating him off the couch.

"This place really is just a carbon copy of Gen's, huh?" Sandy asked.

"Ours, too," Mel said. "There are a bunch of houses like this in the area—all built just after the war."

Rob nodded from beside her. "This used to be an old farm town. Then, as the city expanded, so did the town."

"Seems very nice," Sandy remarked.

Taylor walked back in from the thermostat. "Yeah, but you wouldn't believe the kind of people they've been letting move in lately," he quipped, returning to his position right next to Tom, his hand resting lightly on Tom's leg.

John looked at them. "You know, Taylor, a few months ago, I wouldn't have believed you could be happy out in a place like this, but I have to say this is the happiest I've ever seen you."

"City life isn't all it's cracked up to be," Taylor said. "Turns out I'm a small town boy at heart."

Tom put his hand over Taylor's, holding it. "He just couldn't resist the deal," he said with a smile.

Sandy rose, looking to John. "Well, Johnny, it's time we get moving. Tom and Taylor need to get situated and we've got our own house that needs work."

"Slave driver," John grumbled as he joined his wife.

"We need to be going, too," Rob said. "Mel's mom is watching the kids, but we don't want to tie her up too long."

"Maybe we should go, too," Pete said to Anita.

Tom and Taylor got up to see their friends off. "Actually, could you wait just a minute, Pete?" Taylor said.

Gen and Tom walked the rest of the group out to their cars, chatting as they went about the new house and how convenient it was that they were right next door to each other. Pete and Anita waited inside with Taylor.

"What's up?" Pete asked.

"I just wanted to run something by you," Taylor said, returning to the couch. Pete and Anita both took chairs, facing him. "Are you guys still thinking about moving out here?"

The soon to be married couple exchanged glances. Anita nodded. "Yeah, we were still thinking along those lines," she confirmed.

"Well, you know I got the settlement check for the DDX case, right?"

"Yeah, that must be nice, huh?" Pete said.

Taylor smiled. "It got us a house," he said. "But, I was thinking about doing something more constructive with it."

"Like?"

"There's only one lawyer in town and he's thinking about retiring."

"Oh?" Pete said, interest on his face.

"It would be awfully nice to be closer to home…and I'm kind of tired of the big firm…" Pete nodded, listening. Taylor continued, "I don't suppose you'd be interested in joining a startup law firm?"

"What about John?" Pete asked, realizing their mutual friend might be offended not to be included.

"He's already a junior partner in his firm and, as he just said, he likes the city. We can always ask him later, but it'll take a while to get our feet under us and I think it's better to start with just two."

Pete and Anita exchanged glances. "When would you need to know?"

Taylor sat back into the couch, holding up a hand. "Whenever you're ready. I've been talking to old Hennessey for the last couple of weeks and we have a preliminary deal worked out. He'll stay on for a little while so we can transfer clients over, get the cases under control, etc. I'm planning to do it one way or another, so it's just a matter of if you want to transition."

Tom came through the door, Gen in tow, and caught the tail end of what Taylor said. "You're going to join the firm?" he asked eagerly.

Taylor shook his head. "We're just talking about it. Pete and Anita need to have a chance to think it over and decide what's best for them."

"Hey, Rob and Mel were just saying a house is going up for sale down by them," Gen offered.

Anita smiled, shaking her head. "You guys are bound and determined to have us live near you, aren't you?"

"Stacking the odds," Gen admitted. "It also really saves on travel time."

Pete stood, still looking at Taylor. "Well, we really should go. Let me think about it and let us talk about it and I'll get you an answer soon."

Taylor shook his hand. "No hurry. I just wanted to put it on the table."

Minutes later, they were gone, leaving Tom and Taylor alone in their new house—one they had chosen and bought together. Tom walked up to Taylor, wrapping his arms around him. Taylor returned the hug, enjoying the closeness even as they were drenched in sweat in the warm house.

"No gettin' rid of me now," Tom said.

Taylor gazed into his violet tinged eyes. "What makes you think I would ever want to? It was too much trouble to get you in the first place!"

"Just making the point."

Taylor laughed. "Yeah, well you can't get rid of me, either."

It was Tom's turn to laugh. "Are you kidding? I had to drive all the way to New York to get you."

Taylor nodded. "Hey, speaking of driving," he said, pulling away. "Don't forget to put this in your car—garage door opener." He held out a small black box.

"Did you move my car?" Tom asked.

"Yep—it's already in the garage. Go put that in before you forget."

Tom headed out the back door and Taylor slipped into the kitchen to watch him. The garage was already closed, so Tom pressed the button to open it. Taylor waited as the door rose, slowly revealing the contents. He watched as Tom realized what was behind the door. He walked slowly into the garage, then turned and ran back to the house.

"You bought another Jag?" he exclaimed as he ran through the door.

Taylor shook his head. "I bought *you* a Jag," he clarified. "I'll drive the Jeep for now."

"Taylor!"

Taylor said nothing, simply holding out his arms. Tom walked slowly toward him, into his embrace, and kissed him deeply, their first kiss in their new house and their new life.

Later that night, the house was assembled for the most part. Gen had reappeared a couple hours later and helped put away dishes, unpack boxes, put away clothes and the like. Taylor again commented on how much of a mom she could be, but neither he nor Tom complained.

Mel had appeared a short time after, further aiding the process. She and Tom went around the house, hanging the various pieces of art he had stowed in his apartment. Mel asked whether they would still find him in the bakery and he said he'd agreed to stay on for weekends for a while so Mrs. Caillan could find another fulltime baker. He said Taylor would be coming down to help run the place while Emmy was back in school.

For her part, Emmy had been very excited to learn "Mr. McEwan" would be teaching at her school the coming year. She had even managed to rearrange her schedule to make sure she'd be in his class.

With Gen in the kitchen and Tom and Mel bustling around hanging pictures, Taylor had focused on making sure they had somewhere to sleep. He had then gone to arrange the library, unboxing the many cases of books Tom had brought from the apartment. The task had kept him busy into the evening, sorting and grouping the material while stopping occasionally to read passages in books he recognized.

As darkness fell, the girls said their goodbyes, and he heard Tom come up the stairs. The wood floors creaked as he walked down the hall, stopping in the doorway.

"I wondered why it got quiet up here all of a sudden," he said. Taylor was relaxing in one of his trendy leather easy chairs—one of the only other things to survive Ryan's selective departure months before.

"It's hard to pass up some of these books," Taylor admitted.

Tom smiled. "Good thing you shacked up with an English major, huh?"

"Just shacked up? And here I thought we were living in sin," Taylor said.

"Sin can be arranged," Tom smiled back. "I'm exhausted. I think I'm going to head to bed."

Taylor nodded. "I'll be there in just a minute."

Tom went back down the hall to the master bedroom while Taylor found something to use as a bookmark. As he unpacked, he'd been surprised by the breadth of Tom's reading interest, but was particularly intrigued to see the sequel to a sci-fi thriller he'd read about a year before. He'd lost himself in it before he even realized it, so he wanted to be sure to finish it now.

Turning off the light, he followed Tom's trail, stopping in the darkened bedroom. One light shone dimly from his nightstand. Tom was already in bed, the sheet and blanket pulled over him. Taylor went into the bathroom to take care of business, then returned to drop his spent clothes in the hamper.

He stopped at the closet, pulling a pillow down from the shelf.

"Did I put out the wrong one?" Tom asked.

Taylor shook his head. "No, this is just my regular one," he explained.

As he pulled back the covers to get in bed, he realized the covers were all Tom was wearing. He glanced up.

"I thought it was time to get comfortable," Tom said, blushing slightly.

Taylor nodded, dropping the pillow between them. "Me, too," he said, changing his attire to suit.

"What's with the pillow?" Tom asked. "It doesn't exactly match."

Taylor smiled. "Ah, but it's *my* pillow."

"Your pillow?"

"*My* pillow."

He looked dumbfounded. "So?"

Taylor slid into bed next to him, pulling him close. Tom rolled over to watch him as Taylor told him briefly about the significance of the pillow.

"So it's your pillow," Tom said.

Taylor shook his head. "Now it's *our* pillow. I'm sharing it with you."

Tom smiled. "You'd better be planning to share more than a pillow," he said, resting his head on it next to Taylor.

"By your leave, sir," Taylor said. He leaned over and they kissed as his hand reached slowly back to turn off the light…

EPILOGUE

The Fall Dance

Tom pulled into the parking lot, looking every bit like it was nothing but a normal night. Beside him, Taylor smiled, his hand resting lightly on Tom's where it rested on the shifter. They pulled up next to a car that looked very similar to theirs, only red where theirs was a very dark blue. Inside, the passengers watched their arrival and waved.

Tom and Taylor got out of Tom's Jag, dressed to the nines in three button black suits with tasteful dark colored shirts. Tom's was a deep violet that brought out the color in his eyes while Taylor had opted for a deep maroon that brought out the devil in his personality. Beside them, Gen and her date, Miguel, both got out, similarly dressed to kill.

"Nice car," Gen said.

"You, too," Tom answered. They hugged and both men stopped to shake hands with Miguel. Gen had been seeing him for a little over two months, having been setup with him by John and Sandy, and to all appearances, this time they had a match. They headed toward the pavilion, the cool night air catching puffs of breath as they walked.

"Feels like it might get chilly," Taylor observed.

"We brought jackets just in case," Miguel confirmed.

"It never takes too much to keep Taylor warmed up," Tom said, earning an elbow in the ribs.

"Hey, guys!"

The quartet stopped and turned to find Rob and Mel and Pete and Anita coming up from behind. Like the rest, they had dressed to impress, thanks to Gen's warning that the Fall Dance was a more formal affair.

"Anybody seen Faith?" Rob asked.

"No, why?" Tom asked.

"Just making sure," Rob answered.

They made their way inside and Taylor was surprised by the music. "A waltz?"

Gen nodded. "Just wait 'til you see what they do for Christmas."

Gone was the rock and roll music of summer, replaced by a full orchestra turning out Blue Danube. Gen smiled, turning to Taylor.

"Don't worry, it'll pick up later. They'll do some blues and jazz, too. The best part is it's all live music."

She and Miguel made their way onto the dance floor, followed by Pete and Anita. Rob stood next to Taylor while Mel and Tom went after refreshments.

"So, how go things at the firm? Our little town having lots of legal issues?"

Taylor laughed, turning to the man who had rapidly become a new friend. "No, we're not in too bad a shape, but you should see the stuff we've been getting from Springfield! Christmas should be good for Pete and me."

"Don't forget your neighbors!" Rob said.

"How could I?"

They watched the dancers. Taylor knew virtually nothing about actual ballroom dancing, but the people seemed to be doing a beautiful job holding their own to the music. He never would have guessed there were enough people in town to dance an actual waltz.

"Everything still going okay for you and Tom?" Rob asked.

"God, Rob, they couldn't be going any better. I don't know what I did to deserve him, but I'm not sure I'll ever feel worthy."

Rob nodded. "I know how you feel. I feel that same way every day about Mel. She's an amazing wife and mother, all while holding down a job, too."

Before Taylor could respond, their respective significant others returned, handing them glasses of chardonnay.

"A damn sight better than that beer they had last time," Tom observed.

"Hear hear," Rob answered. He held up his glass. "To happiness—may it continue to shine upon us as we give thanks for its noble work."

Their glasses clinked together as Blue Danube was replaced with something Taylor didn't recognize. Mel turned to Rob.

"I think this is something we can dance to," she said, taking his hand.

Tom turned to Taylor. "It *is* getting a little chilly. Maybe we should try sharing a little heat ourselves?"

"Why, Mr. McEwan, you do know how to sweep a boy off his feet, don't you?"

Tom batted his eyes. "It's a gift." He took Taylor's hand and led him in the direction of the dancers. They all moved in time with the music, each in their own little world of quiet conversation or contemplation.

"Taylor!"

They turned as one, looking to see who called. A gray haired gentleman in a tux rushed toward them, an eager smile on his face.

"I was hoping to catch you sometime tonight," he said, shaking Taylor's right hand. His left hand remained firmly in Tom's grasp.

"Mayor Quigley," Taylor greeted. "How are you?"

"Wonderful, Taylor, wonderful. How are you, Tom?" he said, acknowledging Tom's presence.

Tom smiled and nodded politely. "I'm doing well, sir,"

"You boys have been looking awfully happy, lately," the Mayor observed.

Taylor shrugged. "Things have been okay." Tom glared at him and he laughed. "Okay, things have been wonderful," he admitted.

"Glad to hear it," Quigley said, voice full of cheer. "Taylor, I wanted to ask you something. I'm thinking of retiring. My wife has been bugging me to move closer to our daughter so she can spend time with our grand-daughter."

"That sounds like a great idea, Mayor," Taylor said. "Enjoy spending time with your family—they're what life is about," he said with a glance toward Tom. He felt Tom's hand tighten in his.

The mayor nodded. "I agree. That's why I told her I'd do it."

"Good for you!" Taylor encouraged.

The mayor sighed. "But here's the thing—we're going to need an interim Mayor."

"Oh." Taylor realized what the question was going to be just before the mayor asked him.

"So, how would you feel about being appointed Mayor until we can hold an election next year?"

Taylor's eyes widened and he looked every bit like a deer in the head-lights.

"That's quite an honor, sir, but aren't there other people in town who would be better suited?"

The mayor just shook his head. "I don't think so. The people here like you and they trust you because you've been so open and honest about who you are. You're an attorney, so you understand a lot of the legal aspects."

"I'm an employment law attorney. I don't know anything about run-ning a town," Taylor clarified.

Quigley smiled. "There's not that much to it. It's really just a part time position anyway. You would hardly have to do anything. I know you and Pete Mitchell just bought old Hennessey's firm, so I wouldn't want to screw that up for you. I just happen to think you're just what this town needs. Who knows? You might like it and decide to stay on. I'm sure you'd win election in a walk."

Taylor looked dazed, but Tom positively beamed next to him. "I appreciate all your confidence in me, sir."

"Say you'll do it. My wife will be so relieved."

Taylor laughed. "We don't want to upset Mrs. Quigley, do we?"

The mayor leaned over semi-confidentially. "I hear tell there's a homemade apple pie in it for you," he stage whispered.

"Bribing a public official?" Taylor asked, pretending to be shocked.

"It's sure to bring the press out from the city when they find out."

Taylor nodded. "Okay, I'll give you a conditional 'yes,'" he said. "But I want to meet with you on Monday to make sure we can work out all the details."

"Fair enough. You'll make a fine Mayor, Taylor," he said. They said their goodbyes and he made his way off happily into the crowd.

The waltz had given way to another slow piece Taylor didn't recognize, but Tom pulled him toward the swaying crowd.

"Come on, your honor," he said, "I really am getting cold now."

Taylor agreed—it was definitely not a dance to stand and watch. He caught several glances from the more traditional couples as they made their way out, but no one said anything and no one left, so he figured they were going to be okay. Their friends moved in time over to them, offering a buffer from the occasional stare. From nowhere, Rick and Steve also appeared, giving the occasional gawker something else to stare at.

"Not bad," Tom observed, holding tight to Taylor as he enjoyed his warmth.

"What's that?" Taylor asked, eyes closed, enjoying the music.

"In a matter of six months, you moved, landed yourself a man, and became mayor of the town."

"I'm just going to be standing in as mayor, and that's only if we can work out the details."

"Uh-huh," Tom said, slowly running his hand over Taylor's back.

"Uh-huh, nothing," Taylor defended. "You like it don't you?"

Tom shrugged, swaying to the music. "Living with the head of the town is bound to offer a few advantages."

Taylor moved to let Tom have easier access to his back. "I knew it—you only love me for my wealth and power."

Tom continued to move his hands. "You've figured me out," he said. They continued to dance in step to the music and Taylor held him close.

"You know, you'd better stop that or you could find yourself with more heat than you know what to do with," he said.

Tom slowed his hands, content to just hold him tight. "Found a new secret, huh?"

"Hardly a secret," Taylor said.

Tom turned to stare into his eyes. "Taylor, I'm the luckiest man in the world."

Taylor watched the group with a sense of fascination and warmth. He had come to the town feeling abandoned and alone. A scant six months later, he danced with a group of people who he felt like he'd known for a lifetime. In so little time, he'd found acceptance and love in the last place he ever would have thought to look.

As they kept time with the music, he felt Tom in his arms. He pondered how close he'd come to losing him, never quite sure they would be together in the first place. So many of his friends had tried to convince him happiness was in an endless series of one night stands, one guy after another with no commitment and no support. As Tom held him close and he held onto Tom, he knew, once and for all, that they were wrong.

Love and companionship could be found in the darndest places. He'd found his and he would protect it and defend it with everything he had. In his life and in his work, he'd learned truth was a precious thing and he knew how to recognize it. This place, these people, and this man were the truest things he'd ever known and, in that instant, Taylor Connolly knew it was he who was the luckiest man in the world.

Instead of speaking, he simply leaned in and kissed Tom. It was a simple, unimposing action, but it conveyed the passion of the moment in a way no words ever could. There, in the cool night air, in front of anyone who cared to watch, Taylor Connolly and Tom McEwan showed what it was like to have a love that would last forever.

Afterword

This book may come as a surprise to some people who have been more familiar with my earlier (to date unpublished) science fiction work. To answer the obvious questions in the order they appear, "Yes. Yes. No. No. Yes."

Faith is a quirky thing, and for those of us living an "alternative lifestyle," it's a love-hate relationship. *Finding Faith* was born from the idea that faith might be the most mysterious force of all, sometimes taking physical form to guide our lives in the direction we would least expect, in a time and manner completely outside of our choosing.

In America, we tend to want to label everything—people, places, events, and things. Everything has to be something, but we get confused when it's more than one something. *Finding Faith* is about breaking down some of those barriers. Taylor Connolly is a gay man, but in the end, that's really his least noteworthy quality—even among the eagle-eyed members of the town, his car draws more attention than he does. Taylor could be anyone, and in that way, represents everyone.

In his own right, Taylor is a different class of gay man—neither ashamed and hiding nor loud and proud. He's just a man, like any other, trying to lead his life, in the pursuit of happiness. Contrary to popular belief, there are really far more men like Taylor in the world than the more boisterous and flamboyant gay men of the popular recent media presenta-tions might lead us to believe. These are the men who, like Taylor, could pass by on the street without getting a second glance.

More to this point is Tom, who more or less understands "what" he is, but doesn't see a point in announcing it out without a reason. In applying labels, we often feel we must apply them to ourselves. Tom is the antithe-sis of this belief, living his life openly, but without a banner for the aspects he isn't living. Suzy's comment at the dance is the perfect example—she thinks he's an introverted jock who's not that smart, having no idea he's a college educated writer on his way to becoming a teacher. It's the assump-tions we make that limit us and Tom is the expression of this concept through no one really knowing him for who he is.

Perhaps most importantly, *Finding Faith* should resonate with virtually any reader in the simplicity of its message. The story is as old as time and transcends culture, class, or sexual orientation. It's about betrayal and the faith to press on to the actualization of one's innermost desires and dreams. A pessimist may argue that the love Tom and Taylor ultimately find and share is real only in fiction, that real relationships are never that easy. To the contrary, their relationship is, in fact, the fundamental state we all aspire to achieve. Faith is what drives us forward, and if we're lucky, guides us to our intended destination. In the book, the character of Faith forces Taylor and Tom to admit their true nature and feelings for each other, and ultimately, if indirectly, drives them to each other. Like its fic-tional manifestation, faith won't always lead us down the path of least resistance, but hopefully, the end will justify the means.

For the curious, the theme of faith is a deliberate conceit—none of the characters rely on nor expect the intervention of an outside power. For them, faith is inner strength—Taylor's faith that his move is the right deci-sion, that Tom cares for him, that a relationship is the right direction;

Tom's faith that Taylor will love him in return and validate and support his own revelation; and Gen's faith that the two will work through their issues without losing each other. Faith is not a belief in a higher power, but in the concept that the universe will unfold in a way we find favorable. *Finding Faith* shows faith is our own power. Sometimes, it's the power to believe in a supreme being; sometimes it's the power to believe in the survival of a loved one; sometimes it's the certainty that life will go our way. Always, it's our own inner strength to cling to what we believe in the face of adversity and to grow stronger as human beings in the process.

I hope you've enjoyed *Finding Faith*. If you have any comments or questions, I'd love to hear from you. Please direct email to andrew@andrewBarriger.com and I will endeavour to respond as quickly as possible.

And for those of you wondering what happens next, look for *Finding Peace*, out summer of 2003.

All the best,

Andrew Barriger
November 2002

0-595-26309-7

Printed in the United States
93576LV00004B/48/A